T0129030

Stepping into the Abyss

Choices and Consequences

Concordia International School Hanoi
and The Lutheran Academy

STEPPING INTO THE ABYSS
CHOICES AND CONSEQUENCES

iUniverse books may be ordered through booksellers or by contacting:

iUniverse
1663 Liberty Drive
Bloomington, IN 47403
www.iuniverse.com
1-800-Authors (1-800-288-4677)

Because of the dynamic nature of the Internet, any web addresses or links contained in this book may have changed since publication and may no longer be valid. The views expressed in this work are solely those of the author and do not necessarily reflect the views of the publisher, and the publisher hereby disclaims any responsibility for them.

Any people depicted in stock imagery provided by Getty Images are models, and such images are being used for illustrative purposes only.
Certain stock imagery © Getty Images.

ISBN: 978-1-5320-4814-2 (sc)
ISBN: 978-1-5320-4815-9 (e)

Print information available on the last page.

iUniverse rev. date: 04/20/2018

Contents

Foreword

By

Terry Umphenour

Stepping Into the Abyss: Choices and Consequences is a book filled with delightful tales, through which imagination takes both the reader and the writer on an adventurous tour of the writing experience. This project exposed the minds of middle school student writers from Concordia International School Hanoi and The Lutheran Academy in Scranton, Pennsylvania, to the demanding challenges of writing and refining a 5000-word story for publication. Collectively, the stories printed on the following pages take the reader on imaginary adventures through time and space.

Brainstorming to determine the genre and story parameters started the process. Most students expressed excitement at the freedom to write about topics of their choosing, while some students expressed concerns about writing such a long story and the time it would take. The second phase of the assignment found students struggling to introduce their characters, set scenes, and make characters come alive with individual characteristics. After considerable thought, a first tentative outline, and a brief introduction, each student read and revised a plot and storyline that provided the conflicts needed to bring the story to its climax and conclusion.

Usually the middle school writing process includes an outline, a rough draft, a final draft, and proofreading. *Stepping into the Abyss: Choices and Consequences* required students to write an outline, a character development sheet, an initial introduction, a first draft, and three additional drafts.

After finishing the story's first draft, each student revised their draft, ensuring the facts remained consistent, the story used the same tense throughout the manuscript, and correct paragraph and sentence structure kept the storyline moving forward. Next, each young writer edited his or her own work to make sure the story used active voice and adjectives had the correct tense. The final draft provided an opportunity for each writer to proofread. Proofreading such a long story, one that needed every mistake corrected, provided many opportunities to teach the conventions necessary to publish a story.

Pursuing personal excellence remains one of the expected student learning results at Concordia. *Stepping Into the Abyss: Choices and Consequences* provided students an opportunity to reach this expected student-learning result. However, only you—the reader—can determine the degree of success each of these young writers reached toward achieving that goal. The final stories are printed exactly as the students submitted them and may include errors or even missed comments that should have been deleted. In order to make this work a continuing education resource, no teacher or professional editing was added to the final submitted stories.

It is with great pride that we present *Stepping Into the Abyss: Choices and Consequences* for your enjoyment. Our hope is that you enjoy reading these imaginative, adventurous stories as much the students enjoyed writing and editing them. To learn more about this writing process and its authors or to comment on this work, contact Terry Umphenour at the following email address: terry.umphenour@concordiahanoi.org.

About the Author

The students authors for this book are middle school students at Concordia International School Hanoi and The Lutheran Academy in Scranton, Pennsylvania.

The Trials of the Heart

By

Nora Betts

I lay on my back, the cool wood of the dock against my skin, the summer sun beaming through the trees around me, outlining the branches in gold. The light dances on the murky water of the pond beneath me, and I stare up at the blue sky between the tops of the spruce trees. Without warning, violent images of death flash through my mind. I shudder uncontrollably and blink hard, trying to clear away the unwanted pictures from my subconscious. I've faced them enough.

I take several deep breaths, hold them for a second, and then let them out slowly, trying to calm my racing heart. Then I distract myself from my thoughts and focus on the warmth of the sun on my cheeks, the smell of lilacs around me, and the gentle breeze whispering through the trees. I smile and close my eyes.

I open my eyes at the sound of an unusual rustling in the foliage that peaks my interest. I stand up, brushing my long, golden hair from my shoulders. My eyes scan through the trees but see nothing out of place. As I search the trees one more time, a shadowy figure partly hidden behind the dense leaves of a maple tree catches my eye.

"Um, excuse me?" I call.

The figure makes no move. I peer closer at the shape—tall, a man's height—but his facial features are shaded by the trees. All I can see are his eyes, sort of glowing in the dim light beneath the trees.

"There's a road just over there," I say awkwardly, pointing to my left.

He stays still, his eyes trained on me. A sinking feeling grows in the pit of my stomach.

A hand firmly grips my right shoulder. I scream and turn around, almost toppling into the water. A brown-haired boy looks as frightened as I do. "LUKE! You scared the crap out of me!" I breathe.

"Sorry, Julia," Luke says through his laughter.

I push him. "It's not funny! I'm freaked out." I lower my voice and whisper, "There's someone in the woods, and he just keeps staring at me."

"Where?" Luke asks.

I point to the tall maple tree. "Behind that big tree on the other side of the pond."

Luke shades his eyes with his hands and looks across the pond. "I don't see anything." "There was someone there," I say, growing even more uneasy.

"Your screaming must've scared him away," Luke says.

I sit down on the edge of the dock and run my fingers along the wood. Luke sits down beside me. "Are you okay?" he asks softly.

"Just thinking…thinking…about my dad." An image of my father lying face down on his desk, a gun in his hand flashes through my mind. "I was only seven," I say, my heart growing heavy. Luke moves closer to me, and I turn to look at him.

"I'm sorry," he says.

I give him a sad smile. "It's not your fault," I sigh. "It was seven years ago and there's nothing anyone can do." We sit in silence for a moment, just watching the rippling water beneath our feet. An idea pops into my head. I grin.

Luke runs his hand through his hair and gives me a weird look.

"Do you have your phone on you?" I ask slyly.

Luke shakes his head. "Why?" he asks.

I smile devilishly and place my hands against his shoulders. I shove Luke. For a long second, he struggles to maintain his balance, but gravity wins. Luke falls backward, his arms and legs flailing through the air during the two-foot drop to pond.

"Ah!" he yells just before he hits the water. A huge splash breaks the flat, murky surface.

I laugh uncontrollably as he resurfaces, gasping for air—his grey eyes wild.

"What was that for?" he screams.

"For scaring me," I laugh. Luke tries to glare at me but ends up laughing, too. He swims to the edge of the dock and reaches for me.

"Help me up," he grins.

"I don't think that's—"

The next thing I know I'm in the pond! The cold, wet water constricts my lungs. My hair swirls wildly around my head. I come up for air, and it's Luke's turn to laugh. I wipe long clinging strands of hair from my eyes and splash water at him.

"Oh, you love it," Luke yells. I smile.

* * * *

The sun sits lower in the sky, and a line of red traces the horizon. Luke and I run barefoot out of the trees and across the soft grass, our shoes in our hands. My sopping wet tank top and shorts stick to me, and my hair streams out behind me as I run. Luke and I collapse in laughter on the grass, panting and trying to catch our breath. I lay on my back, my hair splaying out around my head. I cross my arms over my stomach, trying to control my laughter. I tip my head back, seeing the world upside-down, and strain my eyes to see pond through the dense trees from which we have just come. I can just see the glittering water across the small field.

I look over at Luke. He lies on the ground, his arms behind his head. His wavy, brown hair sticks to his forehead, and his face is tilted up to the sky. Luke is of decent height, only three inches taller than my five-foot-six. I admire his broad, slim shoulders and his tan skin, and absolutely adore his strong figure clad in Khaki shorts and a blue T-shirt. They make his eyes seem even more brilliant.

Luke catches me looking at him, and I give him a small smile.

I sit up, glancing in front of me, opposite the direction of the woods. The dirt road stretches as far as I can see before disappearing into the trees. It marks the boundary of his family's house and property and mine. Luke and I stand up from the grass and wait in silence for a second. I awkwardly brush grass from my shorts and clear my throat.

"I guess I'll see you tomorrow?" I suggest.

"Text me in the morning," he tells me.

"Of course."

Luke takes his shoes in his hand and walks across the road. He takes several strides before reaching his house. His house is large, suitable for his big family, and the outside of the house is painted a cheerful yellow color. It has two stories, unlike my one-story house, and has a gravel driveway branching off the road. A wraparound porch covers three sides of the house, and a porch swing sways lazily in the slight breeze. Luke climbs his porch steps and gives me a small wave before stepping inside.

I look away from Luke's house and take my own shoes in my hand. I walk toward my house on this side of the street. My house is small and quaint, painted a cool grey color, but easily accommodates our family of two. A few seconds later, I climb the stairs to my porch and step inside the door. The front door opens to a small mudroom. A few coat hooks hang from the side wall, and a bench sits below them. I drop my wet shoes next to the bench and grab a folded towel from the small cabinet across the room. I wrap the towel around my shoulders and step from the mudroom into my living room.

The living room is mid-sized, with a brown leather couch in the right side of the room next to the TV. A rocking chair sits perpendicular to the couch. A huge, round window takes up a good portion of the right-side wall, and a bench built into it makes it the perfect window seat.

"Mother! I'm home!" I call, walking across the room and taking a seat in the rocking chair.

"Hey, Julia!" she yells cheerfully. She comes to meet me a few seconds later.

Her mid-length light brown hair is done up in a bun, and her smiling green eyes are the same shade as mine.

She hugs me and then laughs when I get her wet. "Playing in the pond again today?" she observes.

I laugh and scoot out of the chair, gesturing for my mother to sit. "Hey, Mother? Do you think you could tell me the story of dad's proposal?" I ask softly.

My mother smiles and sits down in the rocking chair. "Your father and I met in our second year of college. We dated for three years before he proposed. It was in early May when trees were in full bloom on campus. I remember, just as the sun was setting and making the sky glow red, your father led me to one of these trees. He had strung lights from its branches. I laughed at the silly grin on his face as he showed it to me. Then...then he took my hands in his and said, 'Lucy, you are the best thing that has ever happened to me, and I love you more than life itself.'

"Then he got down on one knee. 'Lucy Johnson, will you make me the happiest man in the world and marry me?' It was the best day of my life. I said yes, of course. Five months later, we were married."

My mother's eyes sparkle as she remembers him.

I imagine the two of them—my father with his golden hair and charming blue eyes and my mother's hand over her heart as he pulls out a ring. I smile. "I love that story."

My mother looks down sadly at her hands and fingers her wedding ring. "I miss him," she says.

I stand up and give her a hug, and she holds me tight.

She lets go and breathes a shaky sigh. "Well, you'd better get to bed," she tells me.

"It's still daylight, though!" I protest.

"Nice try, Julia," she says. "It's Alaska in June. The sun doesn't set till well after midnight. Go to bed. It's already ten o'clock."

My mother ushers me across the living room and kitchen and to my room. I laugh to myself about her, well, motherliness.

"You sound like someone's grandmother, not a thirty-five-year-old," I joke.

She fake-hits me, and I run the last few strides to my bedroom door. I push it open and walk into my room. My twin bed sits by the far wall, my dresser and desk on the right side. My walls are painted turquoise, and a soft rug sits at the side of my bed. I grab a long nightshirt and shorts from my dresser and walk to the bathroom one door over. I run through my usual nighttime routine—take a shower, change into night clothes, brush my teeth, wash my face—and walk back to my room.

I take a seat, cross-legged on my bed, and stare out the window at the beautiful sky. Still, a sense of insecurity settles in my stomach when I remember the man in the woods, but I clear the thought from my head, remembering the fun I had today. I yawn and settle down in my comforter, the breeze through the open window lulling me to sleep. What I don't see is the figure standing in the tree line, his eyes glinting with some secret, a handgun in his gloved fist.

* * * *

5

Red and blue lights flash against the brick building, and the cold stings at my wet eyes.

"M-m-mother," I whisper frantically. She hugs me to her chest and pushes her way through the crowd, the sirens wailing around us.

My mother ducks under the police tape and weaves her way toward the open doors of the building.

"Hey! You can't be back here," a voice calls. She hurries on. A hand grabs her arm, and she is pulled to a stop. "Ma'am, you need to leave," the officer says sternly.

"I need to see my husband!" she begs. "Please!"

The man gives her a wary look and steps aside. She whispers a "thank you" and runs inside, holding me tightly to her.

"What's wrong, Mother?" I cry. She stops to look down at me, and I see the fear in her eyes. She gently strokes my cheek.

"It's okay, honey. It's okay," she assures me, but it seems like more of a reassurance to herself. My mother resumes her hurried running through the building, my arms wrapped around her neck. She sidesteps another officer and rushes down the left hallway. She pauses for a second at a door marked with the name C. Johnson. Then with a deep breath, she pushes past the paramedics and into the office.

`My mother freezes. The man lies face down on the oak desk, his right hand gripping the handle of a revolver. A pool of blood collects around his head, and his golden hair is stained with red. A few drops of crimson stain the white of his shirt, and his skin is ghostly pale.

"CHARLES!" my mother screams. She sinks to her knees, pulling me down with her, and sobs. I try to turn my head, to see the cause of my mother's anguish. Her hands press my head to her shoulder, denying me any possible view. Instinctively, I fear the worst. I feel tightness in my chest and burning in my eyes. Police officers and paramedics surround us, my mother's sobs shaking her entire body. Tears stream down my cheeks, and I lift my head.

"Daddy," I whisper.

* * * *

I wake with a start, my hair plastered to my neck in sweat, my face wet with tears. I bury my head in my hands and calm my racing heart. I open my eyes, squint at the light from my window, and look at my clock radio on the nightstand beside my bed—10:33 a.m. I sigh and sit up, my hands still shaking.

I reach for my laptop on my nightstand and open it to my email. I type a quick "good morning" to Luke and hit send. I get out of bed and take a quick shower before pulling on a knee-length purple dress. I grab my laptop and walk out of my room and into the kitchen.

"Morning, Mother," I say.

My mother looks up from her newspaper and smiles.

"Good morning, Julia."

I set my laptop down, and lean down and give her a hug. I take a seat next to her at the counter and take a sip of her coffee.

"Hey!" she laughs. I hand it back, putting on a face of innocence. I open my laptop to my email. Nothing.

"What's up?" my mother asks.

"Oh, nothing. Luke's just not responding." I don't say any more, not wanting to tell her about the man in the woods.

"He probably just slept in," she reassures me.

I glance up at the clock on the wall. I can't shake the worried feeling in my stomach. *Luke never sleeps in past ten o'clock,* I think to myself. I sigh and allow my thoughts to wander away from my insecurities. I look around the room, trying to find something to distract myself.

My eyes land on a picture on the counter. A younger version of my father holds me up with his face tipped up to mine. A huge grin spreads across my toddler face, and my small hands rest on the sides of his head.

I sigh a longing sigh, remembering the fun times I had with my family.

"Do you want some breakfast? I made some pancakes," my mother offers.

I shake my head. "I'm gonna go over to Luke's, if that's okay."

My mother nods. "Just have some breakfast when you come back."

"Yes, Mother," I laugh. I grab a sweater from the back of my chair and half-run to the mudroom. I pull on a pair of cowboy boots and shout a goodbye to my mother before stepping outside.

The sun sits high in the sky, beaming down over everything and warming the earth. A few grey clouds dot the sky, and a strong wind ripples the bottom of my dress. I cross the road to Luke's house and walk up the stone sidewalk to his porch. I pause for a moment, my hand poised to knock on the door. I let go of my anxiety and knock a rhythm on the wood. A few seconds later, the door swings open.

"Hi, Mrs. Fields," I say brightly.

Luke's mother is a slim, friendly-faced woman. Her shock of curly, dark brown hair cascades around her pale face and down her back. Mrs. Fields cradles her baby daughter with one arm and ushers me inside with the other.

"Come in, come in!" Mrs. Fields exclaims. She closes the door and turns to me. "What can I do for you?"

"I don't mean to bother, but is Luke around?" I ask, taking off my boots in the entryway.

"He should be in his room. You can go on up if you'd like."

"That would be great," I agree. "Thank you, Mrs. Fields."

She nods in a flattered manner and flashes me a smile before leaving the room.

The walls in the entryway are a tan color with picture frames and art projects hanging on them. A family portrait hangs on the side wall, where Mr. and Mrs. Fields stand behind their four children. Luke stands in the middle next to his younger and older brothers, and baby sister.

Beside the entryway is a carpeted staircase leading to the second floor. I walk in that direction and mount the stairs. At the top, four doors stretch down the hall. I choose the second room from the stairs. LUKE is spelled out in wooden letters and nailed to the door. I knock softly but get no reply. I knock a little harder and open the door a crack.

"Are you awake, Sleeping Beauty?" I call. He doesn't answer. I sigh and push the door completely open.

Luke's blankets are rumpled in a violent manner and papers are scattered across the room. The white curtains billow from the wind of the open window. Pens, his laptop, and papers are scattered on the floor around his desk. But Luke's bed is empty.

I step around the items on the floor and walk to the side of his bed. His iPhone lies face down on the floor. I take it in my hand and turn the screen towards me. His email is open to my name. In the text box, a single word is spelled out but unsent—HELP.

"L-Luke? If you're hiding, I'm going to kill you," I threaten. I half-expect him to jump out behind me, but nothing happens. The reality is scarier than any fantasy I could imagine. He's gone.

No. This isn't happening, I tell myself. Then I think about yesterday. *He's hiding from me in the woods! He must be. He's joking. He's just trying to scare me.*

My head spins, and my stomach churns. I run out of the room, not bothering to shut the door. I take the stairs as fast as I can, my heart pounding in my ears. An image of the man in the woods flashes through my mind—his piercing eyes trained on me and his broad stature lurking in the shadows. I collide with Mrs. Fields and let out a small scream.

"What's wrong, Julia?" she asks, startled.

"Luke," I babble. "He's... I-I-I don't know where he is." I leave my boots in the entryway and run with socked feet across the road and towards the woods. Mrs. Fields calls something to me, but I ignore her, pumping my legs as fast as they will go. I run across the grass, small rocks tearing into the bottoms of my feet, my dress whipping wildly around my legs.

I near the line of trees around the pond and run harder. I break through the trees and dodge my way through their clawing branches. I skid to a stop where the woods open. My chest heaves from running, and the air stings my lungs. I double over and try to slow my breathing. My heart hammers. I stand and look in front of me. The cloudy water of the pond ripples in the breeze. But the dock is bare, no one in sight.

I collapse onto my knees in the grass. My vision blurs with tears and a sob constricts my throat. *Why? Why Luke?*

The minutes go by fast after that. My mother runs up beside me. She takes my head in her hands and asks me what happened, but my crying drowns out her voice. She pulls me into a hug, and I wrap my arms around her neck the way I had done when my father died. She holds me close, letting me cry into her shoulder. Images of the man in the woods play over and over in my mind, but all I can think about is Luke.

* * * *

I sit up, wiping the tears from my eyes, the sun making me squint. My mother rubs my back and, seeing that I am awake, looks at me, a worried expression on her face. "Julia. *What happened?*"

I swallow hard. "He—" my voice cracks and I wipe at my eyes. My mother pats my back.

"Honey, Mrs. Fields came over and told me how you ran out of her house, whispering something about not knowing where he is. But, honey, what is it that is worrying you? You can tell me anything."

I take a deep breath, and blurt out all the things I had been worried about, all the things I had hoped were not true. "He's gone, Mother! The man in the woods kidnapped him. I don't know why, I don't know how, but I know that he did. Luke tried to tell me. He tried to send me an email. His room is wrecked. He's *gone!*"

I collapse into a fresh batch of tears, and my mother hugs me close to her, stroking my hair.

"Oh, Julia! It's okay... It's okay, honey. Shhh," she croons.

I sit up, burying my face in my hands.

"Julia. This 'man in the woods'. Who is he? If he really did kidnap Luke, we need to find him. Do you remember what he looked like?"

The all-too-familiar eyes flash through my brain and I grimace. "Yeah," I whisper. "I kinda remember." I describe his stature, his broad shoulders, and his piercing, hazel eyes that would haunt my dreams forever.

"Oh, Julia. You poor thing. I'm going to call the police." She pulls her phone from her pocket and stands up. She looks down at me. My mother's expression softens from the mask of worry into a look of pure pity.

"Honey..."

I sigh and give her a as much of a smile as I can muster. A knot of worry clenches in my stomach, and I have to swallow to keep back a fresh round of tears.

She kisses me on the top of the head. "We *will* find Luke. He's strong— nothing will happen to him."

I try to believe with all my might that Luke will be found, but my heart feels heavy. My mother dials 911, and puts the phone up to her ear. She paces back and forth, talking into the receiver, and nervously twisting a lock of hair around her finger.

I stand up and wander my way to the dock, wiping my wet eyes. I sit down on the edge and feel the familiar wood under my fingers. I sigh and rub my head, the thoughts of today too hard to process.

Then I see something out of the corner of my eye. I stand up and walk back down the dock and along the side of the pond. An orange envelope sitting in the grass catches my eye. I crouch down to examine it. I look behind me, where my mother stands, her back to me. I cautiously take it in my hands and finger its surface. My brain whirrs. *Do I want to open it?* With another glance behind me, I decide that I do. I tear the top of the envelope and stick my hand inside. I pull out a single card-sized piece of paper. The numbers 6450'55.6 14703'31.4 are scrawled out in Sharpie on the paper.

I sit back on my heels. *This makes no sense.* I shake the envelope and a scrap of paper falls out. It says, "***WAIT FOR MORE.***"

* * * *

Over the past ten days, I had gone out to the dock, and every day, an envelope had been waiting. I had smuggled them into my room, behind my mother's back. I had been troubled, fighting over what I should do with the envelopes, whether to confess everything or keep it secret. I had decided to keep it secret—I didn't want any more things for my mother to worry about.

Now, ten days after Luke's disappearance, I sit on my bedroom floor, my fingers caressing the orange paper of another envelope. I take a deep breath and tear into it. I pull out two pieces of paper—one marked with a cryptogram of numbers, the other, a message written in the same messy scrawl: *Use the coordinates. Come alone or he dies.*

Luke is alive! A wave of relief washes over me, but soon turns to dread. I look down at the note one more time. *It says to come alone... I'm only fourteen years old! I can't just wander off into the woods.* My conscience battles itself, unable to decide whether to alert the police and jeopardize Luke's life or go alone and face whoever kidnapped him by myself.

Pacing back and forth, I ponder all the different things that could happen depending on what decision I made. Luke's tormented face fills my mind, and I decide on the latter. I can't leave him.

I stare at the note for a second. A thought dawns on me before I can think too hard about it—they're coordinates! I kick myself for being so ignorant and frantically search for my laptop. I grab it from my nightstand and set it on the floor. I dig around in my desk drawer and pull out a stack of the orange envelopes from previous days. *Let's see where Luke is....*

* * * *

I run my eight-year-old hands over the face of the smooth rock and pull my arm back. I launch the rock, and it skims across the water, bouncing one, two, three times. My feet brush the edge of the water, and the cold stings at my toes. The cool wind nips at my cheeks as I pick up another rock. A stick breaks with a loud crack behind me, and I stand up with a start. My eyes scan the trees, and I hold the rock defensively behind my head, ready to throw. I turn in a half circle. A hand taps me on the shoulder.

"Hello?" a voice says behind me.

"Ahh!" I spin around and hit the figure with the rock. I gasp.

The boy crouches down on the ground, one arm covering his head, the other rubbing his shoulder, his eyes squeezed shut.

"Oh! My gosh! I'm sorry! Are you okay?" I ask. The boy opens his eyes—a gleaming grey color that look a little too large for his face—and looks tentatively at me. He brushes dirt from his pants and slowly stands up.

"Yeah, I'm fine. Nice throw," he laughs, fingering his shoulder.

"Oh, I'm sorry! I'm just a bit jumpy, I guess," I sigh. I give him a small smile, and he clears his throat.

"Well, um, I'm Luke. I'm moving in across the street."

"Nice to meet you, Luke." I smile. "I'm Julia. Julia West."

"Nice to meet you too, Julia. So, how old are you?"

"I'm eight—just turned eight."

"I'm eight as well."

"Nice."

I walk down to the edge of the pond and step onto the dock. "Come on!" I motion for Luke to follow me, and we both sit down on the edge of the dock, our feet swinging over the water, our voices and laughter echoing through the trees.

* * * *

I slowly open my eyes, not wanting to be roused from such a memory. But I remember what lies ahead and sit up. I glance at the clock on my nightstand—5:21 a.m. I pull on a long-sleeved shirt and a pair of Capri pants. The outside world is still dark, the navy blue of the sky slowly changing to grey on the horizon.

I take a backpack and fill it with supplies from my room—an extra change of clothes, the envelopes, a flashlight, a compass, and my pocketknife that I used on camping trips with my parents.

Lastly, I grab the sheet of paper I had printed out the night before—a map of Fairbanks, Alaska, the area around my house, with the coordinates I had received.

I quietly open my bedroom door and tiptoe into the kitchen. I stuff a box of crackers, a couple of water bottles, a container of peanut butter, a bag of trail mix, and a box of matches into the backpack. I take the spare flip phone from the drawer and put it in my pocket. I grab a piece of paper and a pen and go to write a note. I stop for a moment, my pen poised over the paper. *I'm really doing this. I'm trekking into the woods alone and unaware of what lies at the end.* My mind whirrs. *Why didn't I just tell the police?*

I shake all worried thoughts from my head and start writing a note to my mother:

Mother,

Don't worry about me.
I'll be back real soon with Luke.
I love you.

—Julia

I set the note on the kitchen counter and sling my backpack over my shoulders. I sneak across the living room to the mudroom. I slip a jacket on and slide my feet into my sneakers. With one last deep breath, I step outside, leaving the last bit of safety I have, and set off into the woods.

* * * *

As I walk through the woods, the sky lightens and turns a pale blue color. This light allows me to see the dark clouds looming menacingly in the sky. *Oh crap,* I think to myself. *This is the worst time for it to rain.*

I walk on for hours, the great pine and spruce trees towering high above me. Little flowers peek out from under rocks and through the grass.

I pass a small creek, hopping onto stones to get across. As I get deeper among the trees, the grass grows longer, and the trees get taller. My feet start to ache from the walking, but I ignore them. I pull the flip phone from my pocket, and it tells me that it is almost one o'clock in the afternoon. That's when I feel the first raindrop on my neck.

The air smells wet, and the breeze shakes the tree branches. I check my compass against my map and assure myself that I am heading in the right direction. Then a heavy gust of wind blows the paper from my hand. I panic. *No, no, no!* I chase after it and snatch it out of the air before it gets too high.

I breathe a sigh of relief and continue my walk. A few minutes later, though, it starts to really rain. First, little drops of water fall from the sky, and I absently wipe them from my face and neck. Soon, the drops get larger and come faster, in shorter intervals. I pick up my pace. A clap of thunder echoes through the sky, and the rain starts beating down. I take my jacket off and use it to cover my head and backpack. Water streams down my face, and my shoes fill with it. *Keep going,* I tell myself. *It's just a bit of water.*

I trudge on through the mud, my feet getting colder every step. Thunder roars and lightning lights up the sky. I wipe the water from my eyes and gasp. A raging river winds across the horizon, as far as I can see. *There was never a river in this direction!* I think. I pull the map from my pocket and peer closer at the route I had traced. A faded blue line winds across the map. I mutter a curse word under my breath. I tuck the map back into my pocket and groan. I'll have to cross it.

I walk tentatively to the riverbank and with a deep breath, wade into the water. I gasp as the freezing water hits my skin. The current is stronger than I expect, and it almost sweeps me away. I regain my balance and trudge through the waist-deep water. The cold chills me to the bone and I shiver uncontrollably. On the other side, I stand shivering and dripping, the sky only growing darker. I search the trees for a dry enough space to stop. A giant spruce tree a few hundred feet from the river catches my attention. I half-jog to it and take shelter under the boughs of the spruce. It pretty much keeps the rain out, and luckily the rain starts slowing down. I take my backpack off and unzip it. I search around the base of the tree for dry twigs to start a fire. Once I collected enough, I pile them up and strike a match. The twigs glow red but go out. I try again, and it works. I find a few dry sticks and logs and pile them up to feed the fire.

When I get the fire going steady, I undress and change into my spare pair of pants and shirt. I pull on my fuzzy sweater and put my waterproof jacket on the ground to keep myself dry. I sit down and hug my knees to my chest, the fire warming me. I check the time—6:35 p.m.—and lie down. I drift off into restless sleep, pictures of the man and Luke playing on repeat in my mind.

* * * *

I awake to the sound of birds chirping and the roar of the river behind me. The air is warmer, though the ground is still muddy. My stomach growls, and I realize that I had barely eaten anything yesterday, besides some trail mix. I eat the sleeve of crackers and take a few globs of peanut butter before packing up. I stomp out the fire and zip up my bag. I walk through more and more trees, the same almost monotonous scene. Hours later, I stop to rest my aching legs and to make sure I'm heading in the right direction. I pull my compass from my jacket pocket and fish around in my pants pocket for the map. What I pull out, though, is a pile of soggy scraps.

It got wet! It's ruined! Tears make my vision blur, and I angrily throw the shredded paper as far as I can. It gets picked up by the wind and blows off into the distance. I sit down on a rock and cry because my map is ruined and from my pent-up anxiety and worry alike. I take a shuddering breath and think a terrible thought. *I'm never going to find Luke. My closest friend for six years, and the only person that can comfort me is going to die... because of me.*

I take a deep breath and shake that thought from my head. *Just think, Julia.* I look around me. A gigantic cottonwood tree sits a couple hundred yards from me. I stand up and make my way towards it. When I reach it, I drop my backpack and climb its branches until I can't any more. I peer out over the landscape, the pattern of pine trees with rivers and streams meandering through them. One particularly large river catches my eye, and it somehow soothes me.

Rivers lead to civilization.

I carefully climb down and don my backpack, heading toward what I had seen. As I get nearer, the sound of rushing water fills my ears. I come to a clearing. A waterfall flows over a steep drop and into the river below. Next to it, on the right side, sits a curious-looking cave. I walk slowly toward the mouth of the cave and peer inside of it.

I throw a rock into it to see if it is inhabited. Nothing responds. I take my flashlight and step into the cave. A soft dripping noise echoes off the walls and puddles collect on the rock floor.

"Hello?" I call.

A cough from farther inside makes me jump backwards and nearly fall. "Who's there?" I shout. "Show yourself."

"Julia?"

I hold my breath, my brain not wanting to believe what I had just heard. "Luke?" I run into the cave, shining my flashlight over all the walls. The beam falls upon a single figure in a metal chair in the center of the cave. The boy looks up, and I immediately recognize his messed-up hair and tired facial features. An expression of total disbelief fills his face.

"Luke!" I run toward him, and wrap my arms around his neck. Ropes bind his hands and feet and a rope wraps around his middle and the chair. I pull my pocketknife from my pants and start sawing. "I thought I would never find you! Are you okay, Luke?"

"Julia. You need to leave." Luke's face is gravely serious with a hint of fear in his eyes.

"L-Luke, I can't. I'm not leaving you!"

"Julia! You need to leave! JULIA!"

A rag covers my mouth. The pocket knife slips from my grasp and clatters to the floor.

The world goes dark before I can react.

* * * *

I bolt upright, my heart pounding.

Where am I?

I search frantically around. The smooth rocks under my hands are slick and wet, and rushing water roars in my ears.

The waterfall.

I stand up, slipping on the rocks. "Who are you? Come out!"

"There's no need to get all worked up about this." The man's deep voice sounds from my left side.

I whip around. He is tall, with broad shoulders and a menacing face. His hazel eyes glint evilly, and his red hair glows in the light. *The man in the woods.* The man strides in front of me, his features smug and calculating. "Julia West. Daughter of Lucy and Charles West."

"How do you know me? Who are you?"

"You don't know me? I'm Joseph Gray. I'm actually a bit surprised that Lucy didn't mention me to you." He paces back and forth.

"Why should I know you?" I growl.

"You shouldn't! But that is why I brought you here. Your mother... Lucy. She is my true love."

"What are you talking about? My mother does not love you! She loves my father and no one else!"

"Oh, my dear child. Must I explain to you everything?" Joseph looks me over and chuckles. "Alright. I guess I must.

"Lucy and I were high school sweethearts, and I swore I was going to marry her one day. I loved her—do love her—more than anything. On our second year of college, though, some new kid messed everything up. Can you guess what his name was?"

"Charles West," I mutter.

"Lucy and I were perfect. And Charles ruined that. He *ruined my life.* He won Lucy over with lies and false love. No one deserved her except me. Your father stole my true love, and he paid for it...Do you understand what I am saying?" he asks slyly.

"No," I breathe. "It can't be true."

"Oh, but it is. It took me a while to find him, but eventually I did. The day after you were born, I found your house. Your father was vulnerable, an open target. All I had to do was pull the trigger. But Lucy was there. I wouldn't do that to her. So I kept planning. It was years later, seven to be exact, that the time was right. He was alone at work. I took out the security cameras and tortured him. His last words were, "Don't hurt my family." Then I shot him in the head and placed the gun in his hand. Everyone believed it."

I sob, tears running down my cheeks, my body shaking. "You are a monster! My father did nothing!"

"HE DID EVERYTHING!"

"Why are you telling me this?"

"Because you, my dear, are going to suffer the same fate your father did. Death."

"Why me? I never did anything!"

"You are the only thing keeping me from Lucy. She loses her daughter, I swoop in and save her from her grief and everything is the way it should've been." Joseph grins. "Now let's go. Tick, tock!"

He grabs me by the arm, and I try to wrestle away from him. "NO! Stop!"

Joseph pushes harder. The rushing noise of the water below makes my heart hammer, and my feet skid against the wet platform of rocks I stand on. Joseph's strong arms push me closer and closer to the edge. Tears stream down my face, and my chest heaves.

"If you kill me, you kill Lucy!" I sob.

Joseph stops for a second. His eyes scan me, full of curiosity. I spot Joseph's vulnerability and continue to speak.

"When my father died, she didn't speak to anyone for weeks. If you kill me, my mother will never open up to anyone again, especially you! Please! You don't want to do this. Just let me go."

"You're a liar," Joseph snarls. "A LIAR!"

He pushes me nearer to the edge of the waterfall and my feet slip on the rocks. I can see the hatred and bloodthirst in his eyes.

Joseph gets me a few feet from the drop off. I cry, trying to fight him away, but he is much stronger than I am.

Just as he goes to take the final shove, he releases his grip on me and whips around. "You idiot!" he screams. He puts his hand on the back of his head, and it comes back covered in blood. Luke stands on the rocks behind him. His arm is poised from the throw, another rock in his left hand.

"I have waited fourteen years for this moment," Joseph snarls. "I will not have it ruined by a rock-throwing *child*."

Time slows down. Joseph clenches his fist and pulls his arm back. He takes a long stride forward, towards Luke. I see Luke's eyes flash with fear as he tries to take a step backwards.

"Luke! Watch out!" I yell, but I'm too late. Joseph strikes him in the head with a force that makes him crumple. I scream. Joseph lets out a guttural laugh, and adrenaline and anger like I had never felt before courses through me.

Before Joseph can turn around to face me, I quickly duck underneath his arm so he is closer to the edge. I slam into him, and he wavers for a second.

"Don't do this!" I shout.

Joseph takes a swing at me. His fist hits me in the face, and a sharp pain fills my head. I double over, but quickly regain my strength.

"You are killing Lucy, and you know it! *You* are the liar!"

Joseph's eyes flash with anger, and he takes a swipe at me. He misses, and I ram my body into him. He opens his mouth in surprise and tries to regain his balance for a moment.

Anger surges within me. "This is for my father." I shove him.

His feet slip a few inches backwards, less than a foot away from the edge.

"This is for my mother." I ram into him again.

His arms waver, trying to keep his balance.

"This is for Luke," I shove him again.

His feet slip on the rocks, and I see the fear in his eyes.

"And *this* is for *me*!" I give him a final shove.

His foot slips, and he falls, arms flailing, a look of utter disbelief on his face. Joseph lands with a crack on the jagged rocks in the river below.

I turn around and run towards Luke's side. I get down on my knees where his lifeless body is, and take his head in my hands. "Luke. Luke, wake up!" He stays still. Blood trickles from a gash in his head. I cry, caressing his face, tears streaming freely down my cheeks.

"No, no, no. Please. Luke, I'm sorry. I'm sorry," I whisper. I go to stand up, wiping tears from my eyes. "No. Luke. Please don't do this. Please." I slowly back away, tears blurring my vision. I turn back toward the cave.

I hear a gasping breath from behind me and a loud cough. I turn around. Luke opens his eyes and stands. I shout out in joy and run into his arms. He pulls me close, and I kiss him. When we pull apart, Luke flashes me a smile that makes my heart flutter.

"Luke! You saved my life," I say.

"You saved mine first. Besides, I couldn't leave you. I love you, Julia." Luke smiles. My heart soars, and I hug him tight, whispering, "I love you too," into his ear.

I feel him smile. I put my head on this shoulder, and he puts his on top of mine. I grin. "How did you get out of the cave?" I ask at last.

"Your pocketknife that fell? I used that to saw my way out." Luke rubs his brow. "Um, I missed a lot. Can you fill me in on what happened?"

"Yeah, sure. Let's call for help first."

* * * *

Luke and I enter the police station, my mother trailing behind us. It is a day after we had been rescued. Blurry memories of the day before flash through my mind: the sound of Joseph's body hitting the water below me; a medical helicopter taking us home; Luke and I getting our wounds dressed; my mother's sobbing as the police car pulled up into the driveway; the frenzied hugging and scolding that ensued. Luke and I take a seat in the wooden chairs on the opposite side of a desk, my mother next to us. A police officer enters the room and shakes our hands. He introduces himself as Officer Owens. After sitting down at the desk, he motions for Luke to start. Luke clears his throat and tells the officer about his kidnapping. He tells of the strange noises that started at midnight of the night of his disappearance, how Joseph had cut the screen on his window and quietly entered. He tells how he was held at gunpoint and forced to jump out the window to the ground below, where he was knocked out. He tells us of the cold, damp cave where he had regained consciousness. He tells us that he had been tied to a chair for ten days, given barely any food and frequent beatings. He tells us about how he had cut himself from the bindings using my pocketknife. He explains how, when he had seen Joseph trying to kill me, he threw a rock at Joseph's head to distract him, but it ended up resulting in Joseph lashing out and knocking him unconscious. I look over at Luke and my heart weighs down with the sadness and torture he had gone through. *It was all because of me. He was bait in a despicable man's scheme to get revenge for something that made entirely no sense. I had almost gotten Luke killed.*

I swallow hard, and Luke looks at me sympathetically. "Hey," he whispers. "It's not your fault, Julia."

"Thank you, Mr. Fields," Officer Owens tells Luke. He gestures to me and I begin.

I tell him them about my father's murder, how my father had been tortured by a man named Joseph Gray before being shot in the head. I look at my mother across the room. Tears stream down her face. A lump forms in my throat, and I try to compose myself. After a few deep breaths, I tell them about the strange figure in the woods and how he had stared at me, his hazel eyes glowing through the trees. Then I tell them about the message Luke had tried to send me, and about his trashed room. I tell them about Luke's disappearance and all that had happened afterward. "The day Luke disappeared, there was an envelope near the pond by my house. Inside it was a piece of paper with a bunch of numbers on it. I got a letter everyday for ten days. On the tenth day, there was a different note inside it. It said, 'Use the coordinates. Come alone or he dies.' Then it hit me; they were coordinates all along. I typed them into my computer, and the dots traced a route through the forest. I decided not to tell the police." I look up at Officer Owens, "I knew that if the cops got involved, he would kill Luke. So the next morning I snuck out and hiked across Fairbanks. It took me about two days before I stumbled upon the cave where Luke was being held." Then I tell them how Joseph knocked me out, and how I had awoken on the banks of the waterfall. I tell them about the fight between Joseph and I, and how I had pushed him over the waterfall.

Officer Owens thanks us for our time and shakes our hands. "We'll catch Joseph Gray. Just be careful, kids." And with that we leave the building.

The three of us walk to the car as a police cruiser, lights flashing, siren wailing, pulls into the parking lot. The officer hops out. Officer Owens exits the police station and jogs to meet the other officer. They start talking. I slow down and listen.

"I found him on some riverbank in Fairbanks," the first officer, Officer Smith begins. "He was soaking wet and screaming something about a girl named Julia."

My breath catches in my throat, and I see Officer Owens tense.

"When I told him that we should go to the police station, he put up a fight, and pulled a knife from his belt. I had to Taser him to get him to settle down. I'm going inside to question him."

Officer Smith rounds the car and opens the back door. He yanks a man out, a man with red hair and glowing hazel eyes. I grab Luke's hand and gasp. Joseph smiles at us.

"Hello, Lucy," he says slyly.

"You have the right to remain silent," Officer Smith barks.

Officer Owens looks wide-eyed at me. "Is this him?" he mouths.

I nod.

Officer Smith pushes him toward the door of the police station, but Joseph fights back, positioning himself to face us.

"You will never escape, you know," he shouts. "I'll be back!"

"No, you won't," I say, and I truly believe it. As I look at him, I realize that he looks vulnerable. "You don't scare me. I'm stronger than you think."

Joseph's eyes narrow.

I look at him defiantly. "You failed."

Joseph clenches his fists and fights against the police, anger surging through him.

I take my mother's and Luke's hands. I look at each of them, a smile spreading on my face. Then I turn back to Joseph. A spark ignites in my heart, and I feel a newfound power. With unwavering confidence, I say these words, the truest words I could say: "You will never hurt my family ever again."

And he never did.

A Head of Chaos

By

Sarah Bjornstad

Chapter One

There was something unexplainably therapeutic about lying on the floor. When I looked at the ceiling and that was all I could see, it was like everything else went away: all the things I didn't want to think about, all my worries, everything that hurt. I could pretend that there weren't ten family members who wanted to talk to me downstairs in my living room. I supposed that people wanted to see me since I had disappeared for four months.

The clock on my dresser chimed ten times, informing me that it was ten o'clock at night. I felt slightly guilty for having left my parents the task of shooing away my relatives, so I decided to at least go down and help with the dishes.

I sat up from the floor and pain like a sharp knife stabbed at my head. I closed my eyes and decided that it must have been the blood rushing quickly to my head. I then got to my feet and started moving forward. The pain only increased as I walked down the stairs and into the kitchen where my mother stood in front of the sink. Her beautiful face turned to me with an expression of concern etched on her features.

"Leah, are you okay?" She dried her hands on a towel and walked quickly towards me.

I only then realized that I had been leaning on the doorframe for support. Without warning the pain became too much and the world went black.

* * * *

Sterile white walls and an antiseptic smell greeted me when I opened my eyes. I sat up and surveyed my surroundings. A hospital! *This is exactly where I want to be considering the fact that I just got out of one* two days ago! I thought to myself. My mother sat by my side and gently explained that I had been in the hospital for a few hours. Before she could say more, several hospital staff in white coats entered and helped me in a wheelchair. Less than an hour later, the tests began.

The doctors had no idea what was wrong with me, so they wanted to take an MRI. I sighed when I heard the news, knowing that it would be a long night. I got to the testing room and lay in the tube perfectly still when I really wanted to be run and be free. I wanted to run until my legs gave out and then run some more. I wanted to run because running made me feel like I could do something––like I wasn't just a pain in the neck to my parents. I wasn't all that I wanted to be and I knew it. So, I just lay there, waiting for them to release me.

After fifty minutes I was taken out of the machine. "Well Ms. Thomas, I have good news," Dr. Makrie said. "You have what is apparently a microchip lodged in one of your sinus cavities. It looks to be almost exactly like the ones that they use for animals." Dr. Makrie looked as confused as I did, but he was familiar with my history, so he knew better than to ask any questions.

"I'm sorry, *what*? How is that a good thing?" I asked. I couldn't seem to control my attitude, but I didn't care. I had been in and out of hospitals for the past week, and I was exhausted.

"It's a good thing because it's an easy fix. We can get it out today."

My father, who had just joined us a few minutes ago, let out a sigh of relief. After that I stopped listening. I was tired, and my head hurt. All I wanted to do was lay in bed with a pillow and cry. I ignored the conversation around me until a tall woman in green hospital scrubs entered the room.

"Ms. Thomas, Jeanine here is going to prep you for your procedure."

Dr. Makrie said. I nodded and the nurse stepped forward as he stepped out of the room. My mother grabbed her wallet and sweater then turned to me.

"Sweetie we're going to go to the cafeteria to get a cup of coffee but we'll meet you outside of the operating room, okay?" I nodded and attempted a reassuring smile as she left the room.

* * * *

I had had enough drugs that week to last me a year, so I opted for the no-drug procedure.

No pain killers to nauseate me, and no anesthesia to put me under. I just laid on the operating table, my head immobilized. I felt the utensil they were sticking into my nasal cavities as Dr. Makrie poked and prodded, trying to loosen the microchip. Finally, I felt the pressure that had slowly been building in my head release. He grasped the microchip and pulled it out slowly and carefully. I closed my eyes and sighed in relief. My head still hurt, but the pain was nothing in comparison with what it had been before.

The time until I got home passed in a blur––the amazement at the chip that had been removed, questions from the police, heavy discussions about things I couldn't remember, and all the details needed for my discharge from the hospital––and I suddenly found myself on my porch, two steps ahead of my parents. As I ran up the stairs to my bedroom, I held the chip in my hand. When I opened the door, a gust of cold air rushed out. Sitting before me on the bed was a short Latina with long black hair. The Latina, Kristin, had been my best friend since I was five years old. An anxious look took the place of her usually gorgeous features.

"So," she said hesitantly, "how was the hospital?"

I plopped down on my bed and inhaled slowly before responding. "Like hospitals always are, I guess: clean, white, creepy, and bad news." I gave her a side-glance. "But that wasn't what you were asking about, was it?"

She smiled and shook her head. Kristin was the nicest person I had ever met. She was understanding, kind, caring, trustworthy, and overall just a good person, so I knew that anything I told her would stay a secret if I wanted it to be. I told her what I didn't dare tell anyone else, "It was scary. It was absolutely terrifying. Being told that something is lodged in your sinus cavities, something so close to your brain, and not knowing where it came from was *terrifying*." I shook my head and almost started to cry. "I have no idea what is on this chip, and I'm not sure that I want to. All I know is that whatever is on here can't be good."

Kristin enveloped me in a hug, and we sat there in silence for a long time.

Finally, she said, "Leah, I know you're scared, but I think you need to make a decision. You either scan the chip and face what's on it, or get that thing as far away from you as possible." She looked at me and smiled faintly. "If you need anything, just come to my house." Then she left.

* * * *

I spent the next few hours in bed, contemplating whether I even wanted to see what was on the chip. But deep down I always knew what my decision would be, I just didn't want to accept it. At 1:52 in the morning, I made my choice. I was going to scan the chip and find out what was on it. I had been afraid, until then, to take this step toward uncovering the truth of what happened during the last four months. The information on the chip had to have been about my past, otherwise why would it have been stuck in one of my *nasal cavities*? I was still scared, but I knew that I would never rest easily until I found out what had happened. Being only seventeen and the victim of a crime that I couldn't even *remember* was almost too much to bear. My parents had asked the police to let me keep the chip and they had complied. They knew that I needed answers and I needed them soon.

Chapter Two

The time had come. I was going to put the chip in a reader, and I was going to find out what had happened to me. I had spent the day waiting for Kristin to message me back on my phone, to tell me that she was on her way with the chip reader. I had shared my decision with her in the morning so that she would have time to get the reader. I would have bought it myself, but that would have meant my parents going with me and therefore reading it with me. It wasn't that I didn't love my parents and respect their right to know about what happened to their daughter, it was just that I wanted to find out when I was alone so that I would have time to process it before I told them. I also wanted them to find out in the easiest and least alarming way possible.

Ten minutes later, at 9:30 P.M., a quick tap on my window let me know that Kristin had arrived. I quickly walked to the window and opened it to let her in. A moist breeze came with Kristin as she hopped from the tree that stood between our houses into my room.

She smiled at me and simply asked, "Are you ready?"

I sighed. "As ready as I'll ever be, I suppose."

with that, we sat down at my desk and started. Now, Kristin is an actual genius (146 I.Q.), so I, as a person with an average intellect, had very little idea as to what she was doing as she assembled the pieces. Her hands moved lightning fast, and she finished within two minutes. She then put the chip into the reader and the reader into my laptop. We waited in tense silence as it slowly inched its way to 100% loaded. A small window appeared on the screen, and Kristin shakily stood up.

"This is where I leave," she said. I also stood, confused. "Wait, what? Why are you leaving? I need you!"

"No, you don't. I've done my part, but now you have to do the rest on your own. I'm not leaving because I need to. I'm leaving because you need me to."

I knew what she meant. I wanted to figure this out for myself, without anyone else to distract me, so I nodded. "Okay, but when I'm done with this, I'm calling you."

She laughed softly. "I wouldn't have it any other way." Then she walked to the window and climbed out.

I sat back down at my desk and clicked on the file. Another page popped up with a video of myself and a boy who must have been around my age. The boy looked kind of nerdy but not unattractive, while I looked tired but determined. We were sitting at a desk, frozen on the screen. I took a deep breath, and clicked play.

"Hello Leah," the boy began, "My name is Owen."

"And I'm, well, you." Past-me said. I studied her as she talked. The way her light brown hair fell across her shoulders just as mine did and how her brown eyes flickered between the camera and Owen. Everything about her was exactly the same as me; her mannerisms, her voice. Everything was the same but I felt as though I was looking at a different person. I had absolutely no recollection of making this video and it was almost supernatural watching myself talk. I was totally freaked-out, but I continued watching.

"We know that you're scared and confused, but we're going to help you and clarify what happened to you over the last four months. So, here's the short version of what happened," Owen began to explain.

"The last thing you will have remembered is walking to Kristin's house, so that's where we'll start. A man from an organization called The Nameless was sent to kidnap you while you were on your way there. You were then taken to The Nameless H.Q. where you were experimented on when you were there."

I slammed the pause button. I was experimented on? What? What did that mean? How was I experimented on? I was afraid to know, but at the same time, I couldn't not find out. My mind raced with a million questions, and the only thing that could answer them was this video. I pressed play.

"You were experimented on by me, but it's okay!" He looked at Past-Me and smiled. "We're friends now. I was experimenting on you with a chip designed to control a person's actions, but every time I inserted it into your brain, it would malfunction after only a few hours of positive reaction."

"Every time he would take the chip out to improve it," Past-Me started, "I/you/we would be conscious. I would talk to him, and slowly I penetrated his wall of steel." Past-Me smiled at Owen and laughed.

Owen just smiled faintly. "Anyway, every time I took the chip out, it became harder to put it back in. Finally, I just couldn't. I knew what I was doing, working for The Nameless, was wrong before I met you, but I did it anyway. One day after lunch, I walked into the room in which you were being held. You were in your chair strapped down and completely powerless," He smiled. "But that didn't stop you from reprimanding me. You told me how wrong I was to be working with the Nameless and set me straight. You then proceeded to demand that I let you go: you, the person who was constrained, who was in no place to be demanding anything.

"But I knew that you were right, and so we made a plan to get you out. We won't go into detail now, but if you're watching this, then our plan worked."

He turned to Past-Me, and I started to talk. "So that's what happened. Remember, Owen is a friend. One more thing—"

In the background there were footsteps, and Owen and Past-Me immediately jumped to their feet. "We have to go," Past-Me said hurriedly, "but good luck." Then the screen turned black. I sat there in shock, attempting to process the immense amount of information that had just been thrust upon me. It was unreal. I didn't want to believe it, but that was undeniably me in the video. There was no possible way that this could be a prank.

"I have to tell Kristen. And tomorrow, Mom and Dad," I said under my breath. I took out my phone and found Kristin in my contacts. I held the phone up to my ear. When she answered, I told her everything, down to the smallest detail. I was in shock, so it helped to talk it through with someone else. When we finished talking, I understood things even more clearly. I was exhausted and emotionally worn out, so I went to bed. Everything else would wait until the morning.

* * * *

Ever since I had gotten home a week ago, I had become an exceptionally light sleeper, so when a creak came from somewhere close to my bed, I awoke immediately. I opened my eyes slowly, afraid of what I might see. I looked around, but at first glance, there was nothing to see. I was unconvinced so I looked again and saw a figure in the shadows. I bolted upright and the figure quickly moved to my side. I tried to scream, but the man (he had a man's physique) covered my mouth with one hand and turned on my bedside lamp with another.

"Leah! Leah, my name is Owen. I was—"

I recognized him in the light of the lamp so I pulled away from his hand and said, "I know who you are." I stood up quickly, disliking the feeling of his almost unnaturally tall shadow looming over me. I was also both uncomfortable and grateful for my loose-fitting pajama pants and t-shirt. They weren't exactly what you want to be wearing in front of a stranger, but they didn't hinder my movement, so I had no trouble climbing over my bed to put something between us.

"So," he said, "I know that you don't remember me, but I do know that you saw what was on the chip."

"Yeah, I did."

We stood in awkward silence for a moment until I said, "So, Owen, what brings you to my bedroom at," I glanced at my clock, "2:57 A.M.?"

He laughed and ran a hand through his black hair. "Yeah, funny story, I kind of decided to take a trip to the suburbs of Minneapolis and got lost and just, sort of, ended up here," he said in a half-hearted attempt at a joke. In a serious tone he said, "Leah, I actually came because I need your help. The Nameless sent me here to kidnap you and bring you back to them."

I raised an eyebrow, but he held up his hands.

"I'm playing double agent here! I know that there are probably a bunch of questions that you want answered, and I completely understand, but I can only answer what must be one of many of them right now. And that is 'what are we stopping them from doing?'" He pulled out my desk chair and sat down, while I sat on my bed. I was already slightly annoyed that he hadn't let me talk at all, but I kept quiet and let him finish.

"The Nameless wants to get control of NATO's (North Atlantic Treaty Organization) shared nuclear missiles to start World War III," I rolled my eyes.

"I know what NATO is," I muttered, crossing my arms defensively. He waved his hand dismissing my comment. "They think that power can somehow be derived from chaos. I was making a prototype and experimenting on you for a chip that would control humans. They were going to use it to create more destruction by killing millions of innocent people. That's why we're going to stop them."

For some reason, I believed every word he said without a question or a doubt. But, one thing still confused me. "Why did you do it? Why were you working for them?'

A look of both guilt and relief entered his green eyes as I asked the question, as if he knew it had been coming but wanted, and didn't want, to answer it at the same time.

"The director of the organization...she's my mother."

Chapter Three

Well this is slightly awkward, I thought to myself as I stared at him. His mother was the one in charge of a terrorist organization? Suddenly, the thought of what he must feel occurred to me, and I stared at my hands. "I see...so what happens next?" I could tell he was glad that I hadn't freaked out on him.

"Next, you and I get plane tickets to Toronto."

"So, tell me again why *I* have to do this? I mean, there must be plenty of others who could help you more efficiently than I." He shook his head sadly.

"You would think so, right? But there aren't. The only people I know are bad ones who don't give a crap about anyone but themselves. You're the only person I can trust and by doing this we can save hundreds of thousands of lives. So, will you help me? Please?" I sat there for a moment then nodded. How could I say no?

* * * *

We spoke very little as we sat in the car. Owen parked in a nearby church parking lot and bought plane tickets for us.

"Why didn't you buy these when you were at the place you work?" Just thinking the name of "them" much less saying it aloud disgusted me.

Without pausing Owen said, "I didn't want to assume that you wouldn't struggle and cause trouble."

I must have looked surprised because he added, "I mean, if someone walked into my room in the middle of the night and kidnapped me, I probably wouldn't want to go anywhere with them."

He had a good point, so I sat back in my seat in silence. I wondered how he was getting the Wi-Fi to buy the plane tickets since he was using the internet, but I just assumed he had hooked onto the church's Wi-Fi and was using that. Eventually he closed his laptop and started driving to what I assumed was the airport. I couldn't stop thinking about my parents. I felt awful leaving them without a note or anything. I knew that having their seventeen-year-old daughter run away *again* would break their hearts. When we arrived at the airport Owen handed me a passport with a name that wasn't mine on it and a fake I.D. He also handed me a backpack that had a laptop, a change of clothes, and a toothbrush in it. I looked at him, confused.

"Traveling without anything would look suspicious."

"Oh, good thinking," I said. As we went through security I felt my heart racing. I was convinced that someone was going to figure out who we were and arrest us.

Owen stepped closer to me and said as casually as if he were talking about the weather, "Leah, you're looking over your shoulder every seventeen seconds. You need to calm down. We're going to be fine. You just need to trust me and relax."

I nodded and swallowed. We got through security without a problem. When we got to the gate we were just in time to board the plane. Since Owen had bought the plane tickets so late, we had to sit on almost opposite sides of the plane. I, thankfully, had a window seat. I loved window seats because they're the best to sleep on, which is what I did. At the end of the flight, Owen and I met at the gate.

"You okay? Did you see anything suspicious on the way out?"

I shook my head. "No, everything was fine. I didn't see anything."

We then made our way out of the airport and hurried to find a rental car. We rented a comfortable and nondescript black Sedan.

"Did they provide you with the credit card and fake I.D.?"

He nodded but didn't say anything. We drove for two hours on the highway with nothing but forest around us. The trees, beginning to change colors, looked gorgeous, and we kept the windows down—partly because it was a beautiful day but mostly because it filled the silence. After four hours of driving north, passing through Ottawa and a few other cities, we finally stopped at a small house outside of a town called Cheneville, Quebec. It was obviously old as the paint was chipped and dirty, but all of that gave it character. It looked like a home that an older couple would live in.

"This is one of The Nameless' safe houses," Owen said as he pulled into the driveway. Inside was not as beautiful. As I walked through the doors, I saw dust floating through the air and landing on all the furniture. The first floor was scarcely furnished, and as I explored the basement in which the rooms were, I saw guns, ammunition, and hand grenades under every bed and in every cupboard. There were two rooms upstairs; the dining room and the kitchen. The kitchen was the only place that was normal. It had regular appliances, and although everything was painted orange, it wasn't the worst place to be. It had old saltine crackers and canned soup, as well as other canned goods and some dry milk. Downstairs there was one small main room and three tiny bedrooms.

"Well this is quite, uh.... cozy," I said to Owen when I came back from exploring the downstairs.

"It's small, but easily defendable, and it's pretty unnoticeable."

I nodded and leaned against a chair. "So, have you been here before?"

He froze knowing that I had actually asked if he had done a job before. He knew I was asking if it was "wet work," a job that involved spilling blood.

"Yes." He turned and walked into the kitchen, and I knew that the conversation was over.

"There's a room upstairs, first on the left. You can sleep there, but we have to leave early tomorrow morning," Owen stated.

"Okay then," I said. "Thanks."

This was probably the most he had said to me since we were at my house. I actually felt badly for him. He and I had been friends, so I figured that it must be hard —me not knowing him. I went up the stairs and into the bedroom. There was a pair of soft pants and a t-shirt for what I assumed were sleeping apparel. I slipped into the pajamas and got under the covers slowly. They were surprisingly warm and soft. It reminded me of home, and I was thankful for that more than anything. As soon as my head hit the pillow, I was out.

* * * *

"So, what's the plan?" We had only been driving on the highway forty-five minutes, but I couldn't wait any longer. It was six-forty in the morning, and the sun had just risen. Its rays went in and out between the trees, making a pattern on Owen's face. He didn't look surprised.

"Well, we obviously can't do this by ourselves, so I think we should bring in the authorities."

I raised my eyebrows, taken aback. "How is that a good idea?" I asked. "Aren't we kind of the bad guys?

"Let me finish. We call the authorities before we go into H.Q. We tell them that there are ten hostages in the building. You'll be one of the "hostages," and I'll be the captor. I demand money, say that I have weapons, and that I'll kill you if they don't bring fifty grand, or something like that. We'll go inside and then tell the authorities that our captor is releasing two people to show them that he doesn't want to hurt anyone.

Then we get away. When the authorities go into the building, they'll find The Nameless. They may not get every member today, but at least they will be aware of their existence."

Chapter Four

It was happening. It was actually happening. We were thirty feet from the warehouse that held The Nameless H.Q. Owen just finished his call to the police, and we knew they were on their way. He informed me of secret passageways he had created in the warehouse after its construction.

"There are security cameras everywhere, so we will have to be extra careful entering the building." He turned to face me. "Ready?"

My throat constricted when I tried to speak, so I just nodded. He grabbed my arm as a captor would his captive and walked so quickly into the open that he practically dragged me behind him. A guard instantly saw us as we turned a bend. He raised his gun but lowered it once he recognized Owen. He talked into his walkie-talkie, letting whoever was in charge know that we had arrived. The guard opened a door.

We saw another couple of guards, and Owen said, "Tell my mother that I'm going to bring the girl to my studio and then come to see her."

The guards nodded, obviously intimidated by the reminder that his mother was not only their boss––but also the woman who could have them killed in an instant. My heart was in my chest every time we passed another guard, but after many twists and turns, we made it safely to his "studio." I could see why Owen liked the location; it was hard to get to and would discourage many visitors.

Once we were in the room, I looked around. The walls were bare, but there was a table and two seats. The table was littered with tools of all sorts and computers. If that wasn't creepy enough, the chairs went above and beyond. One chair was a simple desk chair, but the other was like the chair that you sit in at the dentist office, except this one had straps. I knew it had been the chair I was in for most of my stay. Owen saw me looking at it and quickly turned away. He grabbed a tool, went to a wall and loosened a screw. One, two more, and there was a door in the wall. Suddenly a loud screaming noise tortured my ears and made them feel like blood dripped from them.

"Come on," he said as he ushered me into a narrow corridor. "Three, two, one..."

"What in the world?" I shouted, trying to be heard over the noise.

"They've spotted the police on the road. This is their alarm." He took out his phone and started to work. He had pre-recorded the message about sending two hostages out to show that he "didn't want to hurt anyone."

"I'm hacking into the police chief's phone and sending it to him," Owen said absently.

I was terrified that someone was going to find us. Finally, Owen put his phone away, and he led me to another door in the wall. He pressed his ear to it, and I knew he was listening for the police outside.

"They're here," he said. "Just one last thing. I need you to punch me."

My head snapped up to look at him, to see if he was joking. But he wasn't. "You want to me punch you to make it look more believable?"

He nodded.

"You're an idiot, you know that, right?"

He smiled and then kind of crouched down so that I could reach him.

I took a deep breath and then punched him in the face as hard as I could. He grimaced but didn't make a sound; whereas, I doubled over and yelled, "Ow, ow, ow! Ouch, that was painful!" I continued saying this for at least thirty seconds until I realized that we had to go. I looked at Owen and smiled. "I'm fine, thanks for asking."

He chuckled and said, "Let's go."

* * * *

Now that I look back on it, I can't remember much about what happened next. We walked out of the warehouse, and the police immediately grabbed us and took us to the ambulance as we both were in obvious pain. Owen exaggerated his pain for emphasis. An EMT immediately came to us and a police officer with her.

"Are you two okay?" She looked at Owen. "That looks pretty painful young man——let me take a look."

The police officer stepped forward and looked at us. "I'm going to need to take you two for quest——"

A very, very loud sound that made me want to close my eyes and pretend that I was back in my bedroom with the covers pulled up to my chest shook the earth. Everyone turned to look at the building, and Owen grabbed my arm and pulled me to my feet. He started to sprint into the tree line hauling me with him.

I still couldn't hear anything after five minutes of running. Even if there had been people yelling and chasing after us, I wouldn't have stopped. Owen was on my heels forcing me to move faster lest he run into me. Finally, we broke through the edge of the tree line and stopped at a random car. Owen immediately produced a set of keys out of thin air. I knew better than to ask him how. When we got into the car, Owen started driving as fast as he could. Only then did I ask the question that had been burning in my mind since we had started running.

"What was that?!" I half-asked, half-yelled.

"It was an explosive. I knew that they wouldn't have let us go easily, that we would have to go to the police station and answer questions and tell them a story that didn't happen. I wanted to skip that part because—no offense—you're a terrible liar. To avoid that I did the easiest thing possible; I used a distraction."

I shook my head in disbelief and started to ask him another question, but one look at his face told me that the conversation was over. We drove for another two hours into the city until we came to Quebec International Airport.

Owen handed me a plane ticket, a wallet full of cash, an I.D., and another backpack. "It's safer for us to split up," he said.

"So, you're not coming with me?' I asked.

He shook his head.

"But what are you going to do, what—"

"I'll be fine Leah. I'll start a new life somewhere else," he gave a little laugh, "one that doesn't involve working for a terrorist organization. I promise."

I smiled and nodded slowly, understanding his choice. "I have just one more question for you," I said. "Why me? Why did they choose me?"

He swallowed, took a deep breath, and answered, "Because you were normal. You weren't amazingly smart or important. No one would look too hard for you. But I know now that that wasn't true. You're brave, smart, and morally upright. I'm happy to have known you."

I was taken aback, but somehow, I managed to reply. "Thank you, Owen," I said, and I meant it.

Then I got out of the car and onto the walkway through the doors of the airport without looking back. Behind me I heard the car drive away. I got onto the escalator surrounded by people going on with their everyday lives. They were probably making business trips, taking vacations, and visiting family. Family––that's where I was going––back to my family and back home. And I was more excited than ever before.

Ring! Ring!

By

Pichapob Kangram

The sound from a bicycle ringtone rang through the woods and echoed out twenty kilometers. A teenager rode his bicycle on a dirt path in the woods of the Glendale District in Los Angeles, Southern California.

The rider, Jackson Dimes, attended Theodore Roosevelt middle school. He had brown smooth hair and brown eyes and would be 175 centimeters tall if he stood. Right now, he wore a red jean jacket to cover his black T-shirt and blue jeans. He carried his backpack along with him on the bicycle, shifting and accelerating his movement downhill, passing shrubs and cedar trees.

Even though Jackson came directly from school, the LED panel on his wristwatch informed him the time was 6:30 p.m. He was late again. He was in the woods to expel all his school problems. Today, he had an embarrassing moment. He fell asleep during algebra class because it was his most boring class in the school. He seemed not to understand it and usually gave up listening to his teacher's lecture. His teacher, Mr. Hazelnut, asked him to solve a simple equation, but Jackson awoke and shouted the wrong answer. His face turned bluish when he answered to his teacher.

"Whoa!" Jackson had shouted when he was awakened by his teacher's call.

At that time, the other students laughed and joked about him. Only one of his friends, Teresa Pennyworth, stared at him sympathetically––like she understood how Jackson felt. He thought more about today's assignment and the chapter test which would come in three weeks.

Jackson wanted to be perfect and get an A+ on the test. But that made him feel more pressured. He rushed and went straight to the sandlot in the middle of the woods.

Jackson stopped at an abandoned construction site. It was deserted. Rusty metal bars and crumbled cement pieces littered the floor. The builder stopped before building the roof, leaving a gaping hole open to the outside world. The windowsill seemed ready to fell apart, and cockroaches crawled out from numerous cracked in the rotten wood.

Jackson knew about this abandoned place better than anyone in the district. He even knew where he might find some Graham crackers in the old RV van parked outside! He hid some of them in the RV to keep sneaky squirrels from stealing them.

He parked his bike near the vehicle, opened the rusty RV's door, and walked to the shelf that had almost broken apart. He searched with his hand up there for a while before grabbing a Ziplock bag filled with the Graham crackers that had all molded. Jackson tried to throw them out the window, but the bag hit the side of the window and splattered all around the room. He walked outside with a grumpy face and got his backpack. Then he opened his book bag and yanked the worksheets out. He rolled a log towards the construction site and sat on a flat rock like a desk. He started to do his assignment, but he had trouble focusing and did not finish.

"Man, I wished Teresa was here to help me out with these questions, but I didn't want to go asked her. I must work by myself and prove to her that I'm a mature guy who can work and learn on himself," he thought.

Jackson worked through the problems for a few more minutes but got nothing. He decided to go back home and work by himself. Before he turned to his bike, a bright object streak across the sky. At first, he thought it might be a firefly. But the object came closer to Jackson, and he saw it clearly. The object seemed to be made from shiny metal, and he decided that it must be a comet. But it looked like two pieces of a metal Frisbee patted together. It had a glowing green neon color around the edges, and it was falling towards him. It suddenly crashed in a ball of heat and flame. The ground shook like a severe earthquake. Jackson dodged the crash and jumped behind an oak tree. He peeked out from behind the tree and saw a big crater created by the impact.

The object, that was obviously not a comet, fit inside the crater. It got damaged from crashing into the ground. Through gray smoke, he saw that the top of the object had been ripped off. Jackson couldn't believe his eyes. He had encountered something called "UFO."

He jumped out from behind the tree and walked towards it curiously. The object's light panel turned off, and something living popped out from the cap on the top. Jackson saw a hand, but it was not a normal hand. The skin was light green in color. The hand had five long bony fingers, like a frog and light blue nails. The creature climbed up from the UFO. It had an oval-shaped head, large black eyes, a small mouth, and ears like an elf. It also had hair, but the hair was in the middle of the head like the tip of a paintbrush. The creature walked on the two legs, which gave it a somewhat human appearance. Except, the creature had a thin neck that supported a quite large head.

Jackson screamed and searched for somewhere to hide. He saw a large hedge to his left and wildly jumped behind it. The creature saw him but did not follow. It simply stared at him for a few moments and then turned and looked in all directions. Finally, it moved to a part of the construction site where tools littered the ground. Slowly, it bent over and wrapped a green hand around a metal bar. Jackson watched it pick up the metal bar and move back to the crater. He saw it jump back on the top of the metallic, saucer-shaped vehicle and use the bar to try open a panel. The creature climbed back to the top of the saucer with the metal bar in its hand. It went down the hole it came out from the first time.

Even though the creature was no longer walking outside, Jackson watched the alien carefully to make sure the creature was about to leave. But then, the same creature climbed up to the top of an old abandoned Turk cab. It held the same metal bar that it took form the construction site. Now, the creature had another object in its other hand. Jackson zoomed closer to see what it held.

He observed that the object the creature held was a belt. The belt had a dial plate with a flat glass plate covered in the front. The belt made from shiny metal and had gaps under and on top of the dial plate. There were four buttons on the dial plate corners. The colors were red, blue, green, and yellow, one in each of the four corners. The creature scanned the metal bars by placing the bars in front of the dial face and letting the green rays from the belt scan through the long shiny metal bars. After it finished scanning, the creature threw the metal bar away. Then it went and sat on a large rock and gazed at the belt it held.

Jackson was amazed that the creature was an alien. He had never seen one in real life before, and he didn't know what should he did when he encountered one. He decided to ask it a question to see if it understood Earth language. But first, he stepped aside out from where he was hiding so the creature knew that he was there.

Jackson slowly stepped out a bit more. Now he was five meters away from the creature, which he felt was a perfectly good distance. The creature turn its attention to him. Jackson froze. He was afraid that the creature would run towards him and attack. But, somehow, he knew that it was too harmless to hurt him. Jackson stepped closer but kept a short distance away. He let the creature know he was in front of it.

Jackson spoke to the creature in a loud, clear voice, so it gave its attention to him. "Who are you, and what's your name?" he asked the alien to test if it did understand the Earth language of English, or not.

"My. . .name . . .is. . .Djin. . .Tzec," an alien voice answered with an unclear sluggish voice.

"Wow! You can speak Earth language?" Jackson asked surprisingly.

"I . . .had. . . learned. . .before," the alien answered back in the same voice.

"Your name was, Djinn Tzec, right," Jackson asked back to the creature trying to pronounce its name correctly.

"Yes, Earth human," he answered back.

Jackson looked at the object in Djinn Tzec's hand. He was curious and wanted to know more about the belt, which didn't look like a belt that he was familiar with, not even like his father's belt. "What is that thing in your hand?" Jackson asked.

"This is an object called Protonitrix. It belongs to me and people from my home planet," the alien answered fluently.

Clearly, Jackson understand that the creature had a big brain that made its head shape like a melon, and the creature also observed how to pronounce words when Jackson speak. Jackson decide to call him the "smart melon head."

"Tell me more about it. Let's have a seat," Jackson verbally invited the alien to sit down, an Earth custom that demonstrated good manners, trying to make the alien feel safe and secure.

Jackson drug two rocks from the woods to the construction site. He placed one big rock for Djin Tzec and a smaller one for himself. They sat and stared at each other for a while, as this was the first time they would be able to learn about each other.

Djin Tzec showed the Prtonitrix to Jackson and started to explain his story. "Our species has built highly advanced technology which is used for working to bring convenience throughout the whole galaxy. My grandfather got inspired by an Earth human's belt. He decided to create a war machine which helped to collect the information of elements to create war armor and named the armor Protonitrix.

"The Protonitrix has powers to scan the atoms of matters, elements, or any living organism and adapt the characteristic power of the object into armor for fighting. My grandfather tried to use the Protonitrix against invaders who wished to use its galactic powers as a tool of war in order to bring chaos and violence to the universe. He buried it and secured it, so that no one could ever find it.

"Before my grandfather died, he said that one day I must be the person who delivered the Protonitrix to the great warriors who lived on the blue-green planet. He would be the person who wore red clothes and blue pants, and he must be brave and heroic. On my way to deliver it, which takes several months to travel to Earth, my spacecraft was attacked by a galactic invader called "Daikaiser." Daikaiser wants to take over the power of the Protonitrix and use it to devour every single planet and every lifeform he met. After my spaceship got damaged, I landed on Earth and almost immediately found you."

Jackson was amazed by the story that his new alien friend told him, especially about the part that the person—the hero who was chosen by the Protonitrix—was like him. He decided to think about being a superhero. He had always wanted to be a hero and dreamed about this moment since he was five years old. But he didn't want to fight or got into trouble with a galactic invader who was absolutely dangerous.

He looked back at Djin Tzec, who now frowned. He understood that Djin Tzec had failed the mission and couldn't find the hero who belonged to this legendary belt. He decided to take the Protonitrix from him and do good, whatever, might happen to him. This might be a ridiculous idea, but it was the last thing he could do for this poor guy.

"I'll take the Protonitrix from you. I promise I will take care of it, and no one––even that invader––will be able to reach it."

"You would?" Djin Tzec asked hopefully.

"I want you to be happy. The person that you talked about might be me," Jackson answered back happily.

"It is your honor to be the hero of seven galaxies," Djin Tzec bowed down and raised the belt to Jackson.

Jackson put on the Protonitrix, and suddenly the belt's dial made a glitching sound and glowed a green color as it recognized Jackson's DNA sample. It also showed a hologram of fire symbols, water symbols, earth symbols, and wind and plant symbols before wrapping around its new owner's hips.

Jackson smiled a little bit and shouted happily, "It's time for an action!"

Morning sunshine lit the sky with a golden, glittery sunrise. The sky changed color from deep blue to orange as nighttime changed into morning. Birds chirped on the trees and made wonderful music for the morning.

The next morning, Jackson in a vest and a pair of boxers. He woke up and went straight to the closet to change his clothes. He grabbed the Protonitrix that he had hidden it in the piles of clothes inside the closet and wore it on his hips. The belt gave an electronic sound––a greeting to the owner.

Jackson went downstairs past his parent's room. He opened the refrigerator and took a small ice cube in his hand. He held the ice cube in front of the face dial on the belt. The Protonitrix scanned the ice cube's atoms and compound molecules. The belt gave a voice message about recognizing the formation of the ice cube and its abilities to build armor.

It processed the data for three seconds before it said that it recognized the ice cube's abilities such as temperature, brittleness, or the ability to turn into solid. Jackson had been attempting to use the Protonitrix by learning how it collected the atoms of an object, as Djin Tzec taught him. Today was Friday, and he still needed to go to school, so Jackson didn't have time to test the belt's power. He decided to get ready for breakfast and went upstairs to pack.

After Jackson finished packing objects for school, he walked down to the kitchen. He hung his backpack on the chair and grabbed a fork and a spoon from the cupboard. His mother was also there. She was cooking a meal for him this morning in front of the stove. And today's breakfast was fried eggs with bacon and boiled green peas.

The smell of the fried eggs filled Jackson's nose as the smoky bacon smelled appetizing and increased his appetite. Jackson gobbled up his breakfast after his mother handed the plate with green peas, cooked bacon, two slices of ham and a fried egg. He couldn't enjoy his meal like normal because his father had to go early for a meeting at work. He wished his father was here with him, but just only for today.

"Mom, I have to leave now. It's time for me to go to school," Jackson said goodbye to his mother.

"Sure, don't forget to feed your cat, sweetheart," his mother replied.

"Thanks for reminding me about that. I'll feed it now," Jackson called to his mother.

Jackson walked to the front door of his house. His Russian blue cat lay on a welcome mat with a food bowl close to its face. The cat slept quietly. Jackson took a pellet bag from the four-foot shelf above his cat. He opened the Ziplock package and poured the pellets into the bowl.

The cat suddenly woke from the sound of pellets being dumped into the food bowl and started to munch the food that Jackson had given. Then it purred. Jackson patted his cat gently to tell it he would be leaving. Jackson opened the door and went to the garage. He put his backpack on the front basket, wore his helmet, and got ready to go.

* * * *

At school, Jackson and his classmates had a basketball lesson in the gym with coach George. They were about to have a small team tournament competition today.

Everyone was set in a position. Jackson had to team up with his favorite friends. He was playing the middle position, while two of his teammates, Roger and Dylan, were in the offence position. The other two, Chai and Thomas were behind him, left and right. The game started roughly. Jackson had to focus on stealing the ball from many opponents. Many times he missed grabbing the ball because the other team was quick. They eventually devised a plan, and Roger stole easily stole the ball.

Because Roger was a big-black muscular guy, he easily scared his opponents. Jackson started to sweat. Breathing roughly and slowly, he stepped over the basketball court lines. Jackson used his right hand to swipe sweat fingers roughly across his forehead. Jackson's face turned grumpy, and a sense of boring frustration showed on his face. He stated in his mind that he shouldn't use his superpowers for today's tournament, even though it was a rough game. But he changed his mind again.

Suddenly, a wall on the left side of the gym exploded into pieces and left a gaping large hole. A laser suddenly burned a hole through the left gym wall and a thirteen-foot tall, gigantic battle droid walked through the hole. It stood about half the height from the floor to the gym's ceiling and was made of black shiny titanium. The head was smaller than its chest but little larger than it hips. The robot had a yellow helmet with a red fin-like tassel on top, like a Greek Spartan helmet. It had four long arms and an elastic cable connected the arms to the body from the shoulders with the left and right arm top being larger than the smaller arms located below the torso. It had two legs and red metal covered its feet in an appearance like wearing boots. The robot also held a weapon in each hand. The top left hand had a long sharp spear. The top right had a big wooden club, while both hands below held an axe.

The robot looked down at the students and then attacked the group of students near it by jab the spear to the left side of the gym floor, trying to kill the students. Everyone ran fast enough to avoid the attack, and nobody injured. The students all gathered to the right side of basketball court. They all grouped together and got ready to run anytime the robot wanted to attack them.

The robot lifted its right foot and stepped nearer the big crowd of students. The students ran for their lives in fear. They were in chaos and ran to their coach. Coach George told them all to go hide in a locker room. All students ran into a locker room, and two of them hurriedly shut the door. Chaos occurred as swarm of students ran away, like worker ants going back to their tunnel.

Jackson dropped the ball and ran into the locker room while his coach and students did the same thing. As the students and Coach George found a place to hide from the robot. Jackson who was supposed to hide and remain silent snuck away and looked down to his hips where the Protonitrix was. He had brought the Protonitrix to school today and hid it all the times in his pants, so no one wondered or knew about the story of the belt.

Jackson unlocked the passcode of the belt by pressing the red button on the top left corner of the face dial, the blue button the below left corner of the dial, the green button on the bottom right corner of the dial, and yellow button on the top right corner of the dial. The dial face showed a symbol of fire.

Jackson looked at the dial and pressed the green button once to unlock its battle mode, but nothing happened. He remembered from two days earlier that Djin Tzec had taught him how to unlock a battle mode. He remembered that he needed to press the green button twice. Jackson pressed the button once more. Then, a yellow flash covered his body.

Many red pieces of titanium suddenly attached to form a shield around his body from his feet to his head, and a mask covered his face. The mask was orange and had yellow goggles that covered his mouth with a red respirator and a yellow breathing bracket. His metal gloves had holes on the palms in it with a metal tube sticking right out from those holes. Jackson felt a little heat from the armor. His body was warm inside. But the external part of the suit was about five hundred Celsius and scorched the cement tiles.

Jackson's fire boots released heat out. He created black-ashy burning footprints on the floor. The transformation was finalized as soon Jackson kicked the door of the locker room and jumped outside to attack the giant robot. He began his first battle using the Protonitrix's power!

The robot saw Jackson approach. It waved the club in its right hand and slammed it hard onto the gym floor. This caused the floor to break apart and left a big crater. Then, the robot swung the club back as Jackson ran towards it. Jackson blocked the attack by catching the club just in time so that it didn't injure him.

The robot pressed more force on the club to squash Jackson to death. As the robot pressed on Jackson's hot flaming armor, Jackson also activated his fiery gloves. The heat from Jackson's hand burned the robot's wooden club and exploded it into pieces. The robot didn't give up. It kept attacking by slicing and chopping the axes at Jackson.

Jackson used the engine inside his respirator to create a smoke. He exhaled the smoke through the respirator to blind the robot's vision. He suddenly he disappeared in the smoke. The robot changed its visual mode into an infrared mode. It scanned through the smoke and captured the heat from Jackson's armor. Then it slashed an axe from two of it lower hands at Jackson. It missed, hitting Jackson's shadow. He hovered in the air with a jet of energy the bottom of his boots.

Jackson volleyed fireballs from his gloves and hit their target. The fireballs hit the robot in the face several times. The robot swooshed the spear from its left hand and slashed the metal barbs in the air towards Jackson. But he managed to dodge the spear by quickly shutting down the engine so that he lowered his height. He dashed through the air downwards toward the robot's left shoulder. With that high acceleration, he cut the left arm off the robot by twirling his body in a mid-air spiral to perform a "drill punch." The robot lost it left arm and fell to the ground unable to balance its body. Jackson landed safely on the gym floor in a bowed down position with his right hand folded into a fist on a floor.

The sounds of the battle from brought the students and Coach George out to watch. Half of the class stared at the robot and the figure in red armor with confused and curious expressions, while half of the class happily celebrated by shouting "hooray." Through his armor, Jason saw everyone looking at him proudly, but nobody noticed it was him inside the armor.

Jackson turned back to the robot who was almost broken apart. He jumped up to its gigantic face, punched its red glassy eye and roasted the whole CPU down with his flames blazing and burning the machine. The robot's face exploded into scrap metal. Everyone shouted happily as Jackson raised his fist. He observed the amazed expression on Coach George's face.

Jackson jumped down from the robot's dead body and ran out the exit door. He wished that he could have more action and fight more, but the fun time was over. By the time he went back into the gym, the tall muscular coach with blonde hair wearing green athletic clothes came to Jackson.

"Jackson, where have you been?" Coach George asked him angrily.

"I ran outside sir, so I could hide," Jackson answered firmly. He did not want to tell the truth. Coach George might ignore his explanation.

Coach George talked to Jackson in a serious tone, "If that thing grabbed you, I would be accused by the school for not caring about your safety. Stick with the others next time." Then he turned back to the students to tell them to depart. "Everyone, grab your belongings and go home!"

Jackson walked back and followed his classmates upstairs.

After the attack ended, the principal paid a group of workmen to carry the robot out. The workers used a crane to carry the robot's body out through the hole in the wall. Many of workers removed small pieces of metal and sharp wood and repaired burned planks. Another group of workers pried some broken planks with crowbars and then put the other pieces of plank back onto the crater. They filled the crater fixed the gym floor. The attack had made the gym unusable and it took a month to repair the damage, which means the students wouldn't have P.E. for a whole month.

Nobody blamed Jackson because no one recognized that it was him in the armor. He smiled and became absent minded, smiling alone to himself as if he were a popular person while the other students discussed the attack and made up their own theories about whether the attack came from an extraterrestrial or it was the result of a mistake from a secret government experiment.

Jackson didn't care about the discussion and theories they argued at. He needed to be ready for the next attack. This battle droid was just an early warning for an invasion of Earth by something from outer space…

"Goodbye," Jackson said to his friend as he walked downstairs to go home.

He walked past the hallway where the lockers were. He saw a shadowy figure at the locker. The figure turned out to be a thirteen-years old girl. She had long blonde hair, white skin, and blue eyes. She wore a green jacket and blue jeans. She had a slim torso, and her thighs were nicely shaped. It was Teresa. She turned back and looked at him, combed her long blonde hair with her hand, and packed up things in her lockers to go home for the day.

As Jackson removed his bicycle from the bicycle rack, Chai and Roger came to him. The tall black guy had short, black hair. The Asian guy took a

CD out of his school bag and walked to Jackson, who wore his gray bicycle helmet and pushed the bicycle tripod ready to leave school. They begged him to go play video games at Jackson's home. But today, he had fighting practice with Djin Tzec in the woods behind the school. He turned his head up to look at Chai and Roger, who held a game CD.

"Jackson, please come and join us today. I want you to try the video games I bought downtown yesterday," Roger said, trying to convince Jackson.

"Why would I? I have a training session today. No time for video games," Jackson answered back.

"Because this is the new edition of 'Special Nova OPS no. 3 Nova Grappler.' The trailer was showed on Youtube last night. Actually, it was cool and looked interesting to play," Chai excitedly explained.

"Whatever, games are just games. They all have the same goals: everyone must win the levels they assign you to play. If you don't mind, I have to leave now. Goodbye, dudes."

Jackson pedalled his bicycle and rode away. He knew that Chai and Roger worried about him.

Chai and Roger saw Teresa walking downwards in front of them. They went asked Teresa to come with them and followed Jackson to steal his secrets.

"Teresa, Jackson kept acting weird this week. He has never come to join us playing video games like before he used to. I am worried about him. Maybe he is depressed," Chai said to Teresa worriedly.

"Or maybe he has a secret that he didn't want us to know. Let's go and see the reason why he didn't want to go play video games. He hasn't been like this before. Normally, when we have a new video game, Jackson would invite us to his house, and we played the game together. Do you think he has a secret that we shouldn't know, Teresa? He said that he had a practice session that sounds important to him, but he didn't explain it to us," Roger added.

"I think he needs to go study algebra today. Don't try to force him to follow you guys. He has his own chores and his own things to do. I suggest if you want to know about his secret, try to ask him individually. This is the best way that," Teresa said.

The three of them decided to follow Jackson. They rode quickly and followed behind Jackson until he stopped to buy chocolate milk for Djin Tzec at the vending machine on the pathway.

Jackson searched the chocolate milk in the vendor machine. He found the correct flavor and inserted twenty-five cents into the coin slot. The chocolate milk can fell into the receiver. Jackson took the can of chocolate milk and put it in his backpack. Then he got on his bicycle and rode away.

Teresa, Chai, and Roger came out from behind the machine. They noticed Jackson riding away. They ran to the roadside and saw Jackson on the road that took him to the woods. Following Jackson exhausted Teresa, but she continued to follow because the two dudes asked her to steal Jackson's secret. Even though she thought it was a stupid idea, she continued the journey.

After a long walk, they finally arrived in the forest. Chai walked in the front, using a pine twig to sweep litter from the path. As the twig swept dried leaves, millipedes and grubs swarmed out and slipped into the shrubs. Along the way, they had to jump across thorny hedges, use a stick to remove a big long king snake on the path without hurting it, and climbed up pine trees to get a better view. It was exhausting. But for revealing Jackson's secret, Chai and Roger would do anything to find out why Jackson rode his bike into the forest, instead of going with them to play video games. Finally, the made their way to the hillside.

They saw an open space in the woods and a sandlot, a bicycle parked on the sandlot, and Jackson carrying the chocolate milk can to a mysterious tent. Roger and Chai were curious about a tent being in these woods. The last time they came here with Jackson, there weren't any tents at this abandoned site. And who was living in the tent sparked Teresa's curiosity.

The three of them slowly took a step down from a hill, which was slippery with soil ready to break down anytime they tripped. Chai stared at Jackson and saw him give the can of chocolate milk to––something. It was a strange figure. He had never seen anything like it.

It was Djin Tzec who came out of the tent and took the chocolate milk from Jackson. The sight of such a strange creature frightened Chai, and he tripped and fell on Teresa and Roger. All three of them slid roughly down the muddy hill and landed in front of Jackson.

Teresa and Roger opened their eyes after falling. In their view, they saw a green humanoid alien with an oval shaped face, big black eyes, and long bony fingers staring curiously at them. In shock, they both jumped back after seeing Djin Tzec, especially Chai. In fear, Chai shrieked and ran around like a crazy person. He bumped into a cedar tree's dark brown trunk.

Jackson stared in confusion trying to understand why Teresa and Roger were screaming as Chai bumped into the trunk and lay on the ground. He stopped the madness by yelling madly and demanded their attention.

"What are you guys doing here?" Jackson asked.

"We came to find out why you are in the woods instead of going home to play video games. I'm concerned and worried about you getting depressed because your parents never allow you to have fun anymore because you didn't do well in algebra," Roger explained.

"Also, it was Teresa's idea that took us here on a long journey into the forest," Chai replied.

"Chai, you are lying, blaming me. That's not nice," Teresa said. She turned and pointed to the alien. "We just need to know who or what is standing next to you. Who is he?" Teresa asked Chai rose from the ground and stood.

Jackson sighed deeply. "Alright guys, I'll explain, but it might sound scummy and too much like fiction. This is an alien from the outer space name Djin Tzec. I firstly met him when his UFO crashed on Earth. He can't go back home and must live secretly in the forest. I helped him build the tent, taught him how to find food, in the woods, and learned about outer space from him. He also gave me the Protonitrix, which is a belt that helps me access armor that has superpowers. I tried to keep these as secrets until you guys came in shrieking and staring at him like he had already harmed you," Jackson summarized the whole story that he had experienced, including taking care of Djin Tzec and where Djin Tzec's UFO was hidden.

Teresa felt guilty. From her perspective, Chai and Roger should also feel guilty. They knew that they weren't supposed to know about the alien hiding in the woods. Jackson was a superhero who saved the other students and their lives when the giant robot attached the gym.

Now that they knew the facts, they thought it was their duty to help Jackson help this poor alien get back home. Jackson saved their lives in the gym. He deserved not to have his secret revealed by his friends who might tell the story to other people. If other people found out about the alien in the woods, and Jackson's alien technology belt, they might send Jackson and Djin Tzec to Area 51 for an experiment that might harm them. Teresa took Roger and Chai into the circle. They brainstormed and discussed what to do next.

Teresa turned back to Jackson and said, "Jack, we think it would work best for us to keep your secret. No one will know about your story. We not wont' tell anyone."

Jackson nodded in agreement. He walked to Djin Tzec and whispered through Djin Tzec's elf-like ears for a few seconds and turned back to Teresa, Chai and Roger. "Alright guys, you're not in trouble. Just don't tell anyone.

While the children and the alien stood together in the sandlot, something appeared from uphill. The something separated into a pack of robot wolves made from metal. Their claws were shiny and curved like hooks and sharp, like penknives. Their eyes were made from yellow glass. In each tail was a sharp edge that pointed up, like a scorpion. The leader of the pack, the alpha, had pomegranate red coloration, while the rest of them had normal metal-like color.

The alpha growled hardly, opening it jaws and showing its ferocious-looking metal sharp teeth. The sounds that the robot wolves made was like a wolf howl, but it was robotic and three times louder. The pack ran down from the hill to the spot where the children stood.

The children ran away as the wolves neared the sandlot. The alpha turned it head to Jackson. It dashed onto him and pressed it paws on Jackson's chest, locked his red jean jacket with its paws, and tried to bite Jackson with the razor-sharp teeth. Jackson heard the growl and the snout close to his face. He used his hand to grab it snout and tried to push it away.

Teresa panicked and screamed. She picked up a rock and threw it at the alpha wolf's head from. The alpha wolf turned back as the rock bounced off its head and look at Teresa. The bright color from Teresa's jacket attracted the wolf's 3D color vision. The wolves left Jackson and then charges at Teresa.

Jackson fell to the ground. He pressed the Protonitrix's green, red, blue and yellow button to unlock the Protonitrix passcode. He swiped the face dial to select an armor to attack the robot wolves. He looked at the ice symbol and decided he should try using ice armor. He pressed the green button two times on the Protonitrix to activated the armor.

Pieces of transparent titanium covered Jackson's body. It built up the armor system starting from the arms and legs, until Jackson's body was fully covered in the transparent titanium. He sensed chilling radiation from inside the armor. The temperature outside Jackson's ice armor was so far below the freezing point that it would freeze everything that touched him. Jackson's mask was different than the last time. This one has a big snow goggles and a blue mask. Jackson also had two pairs of vacuum tentacles sticking out from his back. His shoes turned into ice skate boots to finalize his transformation.

Jackson sprayed a freezing ray onto the ground. The freezing ray pulled moisture from the soil and condensed the moisture molecules to build an ice path. Jackson skated to distract the robot wolves from their attack. The alpha wolf got distracted as it was stalked closer to Teresa. It signaled the other robot wolves to follow its high-pitched radio waves with a frequency that humans couldn't hear. The alpha rushed towards Jackson while the pack followed from behind.

Jackson skated deeper into the woods. He found a big willow tree that stood twenty meters tall. Jackson stretched his vacuum tube and latched onto one of the big strong branch of the willow tree to hide from the pack of robot wolves who hunted him.

The pack arrived at the ice path that ended at the willow tree. Jackson kicked a big branch with his skating boots. The blades under the boots sliced a huge chunk from the branch. It fell on one wolf and literally crushed it into scrap metal. He stretched his tentacles and grabbed a bigger branch above his head.

Jackson came up with a smart idea. He climbed up to the top of the canopy. He saw a stream on a hill west of the sandlot. It calculated the stream was twenty meters wide and eight feet deep down with many rocky ravines and a strong current—the perfect place for Jackson to get rid of these robot wolves. He jumped down from the canopy and then used a jet of freezing ray from his hand to propel himself above the ground so the wolves would not be able to grab him.

Jackson flew back to Roger, Chai, Teresa and Djin Tzec who waited for his return. "Guys, I need your help. The pack is coming closer, and they will chase after me. I wouldn't be able to fight alone. Roger and Chai, ride bicycles and lure the wolves uphill to a stream west of the sandlot. Teresa and Djin Tzec, go hide in the tent for your safety. I'll attack the alpha wolf."

They all agreed with his plan and got ready to work. Chai and Roger sat on bicycles. Roger was the leader, and Chai rode behind with a laser pointer. Teresa and Djin Tzec went into the tent. They silently hid under a large pile of smelly blankets. Jackson saw the hedges shaking, announcing that the pack was coming closer and closer. As soon as all the wolves crashed through the hedges, Jackson created an ice path on the ground. With blasts of his freezing ray he hurriedly skated on uphill on the ice.

While Chai and Roger led the rest of the wolves along a different path uphill, the alpha followed Jackson. Jackson went through the tangled mess of the trees to get to the stream that he saw from the canopy. He rushed more and more but his feet stayed on the ice track or else he would end up having his blades stuck in the ground. The alpha wolf stopped and shot five rockets out of the needle in its tail. Three of the missile rocket flew toward Jackson, and the other two flew to the large branch of an oak tree above Jackson. The missiles exploded in front of Jackson, and a large branch fell and blocked his way. The others exploded behind him. Jackson was burned by the explosion. He lay on the ground and suffered from the pain in his back.

Actually, Jackson would have exploded into pieces if the ice armor hadn't protected him. The wolf walked slowly toward Jackson lifting it tail, like a scorpion. The stinger that used to be a missile launcher now became a long, sharp iron stinger. The wolf stumbled toward Jackson who had lost his track to the creek. It gave a monstrous growl as it tried to sting Jackson to death.

At that moment, Jackson worried about Chai and Roger. He feared that the pack might ripped them apart, or they might drown in the creek. This was the first time that the theme of life and death had filled Jackson's head. He lifted his right hand into the air and shot the freezing ray at the alpha wolf. The wolf's face froze, and frosty ice flakes blinded its vision. Jackson shoved away the wolf's face with a sharp boot blade. The wolf face got a large deep cut on its snout as the blade sliced its face. Anger filled

Jackson. He blasted streams of liquid nitrogen from his palms at the wolf. The wolf froze solid and fell apart. Exploded wires and pieces of metal that were frozen by the liquid nitrogen all crumbled and lay on the ground. Jackson had defeated the alpha wolf. He then used jets of freezing rays to propelled himself into the air and across to the other side of the hill where Roger and Chai were going.

On Roger and Chai's way, they were doing a pretty good job of getting the pack to follow them. Roger and Chai arrived at the stream in time. They gazed up to the sky to see if Jackson there. If not, the pack would arrive soon, and they would be in trouble. Suddenly, a figure appeared in the sky. It was Jackson in his ice armor propelling himself with jets of freezing rays.

As the pack charged from the woods, Jackson lowered his freezing jets and dove into the creek. He used all the armor's tentacles to consume water into his back and jumped up to the shore. Jackson blazed jets of water that mixed with liquid nitrogen to the whole pack. All the robot wolves froze into clumps of ice and exploded into frozen metal scraps.

"Wohoo! Jackson rocks!" Chai and Roger exclaim in joy after the robot wolves were destroyed.

Jackson gave a high five to Chai and Roger. "I think we should go home. It will be dark soon. Would you guys mind helping me throw these metal scraps away?" Jackson asked. Jackson pressed the blue button on the Protonitrix on his hips. He returned to normal human form.

Chai, Roger, and Jackson swept the scrap metal into the stream including a handful of microchip, iron jaws, iron paws, and body pieces. They watched the metal sink in the deep water. Nobody would know there had been robot wolves in the woods.

After their job finished, Jackson rode behind Chai back to the sandlot to pick up Teresa, his bicycle, and backpack. Then they said goodbye to Djin Tzec and headed home.

As sunset approached, the sky turned deep blue. Birds flew back home on the hillside and the trees along the street. Teresa was tired and flexed her sore knuckles. She wished she could reach home and go to sleep until tomorrow, Saturday. Roger and Chai had already arrived at their apartment on West 56 Route District which was close to the front of the woods. Only Jackson walked along with her on the roadside path. It took thirty minutes for Teresa to reach home.

Jackson escorted Teresa to her house. Either Jackson or Teresa both had to walk to their bicycles because Jackson's bicycle chain became broke after. Finally, they both reach house number 5151.

Surrounded by a tall white fence, the house was quite large. It was all white, except the roof, which was a red clay color. There were four windows in the house. Brown lanterns in the garden lighted the way. Moths flew around the morning glory vines that grew on the roof. Teresa took a key out of her pocket, unlocked the front gate, and walked to the door of her house. At this moment, Jackson blushed and asked Teresa for something.

"Teresa, can I talked to you?" Jackson asked with and unconfident voice.

She turned back and answer. "Yes."

"On Monday, we're going to the Natural Science Museum and the zoo for our class field trip, will you come with me?" Jackson asked.

"Sure, see you there, Jack. Goodbye," she said joyfully.

"Goodbye, Teresa," Jackson replied before he turned and walked away. He walked back to his home, which was six blocks away from Teresa's house. Jackson smiled happily the entire way. He decided that he had a crush on Teresa.

It was supposed to be a nice day on Monday, but he was late and worried he might miss the school bus. Jackson road his newly fixed bicycle at high speed. He afraid he would miss the field trip. He hurriedly pushed the pedals and raced through the school gate as quick as a racehorse. Finally, he made it.

Jackson parked his bicycle in the bicycle stand and walked up to the school bus with his backpack. He searched for a seat and founded one left for him. It was next to Teresa. He blushed a little bit at the thought of sitting close to her.

Then Chai and Roger who save him a seat in back for him motioned for Jackson to join them. Jackson dot not want to make his friends angry, but be wanted to sit with Teresa. He paused for a moment and finally made his decision. He walked to Teresa.

"Can I sit here?" Jackson asked.

"Sure, you can sit anywhere in the bus," Teresa answered kindly.

He sat down close to Teresa, smiling happily. Finally, all the students and teachers were on the bus. They took roll, and everyone was ready to go to the Los Angeles Zoo and Natural Science Museum. On the way, the school bus passed through the city. Jackson and Teresa talked about what kind of animals they liked to see in the zoo, especially their favorite animals.

"My favorite animal is the white tiger. It looks ferocious. In my opinion, it is a powerful animal," Jackson said about the white Bengal tiger that he had seen at the zoo every visit since he was five. This animal also reminded him of his pet cat, Gumball.

"Wow! I didn't know you liked a big kitty cat. My favorite pet is the peacock. Its colors are amazing, and this has an astonishing feather pattern when it spreads its tail."

Teresa talked about her favorite animal, the peacock. She thought it was the perfect for girls like her. And, also, her keychain was a peacock which was a birthday present she got from Chai who have traveled back to Thailand and brought the keychain for her. She still kept it nice and neat inside her pocket until this day.

"So, Jackson, what makes you like the white tiger?" she asked.

"My father was born in the year of tiger. Also, the tiger reminds me of my kitty cat, Gumball. He is a Russian blue cat that used to wander behind my backyard. Now I take care of him. He doesn't do much around my house, but when he sees a lizard or mice. He holds it in his mouth and places it on my mom's lap when she watches TV." Jackson explained, as the bus entered the zoo's front gate.

At the zoo, students walked in a group. Jackson walked as close to Teresa as he could. They entered a reptile house. The building was designed like a rocky cave. The roof was made from steel, masonry, and reinforced glass and was climate controlled so the animal could live comfortably inside the enclosure.

Jackson and his classmates stopped at one of the enclosures. Inside the terrarium, there were leaf litter and plastic plants. It has a UV lamp to give the light to the animal that was displayed in the tank. The animal quickly slithered out from the log in the corner of the tank. It was a king cobra, a brown snake with a small white zigzag stripe on its back and a yellow belly. It was quite a long snake. Chai guess it's length and said that it might be about four feet long in length. It displayed its cobra hood in front of the students and made Jackson run back behind the whole group.

As the zookeeper opened the tank lid from behind, the snake bowed down and turned its head back to the open enclosure lid. The zookeeper used tongs to hold a live rat by the tail and place the rat down. The living rat walked around after it got placed by the tongs. It accidentally step closed to the king cobra in front of the clear acrylic that allowed visitors to watch. The cobra respond to the prey by striking the rat on its throat. The king cobra injected its toxic venom into the rat through it fangs. The rat was immobilized and became motionless.

Jackson was shocked when he saw the cobra strike the rat. It happened so quickly, and it also freaked him out when the hissing sound from the snake reached him. Teresa was also scared of what had happened in front of her. She followed her classmates and moved on to the lizard exhibit.

At the lizard exhibit, tanks and cages displayed many lizards. There were green iguanas in the big central enclosure made of clear acrylic glass. There were veiled chameleons in a small cage full of plants. Jackson looked at many lizards.

He took special interest in the enclosure that display the lizards in one large glass tank. He saw a blue necked garden lizard that came from Thailand. It displayed a beautiful blue dewlap throat when Jackson zoomed down in front of the tank. The blue dewlap turned brighter as the lizard crept under the UV light bulbs that were part of the top of the tank. Jackson observed it for a while before he decided to find some more interesting species.

Then, he suddenly spotted a tank that was close to the exit. It was an eight-foot tall tank made of clear acrylic glass. Inside the tank were bamboo twigs, logs, branches, dozens of fake plastic plants, and small cups of water. Inside were eight small lizards perched together on the logs and bamboo twigs. The lizards were light green and a bark brownish color with some small dark blue spots on the sides of their bodies. They all had big heads, big eyes, and slender long tails. Males were all green, and females were all brown. What they all had in common were kin flaps, like a dragon wing folded along their bodies. These lizards basked on tall twigs of a log to reach artificial light from the UV light bulbs on top of the enclosure. They seemed calm to and relaxed. But when the zookeeper opened the enclosure, they all ran quickly to hide in the plastic leaves. Some of them jumped and expands their skin flaps, which helped the lizards glide from the basking area to hide among spathes.

Jackson estimated that the zookeeper was about thirty-five years old. He wore a zoo uniform. The uniform included a sky-blue t-shirt, with the zoo logo on the right of his chest and a small pocket in the left. The man also wore long gray pants with sneakers. He had brown hair and gray eyes. In his hand, he held a large cup of termites, sealed with a mesh net to keep the termites alive. He set the termites cup on a log and opened it. As the termites escaped the cup, the lizards snuck up from their hiding areas and devoured the termites as they ran around in a chaotic manner. Jackson wanted to know the species's name. He turned to the zookeeper after he closed the enclosure lid to prevent either the lizards or the termites from escaping.

"I'm sorry sir, do you know what species these lizards are?" Jackson asked the man.

"They are a species call gliding dragon lizard. Please don't tap on the glass. These little guys can easily die from stress. " the zookeeper explained.

The man exited, leaving only Jackson standing there in front of the gliding dragon lizard enclosure. Jackson decided to try scanning the lizard's DNA sample. Djinn Tzec had explained that the Protonitrix had the ability to scan living organisms' DNA to use their special abilities characteristics. Jackson pointed the Protonitrix dial scanner at one of the gliding dragon lizards. The Protonitrix took ten seconds to scan the lizard's DNA. The Protonitrix displayed a new logo, which had a lizard head with a snake-like tongue, called Reptile Armor. Jackson walked away to join his friends, happy he had received a new kind of armor.

A short time later, Jackson and Teresa stood at the white Bengal tigers' enclosure. While the other students went to see different animal enclosure in the zoo, Jackson and Teresa watched the white tigers. The enclosure was deep below the ground like a well, there was a large water ditch surrounding the tigers' habitat. Many trees and the logs had been placed to make the tigers feel comfortable, like in the wild. There were four tigers in the cage. All of them were sleepy and napping on the bamboo scaffolds. Teresa smiled when all the tigers went to sleep in daytime. Jackson also smiled and turned to her. He felt that they were starting to build a close relationship together.

Suddenly, there was a loud explosion happen behind them. Jackson turned back and saw a figure approach. The figure was a reptilian human. It had green scaly skin covering its body, except for its face. The creature's eyes were yellow, similar to that of the king cobra Jackson saw in the reptile house. The reptilian human was tall and had a lower body like a large green snake body. The creature had arms and five fingers. It also wore a dark purple cloak that covered half its body. The creature pulled the hood over its head to conceal its identity.

Teresa ran behind Jackson, and the other tourists screamed and ran away. Jackson stared at his new enemy, as if ready for combat. Teresa didn't know if the creature would kill her and Jackson or not. What she did know was she felt that Jackson would protect her from harm.

Jackson stared at the reptilian human in the hood, who approached to ten meters from him. The creature hissed like a snake. It opened its mouth, exposing a set of fangs, and the snake like tongue swept up and down in the air. Jackson was now facing a new kind of enemy.

Angry because it destroyed his moment with Teresa, he demanded angrily, "Who are you!"

"My name is Kimnara. I came from the planet 'Reptilia.' Now, Jackson Dimes, I will steal your Protonitrix and gave it to my lord." The creature responded in a sharp, spooky-cold voice.

"I don't even know who your master is, but you have destroyed the peaceful part of the zoo and ruined a lot of people's fun. I will do everything I can to stop you," Jackson shouted at the creature. Then, they both prepared for battle.

Kimnara attacked first. He used his pointer and pointed to a nearby trash can. He lift the trash can with telekinetic power. Then he threw the trash can at Jackson.

Jackson jumped away and managed to dodge the attack.

Teresa was also scared. She froze in place, uncertain what to do.

As Kimnara grasped her hand, she screamed and stomped on Kimnara's snake-like tail. The creature shrieked in pain and released her. Teresa ran as fast as she could. She decided to in the tree canopy to avoid Kimnara spotting her.

Meanwhile, Jackson ran into a nearby telephone box. He quickly slammed the door and turned pressed Protonitrix's switch with four-color button passcode. He swiped through the dial face to see which armor should he use. He found a basic armor, Earth armor. Jackson activated the Protonitrix by pressing the green button twice. A green flash burst from Jackson, and he started to transform.

Brown titanium built up around Jackson as armor covered his entire body. The armor became bigger and bulkier until it made Jackson look muscular. He had a different kind of mask. This mask had a block of brown polygon covering Jackson's head. He got rectangular goggles to see his enemy. Jackson also had blocks of polygon armor on his arms and hands. His metal gloves expanded to the size of an elephant's foot. Jackson finalized his transformation and opened the telephone box, ready to enter the battle.

Teresa observed the action from the tree canopy. She felt relieved that Jackson had courage enough to battle the creature. She knew that he would help her and the citizens of Glendale by fighting against the alien invader!

Kimnara angrily used his snake-tail to grab a block of bricks and threw them at Jackson's earth armor. Jackson blocked them with his arm, encased in brown metal, which prevented any injuries. Kimnara slithered toward Jackson. He punched three times into Jackson's chest, but it didn't hurt Jackson. Jackson quickly smashed Kimnara back using his big fist. The blow squashed Kimnara, but he was still alive. Kimnara was able to use his tail to swipe his at Jackson's legs. Jackson fell and lay on the floor.

Kimnara constricted his tail around Jackson's hips and moved closer to Jackson's goggles. He stared through the goggles to observe inside Jackson's earth armor. Kimnara started to hypnotize Jackson's mind with telekinesis power. Jackson felt sleepy and couldn't control his body or move his hand down to his hips to repulse Kimnara. His hands were too weak, and he doesn't have enough energy to fight back against Kimanra's telekinetic power.

Teresa watched the battle from the canopy. She was now anxious for Jackson safety and afraid that Kimnara would remove the Protonitrix while Jackson was under his control. Teresa decide to do something. She jumped down from the canopy, took the sneaker from her left foot and threw it a Kimnara, who was wrapping its tail tightly around Jackson.

Kimnara felt down as the sneaker smashed into his face. He released Jackson and lay on down on the ground, using his left hand to cover the stinging red mark. Teresa ran to Jackson who was now out of control. She lifted Jackson's upper part of his body.

"Jackson, are you alright?" Teresa asked worriedly.

"I'm fine, Teresa," Jackson responded and rose to his feet.

Teresa also stood.

"He is too strong to defeat with only one power. We have to work together to beat this guy," Jackson told Teresa, unsure about the next step to take.

Teresa looked down and asked if Jackson could to switch to another kind of armor. "Can I switch your armor with some gadgets on your belt?"

"I think, so. Go ahead and try. My arms are too weak to move. Press the green and blue button each time once," Jackson said.

"Let me see," Teresa said while pressing the green and blue button of the Protonitrix on Jackson's hips.

During this time, Kimnara awoke and saw Teresa press the green and blue buttons each once. A bright cyan flash covered Jackson's body, and his armor changed into another form. Jackson now wore water armor. The mask became a helmet with a shark fin-tassel on the top. He wore scuba goggles that connected to an underwater respirator. He wore cobalt blue armor cover his whole body. Blue iron gloves covered his hands, and an oxygen tank appeared on Jackson's back. A pair of flippers covered his feet.

Kimnara slithered toward Jackson as Jackson finalized the transformation. Jackson respond quickly by stretched out his left arm to protect Teresa. He fired jets of water from his right glove. The water blinded Kimnara. Jackson turned his gloves automatically into a water gatling gun and increased his chance of hitting his foe.

Kimnara rubbed water from his eyes. He tried to strike back again, but Jackson quickly volleyed jets of water at Kimnara. He walked close to the front of the reptilian alien as Kimnara stepped back against the fence of the tiger enclosure. Kimnara fell over the protective rail, down into the water ditch inside the tiger enclosure. He disappeared under duckweed that covered the whole surface.

Teresa and Jackson now felt relieved that Kimnara was gone. They looked down and saw that no response from the ditch. Suddenly, something approached in front of them. It was Kimnara. He had become twenty meters tall, and his snake-like tail wrapped into a coiled fist inside the tiger enclosure. He didn't wear his cloak anymore, but duckweed covered his shoulders and his body. Kimnara use his moist reptilian hands to grab both Jackson and Teresa. He pulled them in front of his yellow eyes.

"I think I should literally blow two of you away, like sawdust. Shouldn't I?" Kimnara exclaimed. He squeezed them tighter until Teresa couldn't breathe. No words came from Teresa's mouth; only her body struggled to fight back.

"Teresa, use your feet to kick the Protonitrix. Hit green and the blue button, and I will transform into something that can help us," Jackson shouted across to Teresa.

Teresa didn't respond with words. As Kimnara swung her closer to Jackson and tried to choke her, she swooshed her left foot and it hit both green and blue buttons on the Protonitrix's face dial. Purple flashed over Jackson's whole body. He started to turn into something else. Jackson's armor changed into a new one––the armor he got from the lizard's DNA sample.

Now, Jackson became a purple robot. His helmet was hardened and had V-shaped goggles. On his shoulders, armor plates became purple shaped like the upper skull and jaws of a cobra. He had a metal crocodile head sticking out of his chest and a dragon wing behind his back. Jackson now wore reptilian armor, based on the flying dragon lizard's DNA. Jackson slipped down from Kimnara's hand and jumped onto Kimnara's arm.

Jackson flew into the air using the armor's dragon wings. He clicked a purple button on his wrist that pointed towards Kimnara. A long iron chain bounced out from an opening on his armor. The chain had an iron crocodile head at the tip. Jackson swung it in a circle and cast the metal crocodile head though Kimnara's right hand, the hand holding Teresa.

The iron crocodile jaw painfully locked onto Kimnara's wrist. He shrieked in a monstrously high pitch and released Teresa. Jackson dashed to rescue her. He yanked the chain to brake it, and flew down to Teresa. Luckily, Jackson activated a jetpack on his back that gave additional velocity. Jackson stretched his hand out and grabbed Teresa. She landed safely when Jackson supported her and took her back softly to the ground.

"Thank you, Jackson," Teresa thanked Jackson as she landed on the ground.

"No problem. I want you to stay away from the battle. You can get injured standing there and watching the fight," Jackson said, as he flew back to fight.

Jackson pressed a button on his left hand. A cobra skull-like plate popped out from his wrist. He fired jets of black tar from the nose, which stuck the plates under Kimnara's eyes. He blinded Kimnara with the black tar and landed on the ground. Kimnara waved his hands up and down, smashing the enclosure and scaring the tigers in the enclosure. The tigers all hid in their shelter, shivering like little kittens who saw a big-scary dog. Using his telekinetic powers, Kimnara activated debris from the damaged enclosure and attacked Jackson.

Jackson activated a shield shaped like a tortoise shell. It was flat and wide, made from black metal tiles. Jackson used a voice command to call it from the Protonitrix and place it on the ground. The shield built a large glowing purple magnetic field to protect him from the wood, rocks, cement, and metal bars that flew toward him. Jackson was now very angry. He called a seven-foot-long sword with a purple handle out from the Protonitrix by using voice message mode, same way as he did with the shield.

Using his jetpack and his dragon wings, he flew into the air and attached Kimnara's chest. The purple dragon wings waved as the jetpack keep pushing Jackson from behind.

"Kimnara, you are evil and cause destruction. You should be vanished away from this world!" Jackson shouted as he used the sharp sword he got from the Protonitrix. He stabbed into Kimnara's chest, right into the heart. Jackson stabbed deeper and deeper and activated the cosmic power in the sword. Kimnara shriek in pain and exploded into pieces. Jackson flew down and perched close to Teresa. He turned back to his human form.

Teresa felt thankful. She looked at the enclosure that was literally destroyed. It was filled with green oozing blood. The tigers in the cage came out from their shelter and found their enclosure broken and the green slimy blood all over.

"It's over Teresa. The villain is destroyed," Jackson said. He saw she was exhausted from watching the fight. The battle was over, and it was time to go home. Police and firemen entered the area, and teachers hurriedly gathered students together.

"Let's go back together, Jackson," Teresa replied. She held his hand, and they both walked back together to the bus.

On the way back home, Teresa and Jackson fell asleep on the bus. The both laid their backpack and their lunch bag on their lap and slept with their heads tilted together for comfort and support.

"Wake up, lazy!" Roger shouted as he shook Jackson's shoulder.

Jackson woke up in the confusion. "Where am I?" He looked outside and saw a house with a shiny silver ford in the garage. The house was white and the roof was shiny azure blue. Jackson recognized he arrived at his home. Because of today's zoo attack, the bus was taking students home instead of back to school. He grabbed his backpack and his lunch bag from his lap and say goodbye to everyone on the school bus. Teresa awoke and squeezed his hand as a way of saying goodbye.

He ran down to the front gate, turned back, and gazed the departing school bus. He watched the bus drive ahead to take the other students home. He turned toward the aluminum doorknob on the white front door. He was about going to go inside when he suddenly sensed something in the backyard.

Jackson looked back to his front yard. It was deep dark and cold out in the field with some little chilly winds. He saw the rose bushes and hedges trembling in the wind. Jackson heard a walking noise. Something moved forward from a shrub. Jackson grabbed a crowbar that was near the front door. He held it tightly, ready to smack whatever creature appeared.

Jackson stepped slowly and wait until the shadowy creature moved ahead. He stealthily followed to where it ran in the backyard. Jackson raised the crowbar in his hand ready to smash the creature. Suddenly, it jumped out of the hedges and showed itself. Jackson held back just in time to keep from hitting his cat, Gumball.

Usually, Gumball come in and out of the house through the cat door. But Jackson discovered that the cat door behind the kitchen door was locked, which trapped Gumball outside in the garden. Jackson slowly approached closer and picked up Gumball. He was about to go back to the front door with Gumball, but then he spotted something else lurking near the backyard door, a six-foot tall android standing at the window.

It was look like a female humanoid and had cyan glowing elastic cable hair. It had a slim torso, like Jackson's mother. Its face was oval, and it have only yellow eyes. The face had either mouth nor nose. Its whole body was made of silvery metal. Standing close to the front window, it gazed at a slim woman with long brown hair, Jackson's mother. Wearing her pink apron, she washed dishes in the sink close to the window.

Jackson saw the robot change its hands from normal human hands into large razor blades. Jackson feared it would kill his mother. He hid Gumball behind a nearby peach tree. Jackson put his cat down on the lawn. He hushed his cat so that the female robot wouldn't notice and kill them.

He opened the Protonitrix, pressed the yellow button on the dial to minimize the processing sound to activate scanning mode. Jackson scanned the rays over his cat. It quietly processed Gumball's DNA sample. The glass dial plate glowed yellow light instead of the vocal message because he had turned on the mute mode when he was on the way home. Jackson selected the new cat armor he had just scanned. He wanted to use it to stop the female robot from harming his mother. He pressed green button twice to start the transformation.

Jackson had blue metal pieces covering his body. The armor was azure blue and could glow in the dark. His arms became big cylindrical blocks. Long, sharp metal claws sprouted out from his fist. Jackson got a helmet that was shaped like cat's head. Every part of the helmet was blue, and the hemet had glass goggles for Jackson to see. The goggles were in infrared mode for use during this time, which was dark and gloomy night. The cat helmet had snouts like a real cat, and a yellow-colored band striped its way from his forehead to the snout. Jackson armor finalized the transformation with a blue cable trailing behind him, similar to a tail.

Jackson dashed at the android, who was trying to murder his mother, and grabbed it. Jackson used his blue cable tail to wrap tightly around the android's neck. The long blue tail wrapped around the android's neck tighter and tighter until its head fell from its body.

The headless android grabbed Jackson's tail and threw him aside. Jackson flew above the ground and landed hard on the ground. The headless android ran up to the rainspout with the use of a magnetic field on her feet. She dashed down with her left hand, which had become a cutter. Jackson dodged the attack and pressed his attack by using his iron boots to kick the headless android on her chest.

The motionless android bumped a trash can, but seemed not to be defeated. She stood and wildy charged towards Jackson in his blue cat armor. The android swooshed the cutter against Jackson many times. She knocked Jackson down and stepped on his chest full of scratches.

Jackson used the claw blades on his left hand to slice the android's right feet. He pushed her away and punched his claw at the robot exactly seven times until her body became pruned with big wounds in its metal body. The creature exploded in front of Jackson. He used his arms to block his sight from the smoke that came out of the dead body.

The explosion was loud, and it made Jackson's mother walk out for a look at the back door. Jackson pressed the Protonitrix and turned back to his normal human form. He hurriedly got a shovel to chop the scrap metal into smaller pieces so they could be thrown away. He got the shovel and hurriedly chopped the android's head and body into tiny pieces.

By the time, Jackson's mom stood behind Jackson. She saw wielding a shovel. Jackson rolled his eyes and looked back to his mom. He could see that his mom was simply upset.

"Jackson, what are you doing?" Jackson's mother asked. She seems to be very angry.

"I was out here to grab Gumball. He was wandered outside the front yard and there were many rattlesnake outside ready to bite him. For his safety, I needed drive off the snakes and take him inside," Jackson dropped the shovel and picked his cat who stood near his feet.

"Hmm… Take your cat and come into the house. Your dad is cooking Bolognese spaghetti tonight," Jackson's mother replied.

Jackson, the cat, and his mother walked into the house. Jackson forget that he left the robot outside. But whatever, if his mother didn't know about the robot in the backyard, it would be fine for now.

Monday was a normal day at school. Jackson studied normally with his classmates, but he thought of other things that were out of the lesson. Kimnara's words intrigued in his mind. Kimnara had said that his master was to come to Earth to destroy it and take over the Protonitrix. Maybe the person that Djin Tzec was afraid off had linked with the battle droid that attacked the gym, the packs of robot wolves that hunted him, and the android who tried to assassinate his mother. Kimnara's words formed a conspiracy theory in his head.

At noon, Jackson went to the school garden area close to the woods, near the foothills he had discovered Djin Tzec. Jackson looked around the area and saw students playing card games and chess on tables in the garden. Chai chased and caught a green ugly bullfrog near the fish pond, while Teresa enjoyed the flowers and butterflies.

Jackson looked silently to the woods. He was huffing quietly because it was dusty and hard to breath. He saw a dark, gleaming light that glowed between trees blocked by the school gate. Jackson suddenly heard something moving through the forest, something that made a rustling sound on the foliage. He turned back to the group of students. No one noticed what he was doing. Jackson suddenly opened the school gate, stepped out quietly, and closed the gate.

Jackson entered the woods and saw a figure moving in and out among the trees. Suddenly, the figure approached at him. It was Djin Tzec, his alien buddy who gave the Protnitrix to him. Djin Tzec wore Jackson's old vest and his old trunks that Jackson have given him a week. Djin Tzec carried a long stick on his shoulders. On the stick were dry, wimpy, wrinkled smoked bullfrogs. He also held a basket made from willow branches and vines. Inside the basket, Jackson saw four green bullfrogs. They all jumped and tried to reach the top of the basket.

"Djin Tzec, what are you doing here in the woods so close to school? If my friends or the teachers see you near the gate, you will be in a big trouble," Jackson said.

"I'm finding bullfrogs in the woods, but I got lost and wandered until I met you," Djin Tzec answered.

"Silly, bullfrogs live close to creeks or ponds. In the dry woodlands like this, there are none close to here," Jackson explained why there were are no bullfrogs in the dry woodlands.

Djin Tzec changed the topic. "Also, I have good news for you. Do you want to hear it?"

"What was it?" Jackson rolled his eyes and looking bored, like he didn't care about Djin Tzec's good news.

Most of the time, it would be like he invented new tools from scrap metal, but failed, or like the time when he saw a raccoon monster that had laser eyes and venomous saliva. Jackson decided that it wasn't important for the humans to know, but it was his normal daily life and these facts he already knew.

"I've fixed my spaceship. I can fly back home now," Djin answered happily

"So, now you can fly back home, right?" Jackson asked.

"Yes, but the bad news is, the space conqueror is coming to the earth after he tried to attack you several times with his evil plan, and they failed." Djin Tzec answered. His voice changed from happy into an anxious tone. "I looked at the radar in my spaceship that informs me of things close to the Earth's atmosphere. I believe I saw his spaceship coming closer to the Earth's upper atmosphere. I decided to help you fight back, so you won't have to take care of everything by yourself. It is my responsibility because I brought him here. I would like to fight alongside you."

Jackson gulped when he heard that the space conqueror, who wanted the Protonitrix, was on a flight to Earth to capture the Protonitrix and destroy the world. Jackson felt bad. He was worried about what would happen to the world after the conqueror arrived. Jackson was concerned about his family, his friends, and every important person in his life after the invasion began. He knew that it wasn't just Djin Tzec's fault that the conqueror had come to Earth, but it was his fault that he messed with the Protonitrix.

Jackson changed his mind without a qualm. He did not like to see people suffer because he wanted to be a superhero. All he knew was that he was just a heroic brat who tried to become a superhero without thinking of cause and effect. Suddenly, a flashback appeared in his mind.

Since Jackson had been seven years old, he and his father had gone to the plant where automobiles were tested. Young Jackson enjoyed watching automobiles driven by an operator in the control tower as they raced in a high speed all around the railway. The car had a test dummy inside to test if it the automobile was safe for passengers.

Young Jackson had been eating chocolate wafers while he watched. He dropped the wrapper on the floor, but ignored picking it up. The janitor was cleaning the floor and came to the wrapper and was going to sweep it with his broom, but Jackson's father stopped the janitor. Jackson's his father asked Jackson to pick up the wrapper and thrown it away by himself.

He did what his father said and threw it into the trash can and went back to watch the cars being tested. At that time, Jackson was curious why he shouldn't let the janitor thrown away his wrapper. He went to his father and asked, "Dad, why should I pick my trash up instead of letting the janitor clean it up."

"Because it was your responsibility, Jack," his father answered.

"Why? The janitor cleans the building. He should throw it away," Jackson expressed his opinion.

"Jackson, listen. You do not make people do things that you are responsible for. It is your responsibility to take care of your duties. Look at the janitor. He must clean this entire facility for people to come and watch cars being tested. He must sweep and take out the trash more than usual if the people do not take care of their own trash. I want to see you grow to be responsible for your duties and behave like a good boy. Understand?"

"Dad. I promise I will be a good boy and take care of myself and my duties without another person's help. I love you dad."

A slight cough from Djin Tzec brought Jackson back to the present. Jackson's father's speech still impressed Jackson today. He was thankful for what his father said. Jackson blinked twice to focus. He turned back to Djin Tzec. "I'm sorry dude. It is too dangerous to fight against the conqueror," Jackson said to Djin Tzec in a deep, timid voice. "That's my responsibility, my job, and it's my mission."

"No way! I must help you. You have fought many times for me and your people. I shall help you," Djin Tzec replied firmly.

"I disagree. It's my mission and my responsibility to take him down!" Jackson shouted in Djin Tzec's face.

"Then, I shall still come with you!" Djin Tzec answered angrily.

Jackson twitched his eyes in anger. "Shut up!" He pushed Djin Tzec's chest with his two hands using a great amount of force.

Djin Tzec fell and hit his back on the ground. Jackson stared in silence. He saw Djin Tzec crying. Tears come from his big round black eyes. Jackson started regret his action. He just wanted Djin Tzec to kept away from the conqueror. Jackson stared, he fought to control his heart from beating rapidly after he pushed Djin Tzec down. He tried to stay calm by exhaling all the air from his lungs and breathing in slowly.

Djin Tzec stood and ran away on his two green feet. He ran as fast as he could to get away from Jackson. He now viewed Jackson as a traitor who was deeply passionate about his power and had forgotten about the friendship between them. Djin Tzec zigzagged among the birch and the oak trees before he disappeared behind the woods.

Jackson wanted to apologize for what he had done, but it was too late. He had caused Djin Tzec to run away, and Jackson realized that needed to have Djin Tzech's help and knowledge about how to fight against the galactic conqueror.

Jackson walked back to the park. He closed the gate as he walked toward the school building. Before he closed the gate's metal door, he turned his head back to the silent, plain woods. They created a depressing scene. Jackson closed the gate gently and hurriedly followed the other students into the building.

In the hallway, Teresa, Chai, Roger, and Jackson were walking together as a group. They were going to their lockers to get ready for language arts. Before they took another step in the hallway, something terrible happened. The plants in the flower pots shook, and chairs in the reading area trembling hard. The shaking took place on every floor, except the third floor, where Jackson was.

Suddenly, a huge red laser beam burned through the floor. Explosions from the laser destroyed the whole third floor. Jackson recognized many students that tripped and crashed all the way down to the first floor, which was filled by debris: cement, rocks, and sharp metal.

Jackson hurriedly pressed the button to activate the Protonitrix. He transformed quickly. Within a flash of the green light, Jackson became an earth armor. One of the basic types of armor contained inside the Protonitrix that transformed into big brown and beige blocks of the metal. The brown, hard cubic helmet latched onto Jackson as his arm received a giant beige gauntlet. Jackson, in the earth armor, shot ten thousand tons of sand out from his power gloves. Sand filled the first floor so that it became a big, deep sand basin. Many students landed on the sand. They were mostly safe. Only the few of them cracked their bones or bumped their heads against hard objects.

Jackson ordered Teresa to take the students that were not injured to teachers who were already outside when the building collapsed. Roger and

Chai helped carry injured students out of the building. Jackson looked at the roof that was now cleared. He saw a spacecraft in the sky.

The spacecraft was about ten times larger than a blue whale. Its shape looked like a black marlin in the ocean. The spaceship was cylindrical, and the snout had a long, sharp point sticking out. But the spacecraft also had laser cannons and plasma cannons sticking out from weapon tubes. Suddenly, it landed close to Jackson and the other students. The exit gate on its side opened. As the gate opened sideways, something emerged.

It was a large tall figure, about four or five meters high. It was some kind of a bipedal robot. It was made from dark gray, shiny armor. The hands and arms were large and bulky, like Jackson's earth armor. On its head were five horns——two short sharp horns on each side of its face and one long horn on its forehead. The robot also had v-shaped goggle-like eyes and a black gloomy shawl on its back.

"Who are you?" Jackson asked.

"I'm Daikaiser, the Lord of the Darkness. I'm from the planet Oscur Astonos, and I'm here to take the Protonitrix," the robot introduced himself in a deep metallic voice.

"You destroyed the whole school and tried to kill me and my friends! I won't let you get the Protonitrix," Jackson yelled.

"If you don't give it to me, then I shall destroy you!" Daikaiser fired orange hot beams out from his hand.

Jackson dodged it by ducking down on the floor. He pressed the Protonitrix's green and blue buttons and quickly swiped the pointer on the dial plate to choose the armor he needed. He selected wind armor, which was one he had never used before. Jackson knew that it was one of the basic elemental armors in the Protonitrix, but he had never tried it. He pressed the green button twice until the green flash lit. He suddenly wore an armor made from platinum. His gloves were spiny. His shoulders were covered with sharp hook-shaped spines. Jackson's helmet had v-shape goggles and a big curved fin on top, like a shark's fin.

Jackson shot a small vortex at Daikaiser and pushed him all the way to the wall behind the school reception area. Jackson, in the wind armor, swooshed forward and stomped his left foot on Daikaiser's muscular chest and taunted, "Are you giving up."

"Why should I?" Daikaiser grabbed Jackson's ankle and threw Jackson forward.

Daikaiser stood and kicked Jackson right on the hips and then used his red laser beam from his left hand to shoot Jackson in his chest.

Jackson, injured badly from the fight, pressed the Protonitrix to switch armor. He turned into the fire armor that he used to defeat the battle droid. Jackson's spiny, silvery gauntlet became a red glove with a fire vessel under his wrist. Jackson was in a superheat red armor made from metal. He had his respirator and a jetpack on his back. Jackson blazed fire at Daikaiser who walked towards him. The fire did not seem to cause any damage. Daikaiser's armor absorbed the heat, and it made him stronger.

Daikaiser powered up and walked towards Jackson. He grabbed Jackson's face. He exerted contracting forces onto Jackson's armor. Jackson couldn't breathe. He tried to punch back at Daikaiser, but Daikaiser's big hand make it hard for him to see. Jackson felt as if his skull was ready to explode. Everytime he tried to move, his body contracted hard.

Teresa, Chai, and Roger went to help Jackson, who struggled to fight. Teresa grabbed a flower pot nearby and threw it at Daikaiser. The flower pot accurately hit Daikaiser in the face. He released Jackson and covered his face with his left palm. Chai took an iron bar and smashed it against Daikaiser's chest, but it barely scratched his black armor. Daikaiser removed the hand he used to cover his face.

Roger grabbed a big block of brick from the floor and stood in a position to launch it at Daikaiser. He flung his hand forward, and the brick flew to toward Daikaiser's face. The brick crashed Daikaiser on the injury caused by the flower pot. He stepped back and skittered away from the attack.

Jackson stood after being released and turned his armor into reptile armor. He flew in the air as his armor became reptile armor with dragon wings. Purple flashes covered Jackson. He was now in the purple armor. His shoulder's cobra plate and the metal crocodile jaw in the chest made Jackson look fabulously powerful. His purple helmet had three sharp fins like last time. Two on the side and one on his head. As Jackson emerged from the flash, he punched Daikaiser twelve times in mid-air, swooshing in from left to right. Daikaiser couldn't fight that many attacks in one blow. Jackson angrily punched Daikaiser's face and swooshed onto Daikaiser.

Sounds of two metal pieces banging echoed from the fight, making the students and teachers who were trying to escape from the building turn back and stare.

"You tried to destroy people who didn't even do anything to you. I will thrash you until you give up trying to get my Protonitrix. You must keep your hands off it!" Jackson exclaimed, as he kept punching harder.

"Never, I am a conqueror, and I will never give up to a stupidly weak and wimpy human, like you. The Earth shall be mine. Humans will be my slaves. Ha! Ha! Ha!" Daikaiser exclaimed, as he fought back against Jackson's attack.

"That will not happen!" Jackson shouted angrily at Daikaiser and gave one last hard punch to Daikaiser's face.

Jackson shifted from reptile armor to cat armor. Jackson now had blue cat-shaped armor with the yellow claws and a blue cable tail. He landed on the floor and jumped onto Daikaiser's face. Jackson used the sharp yellow claw blades on his fist to punch at Daikaiser, but Daikasier grabbed Jackson's right hand and threw him onto the floor.

Jackson jumped up and kicked back against Daikaiser's right arm as Daikaiser moved down closer to catch Jackson. Daikaiser grabbed Jackson by the blue cable tail from the cat armor and cast Jackson against the wall.

Jackson bounced off the cracked wall and fell to the ground. He fought back pain and shifted from the cat armor into water armor. Jackson armor turned blue. He wore the oxygen tank on his back and flippers on his feet. Jackson stood and fired jets of water to freeze Daikaiser. But water didn't cool Daikaiser because his armor absorbed heat and turned the water into vapor.

Jackson tried to use gadgets he had with the water armor but accidentally pressed the button on the right of his wrist and activated an orca missile launcher. The launcher was a small cannon made from metal connected to Jackson's wrist. It shot four missiles that looked like mini half-bodied killer whales. The missiles hit Daikaiser and made him stagger. Jackson ran towards Daikaiser. He jumped up in the air and swooshed his right foot toward Daikaiser's face, but Jackson failed.

Daikaiser grabbed Jackson's flipper and smashed him to the ground. Jackson felt a searing pain in his back. Daikaiser walked towards Jackson and grabbed Jackson's feet. Daikaiser was about to squished Jackson's feet but an explosion stopped him.

Teresa, Roger, and Chai stared fearfully at Jackson. They couldn't help him from this situation. Daikaiser was too powerful.

A UFO shaped like two pieces of metal frisbee put together flew over Daikaiser's spacecraft. The UFO glowed a green neon color and shot laser beams at Daikaiser's spacecraft. The spacecraft was cut in half, and the wings exploded.

Jackson smirked happily. He turned his head to the UFO who flew closer. Daikaiser stared at the UFO as it landed. The cap on top opened and revealed Djin Tzec holding something that looks like a flashlight. Djin Tec fired a yellow glowing laser beam at Daikaiser.

Daikaiser grabbed his chest in pain and fell. Jackson stood and ran joyfully to Djin Tzec. He knew that Djin Tzec had forgiven him.

"Djin Tzec!" Jackson cried.

"Jackson!" Djin Tzec cried back.

"I'm sorry for hurting you. Without your help, I would probably have died in this battle. Thank you for be concerned for me," Jackson said.

"It doesn't matter. We must get rid of Daikaiser," Djin Tzec shouted. "Hurry, use the ice armor. I'll slow him down."

Jackson did what Djin Tec said. He pressed the green and the blue button to switch to ice armor. The green flash surrounded Jackson's body and changed into ice armor. He blasted beams of liquid nitrogen to create a path around Daikaiser who was injured by Djin Tzec's flashlight gun. Dazed and confused, Daikaiser stumbled toward Jackson to kill him. He stepped on the slippery ice path and fell. Daikaiser heated his body with heat energy inside him to melt the path. Jackson saw the ice path melt into a puddle of water. He to Djin Tzec who kept shooting laser beams from his gun.

"How can Daikaiser melt the ice?" Jackson asked.

"He is a life form made from dark cosmic particles with the ability to consume heat and kept it inside his dark molecular cells made of cosmic power. If he needs to use the heat, he can release the energy from his body by using thermal radiation," Djin Tzec explained.

Jackson used two tentacles from his armor to grab Daikaiser's hands. He asked Djin Tzec to open the laboratory door, which was close to his current position. Jackson also asked his friends for help. They all ran at Daikaiser, clung onto Daikaiser's lower body, and pushed him into laboratory.

Daikaiser couldn't withstand the force from the humans. He fell and knocked over the UV radiation machine that was used to sterilize the tools in the laboratory. The machine crashed and exploded. The explosion ravaged the whole laboratory. Djin Tzec, Jackson's friends, and Jackson ran from the laboratory as the whole room collapsed.

Roger and Chai saw that the pillar that supported the ceiling crumble. Jackson sprayed liquid nitrogen at the crack and formed a thick ice layer to prevent it from collapse. The kids and an alien survived the laboratory collapse. They felt thankful for the building that collapsed and buried Daikaiser under the debris. They hoped it had killed Daikaiser.

Teresa, Chai, and Roger turned back and walked to the entrance door to exit the building. Djin Tzec stared at the debris with Jackson. He also felt thought that Daikaiser was dead, but he was wrong.

Jackson and Djin Tzec sensed vibration on the ground. It felt like an earthquake. But something rose from the debris. It was a big black dragon as tall as a nine-story building!

The dragon was black. It had a gloomy serpentine head and spine bones that made up the neck. The dragon was a bipedal. It stood upright, like a dinosaur, and had a big muscular chest covered with large white scales. The dragon had green parallel stripes all over its body, except around the neck.

Jackson saw that it also had wings on its back. The wings were big and bat-shaped, with green flaps. The long black, gloomy tail did not have stripes. The dragon had shining green, ferocious eyes that made Jackson anxious. The dragon grabbed Djin Tzec with it big black left hand and grabbed Jackson with it big black right hand.

"I've even stronger than all of you! I'm Dragonic Daikaiser in my ultimate form and will destroy you," The dragon exclaimed and aggressively swooshed it tail toward Teresa, Roger, and Chai.

Teresa got hit and flew into the air. she landed on Roger, who was bigger and taller. Roger flew to the same height and landed on the ground. As he got hit, he lay on the ground and used his hand to grab Teresa's shoulder. Luckily, Dragonic Daikaiser used the tip of his tail to hit. Even though it hurt, it caused no serious injuries.

While Teresa and Roger landed safely, Chai flew two meters into the air and hit the ground hard. He became unconscious as soon as he contacted the ground. He didn't move or respond.

Teresa ran to Chai and shook him to awaken him, but it didn't work. Even though Chai was unconscious, he had no severe bleeding. Teresa prayed that Chai would survive.

Trapped in Daikaiser's hand, Jackson tried to fight back, but he couldn't transform back into his human form because the Protonitrix was wrapped inside Daikaiser's clenched fist. Jackson needed to press it to turn back to his normal form or else he would be stuck in the armor forever.

Daikaiser threw Djin Tzec, in his left hand, to the ground, but Djin Tzec landed on a nearby sheet of sponge. He landed safely and turned to see Teresa and Roger sobbing and trying to help Chai. Djin Tzec rushed to help.

After Daikaiser released Djin Tzec, he used his pointer finger and his thumb, like a pair of pliers, to pinch the Protonirtrix. He yanked the Protonitrix from Jackson. The belt started to fall off. The iron belt chain broke open, and the red neon lights flashed out from the face dial.

Jackson cried in pain. The Protonitrix started to lose its ability to scan DNA or atoms. It stopped recognizing Jackson's DNA, which was the database for it to recognize its owner.

Realizing the Protonitrix was broken, Daikaiser became angry and growled monstrously. Jackson cried as he saw the Protonitrix crushed in front of him. Now it was flat and cracked like a crushed soda can. The dial face that was glass used to switch form was cracked. "Look what have you did!" Jackson shouted at Dragonic Daikaiser. His anger mixed with sadness. Jackson ground his teeth hard, and he shivered. Tears fell from his eyes, like streams of water.

"The Protonitrix is broken. You can no longer obtain its power. Now, I shall make you disappear along with the infinity of its power!" Dragonic Daikaiser looked down and taunted Jackson.

Jackson became even more angry. Not just only was he filled with anger and sadness, but he also feared death.

Djin Tzec moved in front of Jackson. He spread his arms wide and tried to block Jackson from whatever Daikaiser was going to throw. "If you're going to kill him, you must kill me first!"

"Then, I'll destroy you both!" Daikaiser growled. He blasted big neon-green laser beams from his mouth onto Jackson and Djin Tzec.

Jackson and Djin Tzec started to disappear inside the laser beams. Their particles, their cells, and their body were breaking into small pixels by the laser beams. Jackson only had his head left, and he couldn't see much of what was happening. His memories start to showed up, like a film scene in a theater. He saw the time that he spent with his parents on the vacation, the moment he was born, and the time he went to school and met Chai, Roger and Teresa during preschool time. He saw the time he got his first A+ on an algebra test and the time he took Gumball home after he got it from the dumpster in the backyards.

Jackson enjoyed watching his father building robots and racing cars. He wanted to cry, but he couldn't. He wondered what would happen to the Dimes family without him, what would happen to his friends, what would happen to his parents, who were waiting for him to come back home and enjoy dinner together, and what would happen to his community, his home state, his country, and the world.

Jackson turned his head to Djin Tzec. He was dissolving in the green laser light. Djin Tzec shrieked as his green body became small square pixels and faded away. Jackson felt a stinging pain when he saw Djin Tzec fade away. He couldn't do anything to save Djin Tzec. Jackson had only his head left in the beams, and it started to break into small square pixels.

Jackson yelled out from the beams in pain. Many teachers, the school headmaster, janitors, the principal, and students, except his friends, ran off crying. They remembered and knew how important Jackson had been to the school community.

Teresa wanted Jackson to share more good experiences with her. Seeing him fade away inside the laser beam was the saddest thing she had ever experienced.

Suddenly, a bright white flash came from nowhere and went straight to Jackson. It landed on Jackson's head and the last of Djin Tzec's pixels. Jackson turned his head to the light. They were both suddenly transported by the white flash and disappeared inside the in the green glowing laser beams.

Jackson woke after he faded away. His body was exactly the same as before. He was still in his red jean jacket and blue jeans. He discovered that he wasn't at Theodore Roosevelt Middle School anymore.

He discovered the place he was in right now was a white, plain, and huge. Plenty enough space to put many big cities. Jackson looked to the sky. It was also white and had some kind of glowing light at the highest point, which was infinitely far away. Jackson wondered where was he and why he was in this place. Where was his school, Daikaiser, his friends, and the people he loved?

Jackson got the answer soon. He saw a figure walking towards him. He couldn't see much of the figure from at this point, but as the figure walked closer, Jackson saw it more clearly. The figure appeared to be similar to Djin Tzec, but it was a little bit taller. It had green skin and five long slender fingers. The figure also had a longer neck, but its facial structure was similar to Djin Tzec's black round eyes and oval face.

This figure appeared to be much older. Jackson saw a white beard sticking out of his chin. The figure wore a silk robe, like an ancient Chinese emperor. The robe was blue and had a yellow sleeve, and the figure wore a crown that had seven points. The red ruby point in front was the one largest point. Jackson didn't understand why he looked so similar to Djin Tzec and why he was walking towards him.

"You're Jackson Dimes, aren't you?" the old man asked when he came close enough.

"My name is Jackson Dimes, sir," Jackson Dimes answered, his voice low and quiet.

"Great to see you, Jackson Dimes. You are the hero of seven galaxies," the old man said.

"Who are you? Why did you speak to me like my extraterrestrial, friend, Djin Tzec?" Jackson asked the old man.

The old man introduced himself, "He is my grandson. I'm Tacza Tzec, Djin Tzec's grandfather."

"Wow! You're Djin Tzec's grandfather? I had heard from your grandson that you had died many years after you invented the Protonitrix," Jackson said in amazement.

"I understand you have questions to ask, but first followed me this way," Tacza Tzec told Jackson. He clicked his fingers, and a violet swirling portal opened.

Jackson followed Tacza Tzec into the portal. He didn't really want to know where he would go next. Jackson and Tacza Tzec arrived in Hades. The place was filled with dangerous flames, hot magma, and rivers of lava.

Spirits of people were summoned to this desperate land. There were people climbing thorny wooden poles up to the top to get away from the lava. On their way, they get pricked in the heart by thorns and spines. Vulture and the ravens were chewing and munching on the carcass of the people who failed to reach the top. Some people sank in the magma pool. They screamed in pain as the molten rock scorched their bodies, and devils kept pushing them down into the pool.

The devils were human skeletons wearing gray cloaks. They held a scythe and kept slicing those spirits who tried to escape. The image frightened Jackson. He saw chaos, flame, and scared and despaired people running around, and angry devils punishing the people. He wished the he could push the scene from his mind.

Tacza describe the purpose for coming to Hades. "Here are the spirits who come to the Hades. This is a place where sinful spirits are punished. They never made goods things happen in life, and they destroyed and tore apart relationships between people who kept doing wonderful things. Selfish and greedy people are also clumped inside this land for punishment.

Jackson frowned a bit and then shook his head.

"Jackson, I know it isn't time for you to see the Hades, but we're going to the heaven next, and I wanted you to see the contrast and know justice is served." Then, Tacza Tzec touched the lava rock beneath them. The lava rock became an elevator and lift them away from the horrible scene. Jackson saw the whole area of Hades as the elevator rose higher. It was so large with plenty of empty space made from lava rocks and scorching magma rivers.

The elevator slowed. "Jackson, we have reached Heaven." Tacza tugged Jackson's right shoulder.

"All right sir, let's go," Jackson said.

Jackson and Tacza Tzec exited the lava rock elevator. They looked at Heaven.

Jackson's first view of heaven showed a calm, warm, creative, and peaceful place. Many clouds look fluffy, but the puffs were hard and make him think he was standing on solid tiles. Jackson looked at the crowds of spirits and saw them heading to the gates. The gates were golden bars, tall and creatively artistic. Jackson saw many people hurriedly enter the three channels leading to entrances. At the entrances were gray sculptures of Buddha, Jesus, and Allah, all made from limestone. The Buddha was in the meditation sculpture, and he flattened his left hand. Jesus stood and stretched his arms wide, like the statue in Rio de Janeiro. Allah was holding the Quran in his hand and looked down to read its wisdom.

Jackson suddenly spotted someone walking around. It was his friend, Chai. Jackson hurriedly went into the crowd. He bumped many spirits as he made his way to Chai. Jackson grabbed Chai's hand and silently pulled him away.

Tacza saw what had happened and asked Jackson what he was doing.

"Tacza, I found my friend in the crowd! We must take him back home," Jackson shouted while he dragged Chai away from the entrance gate.

"Why did you stop your friend? His spirit needs to go behind the gate to spend his life in Heaven," Tacza said.

A man with golden hair, blue eyes, and white skin, wearing a white robe nudged up to them. "I'm sorry for interrupting you, sir. I'm the toll gate controller. The Lord has reported to me that Jackson Dimes and Chai Lakkamorn need to go back to their world. They are both on a mission to fight against the evil who is causing chaos in their world," the man reported. "Also, God said these two spirits must go back to their home planet. Please take them immediately, sir."

"Sure, my friend, I'll take them back home and make sure they are safe," Tacza said to the man in the robe.

He turned back to Jackson and Chai. "Jackson, it's time to take you and your friend back to your home world. Let's go." Tacza ordered Jackson, who held Chai's hand.

Jackson felt great joy that he would be able to spend his normal life back home.

Tacza clicked his fingers. Everything turned back to the white, plain place where he found Jackson. Jackson held Chai's hand, but he still had questions that needed to be asked before he left.

"Mr. Tacza, why are Chai and I allowed to go back to our own world?" Jackson asked.

"It was the Creator God who told ordered me to take you back. He pulled your spirits out from the laser beams and preserved your spirits here. Your body can be regenerated after he reconstructs your pixels. But if it was too late, you wouldn't be able to get your human form back." Tacza talked about the Creator God who dominated every universe.

Jackson was surprised that the light of the infinite universe was as plain and white as the Creator God's throne. Before he could ask Tacza to show him the Creator God, something came into Jackson's mind. "Mr. Tacza? Do you know where Djin Tzec is?" Jackson asked Tacza in an anxious voice.

"He is fine. Right now, he is following my footsteps to Heaven. God saved his spirit, but his body is gone. Creator God has preserved spirit, his essence in an energy spirit ball that floats through the universe. Djinn Tzec's memories and ability to talk will stay the same." Tacza stopped his speech suddenly. He looked at Jackson and saw Jackson crying. He knew that Djin Tzec was an important to Jackson. Their friendship was so strong. Even the evil monstrous dragon would never destroy them or separate them.

Tacza shined light from the ruby on his crown. Something appeared in his opened palms. The object became solid. "Here is his last present to you, Jackson. Always remember him that he with you at all time. He wants you to remember the good times you had together." Tacza took a pause for the breath and then continued, "I knew that you that you still have many questions and activities that you and my nephew would like to do together. But when there's birth, there always death behind. The only thing that is still stable in our world is prestige and destruction. It would be your choice now to choose which path you will follow, Jackson?" Tacza held the fixed Protonitrix in both open hands. He handed it over to Jackson. He shook his head lightly and told Jackson to wear it. Jackson accepted the Protonitrix, put the belt around his waist, and grinned in joy.

Jackson never heard words or speech like this before. He suddenly understood the Truth of the world. He paused and zoomed deeply into his memories. He remembered the time he first made another person feel better, and many times he saved innocent people form something that was dangerous or evil. He took hold of Chai, who look around absentmindedly, and felt proud. He promised himself to always fight against evil. *"You did well, Jackson. Kept doing it constantly."*

Jackson turned back to the white wall from where he awoke. He waved his hand in delight to Tacza Tzec, and a clear, pure energy orb near Jackson proved Djin Tzec was with him. In an instant, Jackson's and Chai's spirits returned to their world and the important mission that needed to be completed.

Back on Earth, Daikaiser felt glad that no hero or any kind of person could stop him from continuing his plan. He crashed through the front entrance of the building and walked over to a group of people who became anxious with feelings of hopeless.

"To all of you foolish humans. You have lost your hero. I shall claim this planet after I have destroyed all of you!" Daikaiser roared and fired green laser beams at the group of people who didn't know what to do. The green laser beams traveled in the air, suddenly stopped, and changed their direction back to the owner. Daikaiser got shot in his chest five times. He roared loudly because of his injuries and turned his dragon head back to the group of people who stood and used their arms to block the lasers.

Jackson appeared in front of group. Everyone except Daikaiser didn't believe their eyes. They saw Jackson standing in midair, using his hand to repel the laser beams away, like a reflective shield. Daikaiser was amazed at Jackson's power. He wanted to ask how Jackson got such super power.

"Impossible, my laser beams destroy everything they touch. How did you stop them?" Dragonic Daikaiser asked in doubt.

"Evil beings, like you, will never win. I'll show you why," Jackson replied in a deep serious tone. He suddenly tapped his finger on the Protonitrx's face dial. His whole body covered in the silvery platinum. Jackson's whole body became shiny, like a knight in the fairy tales. His shoulder plates became sharp like the spines. His helmet was white platinum with two sharp metal edges that went up like an owl tassel. Jackson had glass goggles with his helmet.

This armor was special. Jackson had a sword that was quite large—about five feet long. It had two parallel black stripes on the blade. The handle was easy to hold, but the attack power in the blade was extremely high. Jackson finalized the transformation with the cape—like an eagle's wings. Jackson went down to the ground softly with the sword in his hand.

Daikaiser stepped back as he saw Jackson's new figure. Everyone cheered and shouted for Jackson. Jackson smiled from the corner of his lips. He turned back to Daikaiser who was nervous as he saw the Protonitrix had been fixed.

"The Protonitrix!" Daikaiser exclaimed. "How'd it get fixed."

"Your evil power will never destroy our will. Be prepare to be vanquished!" Jackson exclaimed, taunting Daikaiser to fight.

Daikaiser use his dragon claws to scratch Jackson and try to knock him to the ground.

Jackson used his cape to fly. He waved his cape to lift his body up away from the claws. The cape separates into Jackson's eagle wings, and he dashed down to the scaly chest of the terrifying beast. Jackson Daikaiser's chest open.

Daikaiser shrieked in pain and used his hand to cover the wound. He moved his hand away from the injury and saw purple smoke bleeding from his chest. The sword's blow was absolutely fatal!

Jackson charged again. He got smacked by Daikaiser's tail and. Jackson crashed into a huge nearby tree. His lower hips landed in the branches with his left hand holding the sword. Jackson lept from the branches without showing fear. He smiled and flew down to the ground. Daikaiser fired laser beams at Jackson many times. But they all got reflected by his platinum armor.

Everyone who watched exclaimed in amazement, except for the principal who didn't believe Jackson was strong enough to fight a dragon. Jackson's armors started to glow with a shiny metallic flash. He dashed as fast as he could with a high velocity that neared the velocity light traveled through the space. People only saw Jackson as a shining white light that dashed through the evil dragon.

Jackson shouted at Daikaiser, who stared and couldn't do anything to defeat his opponent. "This is for killing Djin Tzec, trying to hurt my friends, destroying the peace, and your plan to take over the Protonitrix!"

"N...Noooooooo!" Dragonic Daikaiser shouted in pain as Jackson stabbed his sword to the same place where he had cut before. Daikaiser glowed in green light, exploded into gasses, and faded away in front of six-hundred people around the school. Everyone carefully watched the attack.

They all smiled as Jackson destroyed the villain away. Jackson literally saved the world!

Jackson turned back to his human form and saw many people from his school community smiling at him. Jackson smiled back.

"Jackson that was cool. Hope you are playing well like this in the basketball game." Coach George said.

"Show me that kind of the move. You got it nice man!" Dylan, Jackson's classmate, exclaimed for him.

"I will have rethink how I feel about you. I've always thought that you were some kind of the timid kid who was afraid of mathematics and not very smart. But you have proved to me that you are very courageous and love people," Mr. Hazelnut praised Jackson.

"Whoa, Jackson. Where's Chai," Roger asked Jackson in the nervous voice.

"I'm here." The sound came from behind the crowd. Roger turned back and saw Chai who had recovered from his injuries.

"Chai! You're alive. How did you heal so quickly?" Roger asked Chai and ran to him.

Chai didn't give any answer. The only thing he did was pointed his finger at Jackson.

"Jackson, thank you." Teresa blushed and spoke softly in Jackson's ear. "I mean I love you."

"It seems like everyone love me for now," Jackson replied in his normal happy voice.

"Jackson is our hero! Jackson is our hero!" Everyone clapped in applause and cheered Jackson.

"OK, everyone, thanks to all of you guys. But I have something to do." After he finished speaking, Jackson walked to the broken building that looked like the abandoned construction site in the forest.

The Protonitrix attached to Jackson glowed and gave a voice message: "Fixing and returning damaged objects back to normal." Then it produced a flash and started to fix the building.

The building started to regenerate and turn back to normal form. It took little time to fix the building and stopped when the building was totally fixed. Everyone walked into the building for a sneak peek. They saw the rooms and objects were in the same place as before the damage.

There were no cracks in the wall or floors and no fallen pieces of rubble and debris. The study area was now safe for students to use. Jackson silently stood and smiled at the campus.

"Jackson! It's time to go home. Follow me upstairs to get my backpack," Teresa shouted back from in front of the main entrance.

"Sure, wait for me at a second," Jackson responded back. He turned his head back to the car park where everyone had stood to watch the fight. He saw a white orb of energy floating around. It talked to Jackson.

"Jackson the great, it was fun to stay with you. I learned many new things while I was on this planet. It was also great for you to help me with my mission. I'm so grateful and can't find any words that explain your virtue." The orb glowed brighter. "Goodbye, Jackson the great. You are always my friend. We will be friends forever. Plase kept the Protonitrix along with you, there are still villains who want to come and cause chaos to Earth. The people are in your hand to protect. Keep them safe from all harm and hazards." The orb flew away as it finished.

Jackson let tears run down his cheeks. He smiled and stared where the orb ball flew into the sky and disappeared. No words came from Jackson's mouth as he stood in the car park. Wind flew from the east and patted gently on Jackson's right shoulder.

"See you later, somewhere out there, Djin Tzec."

On the way back home, Teresa and Jackson walked together. Jackson pushed his bicycle and wore the Protonitrix.

Teresa walked close to Jackson. She looked up and saw Jackson frowning. He looked more depressed than she had ever seen before. "Jackson, what's wrong?" Teresa asked in a worried voice.

"I miss Djin Tzec very much. He died and turned into an orb of light. He will not return in body form. I wish he was still here. He was so brave to fly over and come to help me in my fight," Jackson said in a depressed voice.

"I was so proud of you, Jackson. I am sure that Djin Tzec is proud of you," Teresa said in a soothing voice as they arrived in the front of Jackson's house.

"See you later Teresa." Jackson waved his hand and walked into the house. He knew that every life always had hope. He decided to place his memories of Djin Tzec in his deepest core of his head.

Later that night, Jackson lay in bed ready to go to sleep. He wrapped himself in a blanket. Gumball jumped onto the bed. The cat found the best area to sleep. It lay near Jackson's feet and curled itself over into a ball. Jackson turned his head and saw the Protonitrix across sitting on his desk. He wondered where Djin Tzec waw be right now. Was he already reborn as some kind of life form? Was he on Earth, or would he spend his life after death with his grandfather in Heaven?

A myriad of questions kept sprouting from his brain. Jackson reached over to the yellow electric lamp on the shelf next to his bed and pressed the switch. He gently closed his eyelids and saw a dim dark blue scene. In the last moment before he went to sleep, he started to relax and thought about what should he do tomorrow.

A small orb of light appeared above Jackson's closed eyes and a sudden feeling of happiness filled him. *"Goodbye, Djin Tzec,"* Jackson muttered.

In his mind, Djin Tzec's voice answerd, "Goodbye, for now, Jackon Dimes."

Time

By

Luna Kihara

"It shot a bullet at my doll, and I was frightened to death. I just stood there all alone, not knowing what to do. I was lost. My parents were gone. They had left me behind."

Just as I finished, *Fake from The Sky,* I dreamed of feeling what it was like in WWII. I came to look for a cake recipe for my birthday cake since I, Hannah Waltson, was going to turn thirteen next week on September 26th, but I would rather read about WWII than a cake recipe. I was now in *Liberty Library* located at Chicago Lychenberg. Shelves filled with books lined up across the hall. Atmosphere filled with baby crying to girls chatting.

"Hey mama, I want this book," I could hear one girl say. Then I could see Mona's reflection on the glass dome.

Every WWII book I touched felt soothing for me. I looked around for some books to read, first tilting each book. I brushed locks of golden hair from my eyes and searched for a perfect fit, my index finger slipping from one book to another.

Suddenly my finger stopped on a book with ripped pages. The metal and silver strip made me wondered, *how can books be chained when books are normal. I mean it doesn't really make sense, does it? Chained books. Chained books? Chained book!* I tried to think of some books that are chained. It still didn't make sense. Not knowing what to do, I started to open the restrained literature. My heart raced. *It's nothing.* I touched the smooth metal stripe. The sound made clang through the whole library, which made me even more nervous. Then, when I was about to open the book, I noticed Mona wasn't at her place anymore. I squinted my eyes, and saw her trotting around a bookshelf and heading my way. Her curly brown hair dangled down to her waist. I had to admit, she was a beautiful girl. Looking at her sparkling eyes, as precious as diamonds, I felt jealous.

"Hey Hannah, can you check out this for me?" Mona's voice begged as she stared at me with her imitation of cute little puppy eyes.

"Okay, but only this time. Now go back to the children's corner."

"What's that?" Mona pointed to my book Suddenly, she took my book, while I was too late to hide it back behind my back.

"No Mona, give it back!"

"Nana. Nana!" She teased and blabbed her tongue.

I knew what was going to happen. I knew that she was going to open the book. Instinctively, I realized Mona opening the book was not going to be good.

"Mona, give it back. Now!"

"Quiet please. Over there," Shushed Ms. Elka, the new librarian.

I was afraid of Mona opening the book. My heart raced and vision became blurry as Mona opened the book. The papers started to flip automatically. It flipped to page, *203.* The heading read, *Time Slipping to WWII.*

"What?" I shouted.

"Quiet!" Ms. Elka shushed one more.

"Oh, no," I gasped.

Her high heel shoes hit the ground as she walked. Since, the library was a big dome, her high heels sounded someone knocking on the door, but it echoed more. Klick, klick, klick, the sound echoed throughout the library. Kids, teenager, and adults stopped reading; homeless people stopped napping and sat up from the library's comfortable reclining chairs, and teachers stopped thumbing through reference material in the quiet room. All stared directly at me. I had to hide, but *where?* Then suddenly the book swirled me and Mona up and---Bam*!*

We were not in the Liberty Library anymore.

* * * *

"Where are we?" Mona asked with a shiver.

"I don't know…" I had to admit. I did not understand the scene before, which kinda embarrassed me because I always got an A in history classes. I looked around and saw people wearing old fashion clothes. Compared to ours, Mona had a short pants and a short sleeve shirt. I had on long pants and a short sleeve shirt, too. But when I looked around, I saw something different. People dressed in old fluffy clothes that they may have worn in the 1900s. The women wiped her forehead, which looked like she had just finishing from bathing.

"Hannah, Hannah!" Mona's yelling focused my attention on her.

"What?"

"Where are we?" She asked nervously.

Right, I had to think where we were. I needed some help. I walked to the black lady. "Excuse me, do you know where *Liberty Library* is?"

"Liberty Library? Never heard of that." She had a braided hair that dangled to her shoulder. Her tone made me shiver, as if I were standing in a cold winter Chicago wind.

"It's located in the Chicago suburb, Lychenberg, on Thirty-Fourth street."

"Are you joking!" The lady exclaimed.

I was so curious why she thought I was joking with her. Her tone made even more confused. "Ah, no ma'am," I answered, worried.

"This is not even Chicago!"

"What?!" I stammered in a shocked voice. My tone must have portrayed the doubt in my mind.

The woman pointed to a sign that indicated a town in the western part of the United States. "Look at the sign young lady. What does it say?"

I gulped once. "Um…. it says Arizona."

"Right. Now go wander around and find your way home, and stop wasting people's time." She shouted, and passed between me and Mona. I looked at the sign again it did say *Youngberg Arizona*. This place was about a nine-day walk from Chicago. The book had transported us about 1,600 miles from home. Mona jerked on my hand and pointed to a woman and two young girls passing by and then to a group of women setting on a bench at a bus stop.

"Hannah! What's wrong! Why are these people wearing fluffy dresses!"

I gulped in warm desert air to gain a little time to answer a question for which I had no real answer.

"We are not at home, we are at Arizona," I said in a slow thoughtful voice. Mona scrunched her nose and looked at me as one might look at a crazy person.

"What! We are always at the Liberty Library."

"We *were* at the Liberty Library in Chicago. Somehow we have been transported to Arizona."

"How?" Mona asked in a disbelieving voice, but then she looked all around and continued in a frightened voice, "and where is Arizona anyway?!"

"About 1,600 miles away from Chicago. That takes about 64 days by walking."

"Hannah! Stop pranking me!" My sister's voice neared panic. I had to do something; I had to take control of the situation.

I stomped my foot to get her attention. "Mona! Would you please stop asking me! I am telling you, we are not in Liberty Library anymore. We are not at our home anymore! So, would you please be quiet!" I shouted, trying to get my younger sister to give me her attention so that I could come up with a plan of action.

I quickly went to the nearest shop looking for newspapers. Instead of crying and shouting back, Mona held my hands like she did when she got lost in the park. She held it tighter and tighter. It hurt, but I didn't care. What I cared was why she was holding my hands. The tears from her blue, sparkly eyes rolled down her reddish cheeks. I had to admit, maybe I was a little bit harsh with her. I felt sorry.

"Hey, Mona." I squatted down. "I think I was little harsh with you, and I'm sorry."

"We are not at home. . ." As she said the word home, it made me cry, too. I hugged her. Hugged her tighter than ever, and I started to feel her warmth.

"It's okay. I told her. We will get there. It's a long distance, but we can do it. It'll be fine. We just have to get back the book back and go back to Liberty Library," I whispered into her ear. "In order to get back to our own time, we need to get to Liberty Library in Chicago and find the book. It can take us back to our own time-period. Do you understand?"

"Okay." She hugged me back. "But how do we get to Chicago?"

Then an American Indian standing near the newspaper stand caught my attention. I tried to ignore him, pretending he was invisible.

"You kids wanna go to Chicago?" he asked in a Pocahontas tone.

Mom told us to never speak to a stranger even if they ask you if you want candy. But this time it was more than just candy. "Um. . .Yes!" I finally said.

"Then allow me to assist. I can help you get to Chicago."

"Really!" I said in an excitement.

"But there's one promise. *Will you find my three-year-old daughter?*"

I didn't understand. A missing three-year-old daughter? Why?

"I know you might feel this is crazy, but...."

Did he suddenly read my mind?

"I know it's impossible to find her but. . ."

"Okay, I understand. If you promise to accompany us, we will find your daughter."

"Promise?" He said in a worried voice. I could tell by his skin, because he already had goose bumps.

"Promise." This crazy word called *promise* actually made me more responsible. "But, first things first. You have to tell us the story of how you lost your daughter and when you lost her. That might give us clues for where she is right now."

"Okay... On September 10, 1941, we were going to Kiddieland at Melrose Park at Chicago for her birthday. Once we were in the park, we were going around some rides when there was a mysterious sound going over the whole park. Then she disappeared."

Tears rolled from his eyes. I could tell he loved his daughter so much.

"So that's why, I'm going back to Chicago to find her," the man said, still sniffing.

"Wait, wait, you mean we have to go to Kiddieland? I mean that could take us like forever," I said in a nerve-breaking voice.

"Don't worry kid. We'll find a way to go back to Chicago. Perhaps by train, maybe? And tonight, you can stay at our home. There's a extra room for you. It's was my daughter's room before she disappeared. You might not like it, but that's the only room we've got. My house is just right across the street. We will give you a feast tonight, too. Now come along," the man kindly suggested.

All of the sudden his tears disappeared. He was different, and he was now normal––as though saying the words *daughter's room* made him stop worrying about his lost child. I was also thankful for him. I hoped that someday I could repay his kindness for giving us food, a place to stay, and helping us get home. I took Mona's hand, and we followed the man across the street to his house. As we walked, thoughts about how we transported to this time and place make me shiver and wonder whether there was a way to return home.

"Hannah, why are all these people looking at us. Do we look any difference?" Mona sniffed.

"Mona, we are Americans from the future. They are the old Americans. See the differences?"

"Yeah," she answered anxiously.

Soon we were in the front door of the house. The sun started to fall. I was pleased to finally have a comfy bed and proper food. It was already noon and I am already eating dinner by then at Chicago.

"Here we are!" he said excitingly like he was going to have a visitor put on TV. The door creaked steadily as it opened. "Now come along! Sit anywhere you want. Oh! I forgot. This is my wife Withney." A woman came from the larger part of the room strolling toward us. She has medium range curly black hair with pale blue eyes. "Whitney this is Hannah. And the smaller one is Mona. They have promised to help us find our daughter."

"I'm not small!" Mona shouted.

I felt my skin shiver. I signaled her making my eyes wider to get her attention. "Mona!" I whispered. "Watch your manners!"

"It's okay darling. After all, we are not lonely any more. We have company right here. And you've also promised us to find our daughter after all," she said.

"Well, never mind that, after all, you must be hungry from the journey. Withney, please serve them some food," the man pleaded.

I guess Hannah accepted being a little one now because whenever the word *food* came out of someone's mouth, she got excited like she was going to a birthday party. We sat down on the comfortable wooden seat. Then Mrs. Withney opened the oven, and there it was. A baked turkey came out from the oven and smelled delicious. It shimmered. It was glorious. Mona stared intensely at the meal and licked her lips in anticipation. She picked up the forks and the knifes from the table and looked ready as if she was going to be the first one to take it. Before she even could touch the skin of the chicken leg, I slapped on her arm. I knew this would not be a polite manner.

"It's okay dear. Not to worry!" Mrs. Withney said in a very gentle voice.

"I am very sorry Mrs. Withney." I saw her big, wide smile. This place was a bit strange.

After we have eaten our glamorous turkey, we decided to sleep. We walked into our bedroom, founded something fishy. The bedroom was all made from gold silk, and this couldn't just be for a kid. This bed was king size. This was more than a three-year-old need. It's so humongous. The gold silk was smooth, similar to my gold hair. King size bed for a three-year-old. A golden silk, with gigantic mirror, and closet. Mona already stuck her head on the cushion. I knew this lead to something mysterious. It can't be that he lost his daughter. There *is no* daughter in this family. This must be Mrs. Withney's room.

I opened my eyes. Night had fallen, and the bright moon shined through the window. Suddenly, the door creaked. At first I thought it was just the wind pushing the door. Then I saw a hand on the handle. I hid under the bed and pretended I was asleep. Just when I peeked out of my blanket, I saw *him* with a wide grin on his face. I pulled my blanket up and realized, he wasn't just an ordinary man who lost his three-year-old daughter. He must be working for someone, or maybe he was trying to abuse us. I didn't know, but this was not good. The man looked around for a while and then turned and left, shutting the door behind him.

The next morning, I woke Mona early. The sun hadn't even risen above the horizon. We couldn't change because we didn't have any clothes with us. But we suddenly realized there was clothes for us right in front of our bed. They were made out of a golden silk. We had no other choice but to change. I opened the door and saw two people, Withney and her husband. The aroma of freshly cooked French toast came from the kitchen, and I guessed that Mrs. Withney had prepared breakfast for us. I also smelled fresh honey. I got hooked on the smell and made my way to the kitchen. I saw Mona already on her seat.

I saw the man's face with his wicked grin. I knew I couldn't keep standing up the whole time and staring at Mona eating her fresh wheat French toast covered with fresh honey on top and fresh butter. I walked slowly toward the wooden table with a hot and burning fireplace beside it. I sat down slowly, like how an old nanny would have done.

"Good morning, Hannah," Mona rejoiced gracefully.

I could see her wicked grin. I bit my lips, really tight, and though of some good ideas how to avoid eating breakfast, how to avoid this problem, and how to avoid Mrs. Withney and her husband. My mind swirled as my tummy rumbled. My hand trembled. I had to avoid this delicious looking French toast, and really I had to avoid it. Avoid. Avoid. Avoid. Although I keep thinking this, my hand tremble more.

"What's wrong dear? Aren't you hungry? Or do you want something else?" Mrs. Withney asked in her very generous voice.

"No, I'm fine, Mrs. Withney," I lied.

"Oh, you mustn't be. You only have one turkey leg last night!"

"No, I am very...fin––" I couldn't finish my last word. Suddenly, she put the French toast on my plate, and my hand started trembling again.

"Now, go head and eat breakfast, my dear."

"Uhh," I didn't know the next word that should come out of my mouth. "Thank you." I grabbed the shiny, metal knife and fork beside the plate. I cut the French toast and ate it. The food tasted very delicious. As soon as I finished, I slowly stood and tried to sneak towards the door. I need to get out of this creepy place. Suddenly the door slammed. In front of us stood the couple, the liars who said they had a three-year-old missing daughter. I could see the husband's hand in front of my face.

"Where do you think you are going, little one?" Mrs. Withney asked. She didn't seem to notice that Mona was beside me.

"Outside to play!" I was surprised by how quickly Mona responded.

"And you?" Mrs. Withney asked suspiciously.

"Outside to play with Mona." I shivered from head to toe. The couple moved away from the door. The sunshine shimmered across the dark room. As the door creaked, the couple smiled like they had been turned into nice people. Their smiles glowed.

"Goodbye, my dears. Have fun," Mrs. Withney said like she was proud of her daughters.

"Mona," I whispered, "play naturally."

"Hannah! Let's play tag!"

"Okay!"

"Hannah, you're it!"

"I almost gach'ya!" I shouted. "Mona. Get away from the house," I whispered.

She got farther, and farther. We slowed down a bit. The couple disappeared from our sight.

"That was weird," she said.

"We have to get to Chicago. They didn't lose their three-year-old daughter, and we have to escape from them," I said in a furious voice, like I was trying to persuade someone. We walked faster. There was no time. We had to hurry. I saw Mona trying to catch up. We were both exhausted, even though it was still early morning. I paced myself more and more. I heard my chest bumping up and down. I covered my left hand on my chest. Mona tugged my arm, as if she felt like she didn't want to move. I couldn't see my feet. I didn't know where we were walking. I held her hand tighter. We had no time. We *had* to get back to our home.

Hour after hour we walked. The sun started to fall to the horizon. The colors of sky changed. My legs were all shaky. My back hurt, and I couldn't feel Mona pulling my hands anymore. She was barely standing up. Her eyelids were nearly closed. I piggybacked her. As I walked very cautiously, a dark mist covered up the path. We approached a sign, and I looked at it. The sign said, "West Coast Avalanche." We were at the train station.

My smooth hand touched each rough boxcar to find a open one. Finally, I found one. The door was rough and tough. I set Mona down. I tucked my two hands on the handle and pulled with all my effort. The door was very rusty, which might've been the reason why it hadn't opened easily. It was a large boxcar. It almost was like a home. All the dining sets and the materials were set up. It even had a fridge. I heard a loud spinning machine. I don't know what this was.

I opened the fridge to see what was in there. Amazingly, there was butter and a loaf of bread. In between the walls and the couch was a mysterious door. Probably connecting to other boxcars. Curiously, I touched the smooth golden handle that rusted into brown. The door shook when I went near the door, and suddenly an unknown man with a black colored skin stood before me. He had curly brown hair and ginger eyes. His brown eyes made me wonder if he was from Chicago.

"Hey what are you kiddies doing in my house? Ugh!"

"I am very sorry sir. I didn't know this was your house. We just needed someplace to rest. We found a boxcar that was unlocked, and it was rainy, so I opened the door, and there was a lot of food——" I didn't know how to finish my sentence.

His anger started to burn. "So! You can't just take things out of my fridge, you tiny little, idiots! Haven't your parents ever told you not to go into people's houses without permission! Well that's the same here! Now get out'a here!"

"But sir, I have my little sister here, and we really need to rest. Please!"

"No, and when I say no, it means no, so now get out'a here."

I stared into his eyes once more, like what most toddlers do when they're pleading to someone to do something.

"Okay now, only for one night. One night. After that no more."

"Okay," I answered softly. I walked towards Mona and settled her down on an old dusty couch. I still stood, facing the black gangster–looking guy. He sat down at the dining chair, holding his hands together on top of each other. His back was curved like an arc.

"Why you here," he said in a lighter tone. "Why you here," he repeated.

I didn't have the answer. "Umm," I said as my voice started to tremble.

"Answer me. Why are you here!" his voice grew stronger.

My skin rumbled with goosebumps. I felt the intense heat coming from him. "Because." I gripped my hands really tight. "We need to get back to Chicago." To be honest, I never wanted to tell this. I felt sheepish.

"Huh! Chicago, for what?"

"We need to get home. We got lost," I lied.

"Huh. You kiddoes." He tilted his head toward us. "This train is super express. Here's a trick question. You good at riddles?"

"Well, I am good at math, physics, algebra, and geometry. And I got all 'As'," I said proudly.

"Okay, here we go. If the bus goes to Chicago, what would you do?" he asked in a very wary voice, different from first when I met him.

"Of course, I would ride this train because a bus takes forever."

"Okay, if this train does go to Chicago? What would you do?"

"I already told you, I would ride on this train!"

"Then you better pay me ten bucks."

I shrugged. "But I don't have any money." I touched my soothing gray pocket to find if there was anything I could find to pay him the ten bucks. I felt some soothing paper material that I felt.

I took it out of my pocket. "Oh my, what a miracle!" I called out. There in my hand were two ten dollar bills. I quickly curled my fingers around one of the bills to keep him from seeing that I had the money he requested. I slid it into my back pocket. I might need it later.

"Well, let's see. You do have ten dollars." He seemed very concerned, zooming his eyes toward my money. I suddenly got goosebumps and worried about him stealing my money. It was a lot, and it was totally worth it. Totally worth it. I shoved the money back in my pocket and stared at his eyes.

"Hey, remember kid if you don't give me your ten dollars, you are going to get kicked off of this train after one night!" he muttered.

"Okay. Fine. Although, one condition. How many days will you let us sleep here? 'Cause ten bucks is whole lot of money," I asked in a voice like a salesman.

"Hmm. Let me think. How about two weeks," he said in a suspicious voice. "Isn't it a great deal? Don't you think?" He made a wide suspicious grin, that made me remember the past, at the wicked-witch-but-kind-looking-couple.

"Fine," I said, though it was not totally fine. I handed him my ten bucks. It was only him taking my money. "So..." I asked trying to forget all the reactions I had made. "What's your name?"

"Hey man, I do not tell names to strangers."

"Excuse me!" I shouted. "I am not a man, Mr. Know-It-All."

"Look kid, if it wasn't for me, you wouldn't have been in this train."

"Well..." I muttered, trying not to lose my temper against this guy. "I know that. But can't you at least tell me your name. We are going stay together anyway," I said like I was a genius.

"Fine, Casa Mikasa. Don't laugh."

I buzzed my lips what was that? Casa Mikasa? I glanced up through a small open window at the stars, hoping to get back soon to Chicago.

* * * *

The sun fluttered through my eyes. I looked at a glorious morning. Where was I? Was I dreaming? I sat up quickly and found Mona sleeping beside me. She snored softly. I closed my eyes and smelled the steam of roasting bacon and something better that made my mouth water. I opened my eyelids. A man? There in front of me was my servant! Casa.

"Hey, what's up?" he asked as a way of greeting.

"Nothing, just checking what you were doing."

"I made you breakfast."

"I was just concerned about the smell," I said.

"Hey, yo, wanna eat something?"

"Totally."

"Well I don't have enough for you. Sorry kid."

"But you have it in front of me!" I exclaimed.

Mona snored even louder. She tossed and turned as if having a bad dream.

"But, but. I didn't have anything to eat last night!" I complained. I knew I was acting like a spoiled twelve-year-old. I *was* whining, and I had to admit that. "Please, I gave you ten bucks. You do owe me something. Plus, it's only for two weeks. Please?" I shined my eyes, trying to look cute, like the cute little snowball from the movie *Pets*, except I had to admit that I looked more vicious.

"Hey, I have a good deal!" I grinned. I was usually a super genius. I mean who could ever think of this idea! "I will give you an additional ten bucks, if you let Mona and me have breakfast, lunch, and dinner every day, and when I say every day, I really *mean* every day. For two weeks. How's that!" I made my super genius smile. "Isn't that a good deal?" I knew he must be frustrated because I could see he had no idea how to handle money.

"Fine."

I saw how he finally had to agree. I handed my ten buck to his hand. I was worried, but I still couldn't change anything. A deal was a deal.

* * * *

The morning started to pass. Mona, finally managed to wake up. We were all getting along with Casa. Actually, he was positive on the inside. He was also really good at cooking. Then, I started to remember about Mom and her very tasty brilliant, blue-blueberry-pie. In the morning, Casa always made us scrambled eggs, and at lunch we would go out picnicking whenever we stopped at a train stop. One thing we always had to be careful of was to not get caught by the station master, and finally at dinner Casa made us meatloaf. For dessert, he made us the pumpkin pie. Days went by so fast that I couldn't count how many times, we saw the sunset and sunrise.

Sometimes, I wondered what it would be like when I met my mom again. What would she be thinking? Would she get really worried and call the cops? Would she get mad at me? Would she leave us? And then I remembered that something had changed me: the necklace. I touched my collar and found it was still there. I opened it and discovered a folded piece of paper, a wondrous paper. I quickly stuffed the it back into the locket so Casa and Mona wouldn't be able to see it.

The stars twinkled, another day has already passed. Sometimes I just wished the twinkling night sky would stay forever so that time wouldn't pass, and I could keep this memory forever. Finally, when Casa slept, I reopened my locket and took out the folded piece of paper. I wondered again if the paper was a wondrous sign from Mom. I saw a ink splash at one corner and quickly opened it. Inside, I discovered a letter from my nanny, Nanny Stacy. The note was addressed to me.

Dear Hannah,

I'm very sorry this happened to you. I tried to protect this from you. Please forgive me.
Nanny Stacy

P.S say, "Mahamba yetulaykaya," when the number 203 comes up.

What was she thinking about? I mean she trying to protect me from what? I had never had expected this. What could I do? I mean I couldn't just say I found a letter from my nanny, and she said she was trying to protect me! Casa and Mona would just think I was a weirdo! I gently folded the paper in half and put in my locket. Every time I touched this paper, it was like my nanny's spirit was inside me. Every feeling was in it, all my regrets for what had happened and much hatred for my myself and my nanny.

The next morning arrived, and I calmly sat at the dining table. I pretended everything was normal like the way it should be. I put my golden heart-shaped locket around my neck so Mona couldn't just grab it and take it from me, like she did when she put our lives in danger. I knew I had to tell this to Mona or Casa.

"Hey, I made you scrambled eggs today." Casa said.

"Oh, um, Thanks," I said comfortably. I grinned like I would normally do.

"Ooo! Yay! Casas's original scrambled eggs!" Mona cheered.

I freaked out. What did she just say? "Casa's original scrambled eggs?" What is this? We are not a family! I felt my mind getting crazy. The more I about Casa's original scrambled eggs, the more it made my mind feel so much worse. I stabbed my fork into the scrambled eggs and squeezed the ketchup endlessly. I saw Casa and Mona staring at me with their eyes wide.

"What?" I asked curiously. They stared at "my" scrambled eggs. "Oops. Maybe I used too much ketchup! "Ha, ha, ha," I purposely laughed, although it didn't mean my anger was gone. Weird things were going around in my head. I felt hopeless. What was I going to do? I saw Mona and Casa enjoying themselves, while I was trying to figure out what had happened and how to get back to our own time. Seriously! What was I going to do?

At that moment, the train suddenly stopped. The wheels squealed, and we lurched forward grabbing onto furniture to keep from falling. What was this? The sound waves that came through my ear hurt. Casa glanced through the window.

"Hm, must be some urgent parking." The weird thing about Casa was that he always pretended to stretch out his beard, and he didn't have a beard.

"Hey, Casa, why do you live in a train?" Mona asked.

"Once, my dad was a secret agent. He owned this car so he would be safe, and people wouldn't find him. Until one day, he discovered that one of his co-workers was a traitor and worked for another secret agent. My father didn't believe in killing. However, the other secret agent believed that murdering was okay, so my father tried to stop him. He fought day and night, from dawn to dusk. My father asked his coworkers for help. He even tried to persuade one of his bosses to deal with the other secret agent. But he failed. Until one day he found out that his boss was incorporated with the murders, too.

"At the same time, he found good news. His great, great grandfather was part of this agency. In fact, when my father went to the attic, he found a picture of his great, great, grandfather standing in front of the sign of his company. He was stood in front of a giant ribbon. *The S21 Secret Agency.* He realized his great, great, grandfather was the founder of this company. Soon, he searched around the attic and found a message in one of the toy carb boxes that told about a secret train.

My father forced me to join his agency, but I refused. Instead I told him that I would live here. He still kept on working with his agency until he was killed. The murders still own the company. My father wanted to protect me, so he never told them this place existed. And they still don't know."

"Wow, that story is so awesome!" Mona said.

"Yes, it does sound like an adventurous story. You might be right, young lady."

I opened my mouth but found no words to speak.

Casa looked out the window. "Now let's get ready for the next station. We have to get prepared so one of the engineers doesn't find us."

I saw that Casa and Mona bonded really well. Mona prepared a basket while Casa prepared fresh wild strawberries we had picked from a field near the last train stop. He squashed them and ruby red juice splashed all over Casa's face.

"Why are you crushing the strawberries. You are being very wasteful."

"Hmm, let's see. Mona, could you grab the sugar over there and hand it to me? It's on the right top shelf," Casa continued, like I was invisible. Mona gently set down the sugar, though the shining jar beamed in light from the setting sun, hinting at a beautiful sunset.

"There, all done. Wild strawberry jam!" he exclaimed. Casa held up the strawberry jam in front of me. "See, this is Casa's original strawberry jam!"

I didn't know if it was original, or organic. It more looked like nature's original jam.

"Ooooo! Another Casa's original jam! It looks so pretty," Mona said.

I had to admit, yes, it was pretty. It did look delicious, but what I did not like was, Mona's googly eyes staring at me, like she was ready to eat the whole thing, even the bin.

While they enjoyed themselves by getting ready to eat, I quickly peeked inside the basket. It was full of food: muscut grapes, sandwiches, bread, butter, sugar, salads, and wine, probably for Casa. The food itself looked so gorgeous. It was like a precious gem.

"Okay, all set." Casa handed me the jar of fresh strawberry jam.

I placed it in the wooden basket and quickly close the lid. The train's horn blew, indicated a stopping point.

"We are almost there. Casa's low voice made me sink down. The train stopped. For a moment, I heard nothing but silence. The setting was beautiful. "Shh. we can't let the driver find us," Casa whispered.

Quickly, we tiptoed through the door and out to the beautiful, fresh green valley. The clean brought back memories from the past. There was long river bank that ran almost to the train station. Mona ran all around like, forever. Casa and I walked gently on the grass. The warm wind that reminded me of my mom passing by. A sudden gust of wind tugged at my collar and may necklace slipped into plain sight. When I tried to shove it back in again, Casa's catchy eyes caught on my necklace.

"Hey, what'cha got there?" I saw his eyebrows rise up, meaning he was curious or suspecting something. It reminded of a funny moment when once Mona took the Cookies and Cream ice cream out of the refrigerator. I blinked my eyes, as though I was daydreaming.

"Nothing, just a plain old necklace," I answered. I gently sat down on the soft green grass. He stared at me suspiciously, but I didn't care. He doesn't know who my mother was, and he shouldn't go into people's private business. I breathed deeply and took a sandwich out of the picnic basket, ignoring Casa. The sandwich was a mix flavor of the wild jam, and peanut butter. The flavor, was so sweet, I could've eaten more than thirty of them.

I smiled. Mona was around the corner trying to catch the monarch butterfly. We silently ate. After Mona caught the butterfly, and we quietly walked down to the train without saying one word. Casa said today's dinner was going to be leftover sandwiches. Then, without a word, Casa just left us and went into his bedroom.

"What's wrong with him?" Mona asked, stuffing a large piece of sandwich into her mouth.

"I don't know, but he will probably feel better by tomorrow," I said. I also took a sandwich and stuffed it into my mouth. It did look like we were playing chubby bunny. As we were getting ready for bed, something strange had happened. It felt as if something was burning inside the train car. Strangely, the stove was already off. The scent suggested that it was, probably, the torch in the front boxcar. I felt, it was stronger than that. I ran into Casa's bedroom and woke him by spilling a bucket of freezing water on his head. Then he looked through the peeker, which you can peek through to the other boxcars. In a moment, we quickly realized it was something big.

"BOMB!" We both shouted. We quickly packed all the stuff needed for an emergency. Suddenly, my necklace dropped. I tried to pick it up, but it was too late. Casa screamed into my ears.

"HANNAH! YOU HAVE TO COME NOW!"

"WAIT! I HAVE TO GET MY NECKLACE!" I screamed back.

"YOU SAID IT WAS JUST AN PLAIN OLD NECKLACE! IT'S TOO LATE NOW HANNAH!"

I also knew it was too late, but I needed my necklace. Nanny had left me a precious note, that I didn't even understand. I couldn't even tell Mona, and Casa the truth. What was I supposed to do!

"HANNAH COME NOW!" Casa extended his hands to me. I had no choice. Mona was up on the roof staring at me, worried. I quickly grabbed his hand. He pulled me up. The twilight shining was beautiful, but there was more happening in front of me. We quickly ran across several box cars toward the back of the train. The fire from the bomb was closing on us. A train tunnel approached. We were almost in the train tunnel and had nowhere to go. Empty fields lay along both sides of the train.

"We are going to jump off to that field," Casa said, urgently pointing to a field on the right side of the train.

"WHAT!" Mona and I both yelled. The sound of the fire coming close by, made me even more nervous.

"JUST JUMP!" I couldn't believe what just happened. Mona jumped. I followed her. and for a second her head didn't appear. I thought she was dead until...

"I'm okay," her shaky voice, made me wonder if she was ever hurt. The cool and breeze wind slapped my face. I had, gently, landed on the field. Then I saw Casa walking toward us. We were safe. The train raced into the tunnel, and we heard a loud crash. Fire and smoke belched from the mouth of the tunnel.

"Hmm, wonder why there was a bomb," Casa said in a firm voice.

"Oh, no," I gasped.

"What's wrong?"

"I lost my necklace."

"Oh, I'm very sorry," Casa said in a mocking voice.

I wanted to scream out that it was his fault. But, I had to admit, if it wasn't for him, I wouldn't be alive. I felt so empty. The message Nanny Stacy wrote was still a mystery.

"Now, how are we going home?" Mona whined. She sat like a two-year-old baby.

"I've heard there's a village right below this valley. Maybe we could take a night out there."

I hesitated. All the things we had are lost, and now we don't have anything. We steadily walked down the valley. The beautiful sun was starting to set down. I was already exhausted. Mona, fell every time we stopped. I had to admit we were all tired. Another hour finally found us in front of the village. The night was a clearing, and the stars shined. Suddenly, something we discovered something totally unexpected. The village was empty. There were broken trees everywhere. The stones were lying everywhere. The people were *gone*.

"What's wrong?" Mona whined.

"Somebody must've attacked the village," Casa said in a deep voice.

The trees rustled. I felt like the trees were surrounding us everywhere. Then a twig cracked. We all turned. There was nobody. Another twig cracked. We all turned our heads. I saw nobody. It was funny how we turned our heads at the same time. I felt something bad was about to happen. I knew it was something strange. Then in a moment, everything went black.

* * * *

For a moment, I felt something comfy. I instantly opened my eyes and discovered that I lay on a bed. There in front of me stood a slim woman wearing big white fluffy dress. The women had a dark black hair a curl at the bottom tip of her hair. In a single motion, I quickly stood. I saw Mona lying on a bed beside me. Quickly putting on slippers that lay at the food of my bed, I stepped beside Mona. I shook her but she did not open her eyes.

"What happened to her!" I shouted.

The black-haired nurse stood in front of me. She knelt low. "Don't you know? The Nazis attacked you."

"The who?"

"The Nazis."

I did learn about the Nazis in my social studies class. I got an *A*+ with thirty bonus points.

"Luckily, one of the guy who was standing beside you, carried you all the way here."

"Casa," I gasped. "Where is he!" I shouted.

"He is in the operation room right now."

I quickly approached the nurse and grabbed her arm.

"Where Is the operation room?"

"Darling, we have consequences here."

I ignored her threat. "Tell me! Where is the operation room!" The look in her eyes told me I would get no answer, so I ran away. I looked at all the signs. By sheer luck I soon stood in front of the operation room. Since it was a lot different from an operating room that one in 2017, it didn't have a glass window on the operation room door, only a glass window in the form of a half-circle high above the door. I tried to see what was going on, I even tried to leap. But it was too high. I gave up. Then I backed up and prayed to God for Casa. I was hopeless. Everything I did seemed so useless. Once more, I put my hands together and prayed. Time seemed to pass slowly. Suddenly, a man came out of the operating room.

"Um," I didn't even have the nerve to talk this guy. He just passed by me like I was invisible. Then in a moment, I knew that I was just a useless person who always bragged about my grades. A person who only cared about myself. I stepped forward. Then, this there was a light tap on my back.

"Hey, do you know what happens, when you lose one of your best companions?"

"Yes. I lose control of myself, and I start to think negative things about myself," I said and then turned around. There was Casa. Casa was my best companion.

We walked together without saying a word. This felt so awkward. I still pleaded with God for this to end soon so Mona and I could get back to our own time. We went to Mona's bed, and soon she was awake. We held hands. The nurse seemed pleased to see we were all fine. We stayed at the hospital for nearly a week. Then it was time to go.

After we thanked the long, slim, black-hair women, we walked out of the hospital. The problem was that we didn't have any place to go and had no food to take with us. Soon we were hungry. We quietly walked without even saying one word.

"Where are we going!" Mona whined.

"Hmm," Casa said intelligently.

"We've lost our car, and now what are we supposed to do?" I asked impatiently.

"I'm hungry!" Mona whined once more.

The thing with her is that she always whines and never gets into the conversation. "What about the valley over there?" I suggested.

"Although, that is a good place, we still need our materials to build a new home."

Casa was right. After all, we didn't have the materials we need, so how were we going to build a new home? I mean, we already lost our train car and all the things. Then the black slim women from the hospital walked up from behind us.

"Oh, my darlings. There you are. Including you, handsome boy!" she exclaimed.

I thought she must have gotten insanely in love with Casa. She spoke with a British accent. Casa pointed his index finger to himself. I guessed he felt a little embarrassed.

"I was a little worried that you have nowhere to go, so I thought you would like to come to my house and live with me. Huh? Good deal isn't it."

"Oh, is that really okay?" I asked in an excitement.

"Yes, but under one condition."

"What?" We all said at the same time.

"You children including you––handsome boy––will have to help at the hospital, meaning you will probably have to work down at the reception desk. Oh, and you little one, will never be able to go upstairs under any circumstances. You are too young to see bloody bodies."

I just wished, she hadn't said *bloody bodies.*

"Aw, why can't I go upstairs. I want to see the dead bodies, too!" Mona whined.

"Ha, ha," she laughed lightly. "You, my young lady are too young to see anything like that. Now shall we keep going? My house is on the other side of the valley."

As we walked, the sun started to set, and I remembered all the setting suns we had seen from the train car. We were now in front of a big wooden cabin that seemed really familiar to one I had seen before.

"Hey, haven't we seen this one before?" Mona said in an old-meanie-fake-mom's voice.

I giggled softly.

"No, no, darling this is the only house of its kind in this valley!" She stood proudly, like she was trying to show off the amazing structure. "Now, come in. Come in!" She unlocked the door, and it swung open.

The room was filled with decorative things, such as a classical ballerina stature and mini ships that are inside a large clear jar. In front a large fireplace. She quickly made a fire in it. Beside the fireplace was an old fluffy couch, like most cartoons have. There beside it was a old vintage tables like what most old classic houses have. I turned to my right and saw another room, probably her bedroom.

"Now, come in, come in! I know you must be very cold."

Well, true. We were shivering. It was winter after all. We stepped inside the house. The long, slim, black haired lady took off our coats. She was especially carefully with Casa's coat. "Aa… what would you like darling? Hot coco? Milk? Tea? Coffee?"

"Oo! I will definitely take hot chocolate!" Mona said.

"And you?"

"Oh, umm, I will take tea. Tea please," I said.

"Oooo, and you my darling?" It looked more like flirting than asking for some drinks.

"Aaaa, excuse me, I wouldn't need any," Casa finally said.

"Oh, really? I think you are shivering cold. Here, I will serve anything for you."

"I'm really fine madam. Thank you for your offer."

I knew Casa was annoyed by this flirty-lady-person.

"Well, okay. You guys can use whatever you want."

She looked so upset about Casa denying her offers that I had to admit I felt kinda sorry for her. For her, was basically like confessing a person that she liked him, but then the boy rejected her. "Good night."

"Wow! That was so close." Casa looked so relieved.

I wanted to slap his face for embarrassing the flirty women who had helped us. I wanted him to know how she must have felt, but then again, maybe she was too flirty.

Casa moved over to the small kitchen area and reached for the handle on the refrigerator. "Hmm, I wonder if there's anything inside..."

Just before he could open his refrigerator, I slapped his hands.

"Hey! What are you doing?" Mona interrupted.

"You guys can't just take people's food without asking!"

"Wow, wow. We need food to survive, and hey, if we don't have food to survive, what do we do?" He snapped and pointed his index finger towards me.

Ugh! This guy! Without listening, he opened the refrigerator. As the cool breeze from the refrigerator passed by me, Casa and Mona started to take almost everything that was in the refrigerator, except, veggies.

"Ooo! Casa look what I've found!"

Then, in a moment... "Peanut butter jelly time!"

My jaws dropped to death. What was this girl thinking?

Then, in another moment... "Huh? Peanut butter jelly time?"

Thank goodness Casa didn't know what she was thinking about. "That looks terrific! I'll join you!"

"One, two, three, four!" Peanut butter jelly time, peanut butter jelly time!" they both screamed.

"SHH! YOU GUYS ARE GONNA WAKE THAT NURSE!" I whispered fiercely.

"Oh, right! I forgot that this was that nurse's house! Sorry! Anyway, let's keep digging for some food, so we won't starve to death," Mona said.

"Right," Casa responded. They were the worst collaborators! How could this possibly happen? Now, guess what? They started stuffing all the foods into their mouth! I mean whoever does that? I slapped my hands right into my face. I wondered when this would ever end? I hoped soon.

The next morning arrived, and we were still sleeping on the dining room table. I gently woke up. I had several butterflies in my stomach, and I was hungry. I had not joined those stupid collaborators. Mona slept on my right, and Casa slept on my left side. I shook Mona's body to wake her. Before Mona opened her eyes, the nurse entered the room.

"WHAT IS THIS MESS!" she screamed. "YOU WILL CLEAN THIS MESS! YOU WILL ALSO WORK AT THE HOSPITAL FOR EIGHT FULL HOURS, UNDERSTAND?"

Wow, this nurse was more than fierce than I thought. Her face was red, and she stomped back to her bedroom. The harsh woke Casa.

"Wow, that nurse was angrier than I expected."

I stared at Casa and Mona for a long time. I totally ignored what Casa said. I just kept staring at them, so they would feel guilty. Mona simply yawned and started to lie back down.

"What?" Oh, my gosh. This tiny little brat didn't understand a thing! "You guys are guilty and not me. You guys are the one who said, if we don't eat we won't survive! You are going to clean this mess while I will work full hours in the hospital."

The nurse came into the room. "Now, shall we go? They can clean up the room." She quickly opened the front door. "Huh. New fresh morning. Shall we?" The bell the door dinged, and it creaked as she closed it. She was right. It was a whole new morning.

The walk seemed like forever. She chatted for so long. I was so relieved when we were finally at the hospital. She introduced me and showed me how to welcome people when they came to the front desk. I had never worked as a receptionist before, and for sure, I was nervous. I was even more nervous when the first patient arrived.

"My son is dearly sick."

"Um, okay, ye..." I was even so nervous that I couldn't remember the last time the nurse told me what to say and do. "Umm, please just wait for a moment." I scampered around the whole hospital to find that nurse. I didn't even know her name. This was totally not great. Finally I've found her. I think probably the probably left.

"Oh! How was your first patient?" She asked.

It was amazing how her face expression was like expecting me I had done well. "Well, not "so" good. My nerve broke, and I forgot the last thing you said to me. Sorry." I caught my breath when she hesitated.

"It's okay darling. After all, you've tried." She grinned. I kinda felt sorry for her. Then, suddenly, the ground shook, and the building began falling apart. We both nearly fainted. We hurried downstairs and checked to see if the patients were okay. We found that the building downstairs was all ruined. The nurse quickly searched all the ERs in the hospital and began helping the doctors. She turned to me. "Go back to the house now, and warn your family!"

I quickly nodded my head. The one word I wish she hadn't said was the word *family*. Yes, Mona is part of my family. Not Casa though. I quickly ran across the halls. I know it was not appropriate to run at a hospital, but I *had to*. Finally, when I was out of the door, I noticed that the sky had turned extremely gray. Diesel oil field the air. Without thinking, I ran and ran. I ran until… there I was in front of the house. I banged the door open. Both Mona, and Casa opened the door and stared at me surprised.

"The hospital… The hospital…" I couldn't say the whole sentence. My breathe was cold, and I couldn't catch every word I was saying. I guess Casa did.

"Fire? Fire…right? We have to help them out. You guys stay there. I'm going to get more people to help." Then there was another shake. Casa disappeared in the dust and never returned. Mona and I fell to the ground.

I quickly opened my eyes. It seemed as if we were in a full new world. I had no idea where I was. Mona lay beside. My eyes still blurred, not able to catch a single thing that was going on around me. This time, I was gloomier. I was not able to get off my back. I couldn't run all the way to get Casa again. I rolled over and discovered lots of men lining up in front of the door. They all wore camouflage suits. Finally, I had enough energy to wake myself up. It was totally not a hospital. We were in a military camp.

There were only two nurses taking care of people who lay on cots. Both were different from the black-haired women. There were more injured men around us. Then, one nurse quickly glanced at me.

"Oh, you are awake! We are short on cots. The next man will soon come here to sleep, so could you must take turns. So umm, chop, chop!"

I walked like an old man, trying to stand up like I hadn't been awake for years. I suddenly blinked my eyes wider open. Yes! I did forget about Casa.

"Where is he!" I shouted.

"Where is who?" the nurse asked me.

"Where is Casa, the man who went to get help?"

"Well, many people are in the hospital... Umm, you should know darling. Many people passed away. There was a bomb from the Nazis. I mean the Germans. That's why, the American soldiers brought you here. We've found you laying under the house. Maybe your friend died trying to get help."

I bit my lips tight. Casa passed away? It was unimaginable. The muscles in my back tightened. I had no one to hold and me keep up my back in times of trouble. Not only was it going to be hard for me but also for Mona. I blinked back my tears. Finally, when Mona first opened her eyes and blinked, my stomach filled with butterflies. I didn't know what to say except that Casa might be in the heaven.

"Oh, hi Hannah," Mona said weakly.

What was she even thinking? Wait, did she officially lose her memory? She greeted me almost like I was a stranger.

"You know, I was thinking of this dream that wherever Casa goes, he will still be with us," she said.

I pursed my lips again. She was right. Wherever we go, Casa will still be with us. I had to decide whether I should tell her about Casa's death, or I shouldn't.

"Hey, Mona, remember when you had great times with Casa? Well that spirit will still be in our heart, and I need you to know one thing: Casa is still with us, even today." I said. I did decide to not to tell the truth, but the truth was that, wherever we go, Casa would still be with us.

One of the nurses noticed our conversation. "Oh, my child, you are awake. Other men need to get health care. We need that cot as soon as you are feeling better."

"I think we are both fine," I said. "Is there anything we can do to help?" I picked Mona up, carried her to a spot near an empty wall, and settled her down on the floor.

"Yes, yes!! Of course! We need you darlings to collect as much food as you can from the other side of the tent, and bring it back here. These men need nourishment, or they might not survive!"

I nodded my head quickly. "Mona, you stay here while I get food for the soldiers. Get it? It's like capture the flag, but you have to stay in your own territory."

"Yes sir!" Mona saluted. I ran. I ran like the past times, but this time, I had more courage. I was not going to be scared anymore. Bombs flew over my head, as the same diesel oil odor filled my nose. More bloodied men were carried into the tent, and fever soldiers were left to defend our territory. I still heard the *boom* and *whack* and artillery shooting everywhere. The hot flame from an explosion touched my cheeks, and the sound hurt my ears. I kept running until I saw the camouflaged food tent. I rushed through the open tent flap, knowing I was finally here. I scooped up a stack of food and again ran across the open field. These wounded men needed them. The nurse waved her hands at me, motioning me to come quickly. It was a very dangerous moment.

"You have to get more food. This is our last battle. If we win today, August 28, 1945, we win the war!" I once again ran all the way across the field. The more food I got, the more tired it made me. Finally, I delivered the last stack of food. Dusk was already setting upon us, and the glory of the sun started to set. I remembered every time when Casa made meatloaf, and we watched the sun set.

"Good job, darling. I'm very proud of you." The nurse grinned at me.

I was proud of myself too. Mona was already dead asleep. "Ha, I guess the day is over. I guess we owe you a ride back to your hometown," she said. This West Virginia. Where do you live?"

"Chicago. At a place called Liberty Library."

"Hmm, I've never heard Liberty Library, but I guess you can guide the soldiers."

We both looked at each other. I could see even if we had been together only only few hours it was really hard to leave. I awoke Mona, and she hugged some of the soldiers who she had played *hospital* with. I hugged the nurse and blinked back tears.

"Thank you. Thank you for getting us safely home."

"That's our pleasure. Now, the trucks should be ready. Good bye!"

We both looked at each other and nodded our heads that we will see each other again. I stepped into the camouflage trunk. Mona seemed unable to move. I couldn't tell if she was asleep or awake. She seemed to be both. I guessed she couldn't walk. I piggybacked her, and she was heavy. I once more looked at the nurse, and she waved. It seemed to be that the nurse was more concerned about me, than I was about her. She blinked her eyes and walked away into the gray fog. The truck was small, although it did have some seats to sit on. The soldiers welcomed me aboard.

"We would like to go to Chicago," I said exhaustively.

I set Mona on a chair, and she slept. I was exhausted, too, from all the running across the fields collecting food while fire was shooting above me. Without even knowing it, I closed my eyes.

* * * *

Morning arrived. The glorious sun was rising again. Mona woke after we hit a rough bump in the road. Three days had already passed.

"Umm, ma'am we are in Chicago. Where would you like us to stop?"

I blinked my eyes wide. We were in Chicago already? I was so happy to see my hometown. Except it did seem a lot different.

"Ah, yes. Umm, could you please go to 34 street and Liberty Road?"

"Yes, ma'am."

It was so different of how these people treated women. I kinda felt sorry because it was like I was bossing other people. Mona glanced through the window like a dog.

"We are here ma'am. This should be it. Thirty-Fourth Street and Liberty Road." The soldier opened the door. The city was scattered all around, and it did seem so different from the present-day Chicago. We were at the intersection of 34th Street and Liberty Road. We were at *home*. Mona ran across the street and looked everywhere. I walked away from the truck and turned all around until I saw a small sign that said, *Library*. I wiped my face again. It actually did say *Library*.

"Thank you very much!" I shouted to the soldiers in the truck.

"It's our pleasure. Now, we must go quickly. Others will be waiting," said the deep voice of the soldier in charge. He saluted, and Mona saluted back. I watched the truck go by.

"Mona, we found our home!" I shouted.

"You mean this broken house?"

"No, the library. We found the library!" I jumped up and down. My heart was full of different emotions. "We have to get there quick!" I shouted. I took Mona's hand, and ran across to the direction of the sign. My heart raced. Will I ever find that book again? Suddenly, the sign was gone, and we were in front of a small building.

"Do you mean this?" Mona asked as she pointed towards the small building.

"Maybe, I don't know. Let's go in."

She narrowed her eyes. I could see that something suspicious might happen. I took a deep breath and walked towards the building. I pushed the wooden door open, and it screeched from bottom to the top. An old woman stood there organizing her books. After she took a quick glance, she quickly shook her head, maybe unbelievable that I survived or something. "Sorry, is the library open today?" I asked.

"Umm, yes. Please come in! Come in!" she urged. "Now, what kind of books would you like? Fantasy? A Novel? A Report?"

"Oh, um, I think we can look for a book for ourselves. Thank you."

She glanced at me again, probably to make sure I knew where to go. I walked steadily. We were in the section that would become the part where WWII books would be placed. I took a deep breath and remembered the time I chose the book. I closed my eyes. The library was so quiet and cold it almost felt like the Snow Queen's palace in Narnia. I ran my fingers from book to book. My fingers stopped. I pulled a book out and finally opened my eyes. It was the same book. I opened it to page 203.

"Amahamba yetulaykaya," I said. Lights shimmered. We swirled just like we did at the beginning. We were back in Chicago. We were back at home.

Mona and I looked around in amazement. The same people were in the library, and it seemed like only thirty minutes had passed. I took Mona's had and walked quickly to the door. Outside the library, everything was the same as before our journey. Mona smiled at me, and we raced home.

The next morning arrived. I felt strange, as if something unusual had happened. I knew everything was back to normal. Though, something did seem missing, Casa. When I heard the knock on the door, I knew it was Mona. We both grinned from an amazing adventure we had shared. We quickly changed and ran outside to the yard.

"Hey, Mona," she asked. "Do you think, Casa is still alive?"

"Why do you say that?"

"Because, he seems to not be here with us."

I patted my heart. "Mona, Casa will still be here with us wherever we go."

"Okay. Maybe we can plant a small flower for him in the backyard!" Mona exclaimed in excitement. "For Casa!"

"Sure." I shrugged. I did miss him so much. We went to a small flower shop on the corner and bought some flowers. We dug up some dirt and tapped something metallic. I knelt down and ran my fingers through the loose dirt to see what it was. In amazement I picked up the small dirt covered object; it was my necklace. I dripped tears onto the dirt, as I prayed this was not a dream. I actually found my necklace. I actually found it. For all the journeys we've made, I still couldn't believe how my necklace ended up here. But I was happy. Instead of taking it out, I decided to set in place.

"Hey, Mona, hand me the flowers."

She quietly nodded her head. I held the necklace tight, still dreaming of the journey we had. When Mona came skipping back again, her hands were full of flowers, all kinds: daisy, lupine, and violet. We gently planted them in the silky dirt. I held my necklace tightly. But I knew Casa deserved it more. As Mona used her soft hands to plant the flowers, I placed my necklace above the dirt as well.

"Hannah, isn't that yours?" Mona asked curiously.

"I know, but you know what? I think Casa deserves it more," I said proudly.

She quietly nodded her head again, and I slipped my Nanny's necklace, as the gold chain slipped from my hands. We covered it with the silky, smooth soil again. The sky was so bright all blue, without one speck of a cloud.

For a moment, we were again in August 1945: a day Mona and I shall *never* forget.

A Bizarre Mountain Camp

By

Hojin Lee

"Splash!" Startled by the sudden sound, Michael quickly turned his head to look back. He noticed his friend Josh muttering with his feet in a muddy puddle, leaving Josh's dark skin brown because of the muddy water covering his legs. The waterfall showered lots of water from the cliff high up on the mountain, making a huge puddle beside the stream where it landed. Josh unfortunately stepped his feet into the soupy mess. Josh, despite being a healthy dark-skinned boy who had bright eyes with good eyesight, often carelessly stepped into things like the puddle. The mountains where they walked toward their camp towered massively above the narrow valleys below them, and the huge biome of trees made it easy for campers to lose their way. Michael saw Josh struggling to wipe the muddy water off his shirt, but their coach didn't seem to know about this situation, so he walked on without stopping. Josh had no choice but to follow him, trudging heavily because of the injury by slipping and also because of his short legs. Michael tried to call on other kids who were in the camp for assistance, but they were too far away from the group for them to hear the sound.

Michael, who was Josh's best friend, came to his aid and also asked his twin, Liam, to help. Liam groaned a breath of annoyance and intentionally walked slowly. Michael groaned an angry breath of annoyance at his brother's laziness and made an annoyed gesture to Liam to come over faster. Liam pretended not to notice and sat there, slowly pulling out his Snicker bar.

Gosh, I am so embarrassed that he's my brother, Michael thought. *He's so different from me, just too annoying and lazy.*

Having white skin, dark eyes, and brown hair, Liam and Michael looked exactly the same, from their shoe size to the black spot right next to their ear. However, their personality was just the opposite. After finishing eating the candy bar, Liam went a little faster, pleased with his work at annoying Michael, but his shoe struck a tree root that came out above the ground. Unfortunately, when he pulled his foot out, his shoe slipped off and landed in the wet pool where the waterfall showered huge amounts of water.

Liam grunted, clearly annoyed by the accident, and rushed over to get it. He also got his pants wet waded into the water in order to retrieve it.

"Hey Josh, here's a towel." Liam handed Josh his towel for him to clean himself up.

Josh took the towel from Liam's hands, smiling. "Thanks."

Michael looked around the forest as he circled around the waterfall. Then he noticed something strange. *Hey, where is everyone?* He glanced around, looking for the coach. There was no one except for them. He tapped Josh and Liam on the shoulder. They too, had noticed the silence.

"Wait, what? Where is everyone?" Josh said, with a worried tone.

Alarmed etched on his face, Michael looked around and saw nothing but tall, green trees lining the trail. He also saw that the trail suddenly disappeared a few meters ahead because of a large rock blocking passage. There was nothing that told them the way. Going back was not a choice because they had already walked at least thirty minutes on this route. They might have a chance of getting more lost than they were, if they turned back.

Josh kicked the ground in frustration. "What are we supposed to do now?"

Liam shouted, "Hello! Can you hear me? Where are you?"

No response came back to them, only echoes of his voice.

Josh shouted louder than Liam, "Come back! We're lost!"

Neither shouts nor friendly faces came back from the dense, forbidding forest. Creepy silence filled the air, and Josh realized the seriousness of their situation. He pulled out his cellphone to see if he could get a signal and discovered his battery was out of energy. He took a quick inventory of their assets and found no supplies, no map, and no way to communicate with his coach or anyone else. They also did not know the forest of tall trees around them, which surrounded a vast area of the mountain.

Michael saw a steep cliff on the left side of the trail, and he also found a sign that said, "frequent landslides, travel on your own risk." Additionally, the sky grew darker by the minute, making it hard to see things more than a few yards away.

"I shouldn't have wasted battery playing games on the bus!" Josh shouted, looking desperate. Without their coach, they had no easy way of finding camp or a way off the mountain.

* * * *

The sunlight shone through the glass panes of their apartment as Michael sat on a cushioned sofa and watched TV. *So excited for this.* Michael thought. *My parents are finally going out into space!* Michael's dad and mom were astronauts that worked for NASA, and today, they would be on a mission to test out a new space module, the Endeavor II, that was confirmed safe to launch just a day ago. However, the schedule said for Michael's parents to go to NASA at about three o'clock in the afternoon, but he saw that they were leaving now for some reason, at only 9:30 a.m.

Why are they getting the car right now? There's simply no reason to get their car to go to a market that was only thirty meters from our house. They wouldn't be going to the department store also. Why should they be buying things right now? So out of confusion, Michael ran to the door and asked them, "Where are you going? You're not going out now, right?"

"No, it's for a different reason. We'll be back in about…three hours or so." Michael's mom replied.

Michael thought about this for a second. *Three hours? That is one heck of a time spending outside. So, they won't be going for shopping or things like that. Well, at least this is something for me to spend time with while they are away.* It could be grandma's house or a camp… a camp! Michael's brown eyes shined with excitement. *Maybe they're just hiding this for a surprise.* So, Michael decided to see what they prepared, and he just replied, "Okay, bye." But he noticed that they had already left.

Michael rushed to Liam, his twin brother's room, and discovered he was still fast asleep. He took his phone out, placing it right next to Liam's ear, and turned the media volume to full. Then he turned on his favorite rock music.

The first second the music turned on, Liam shrieked, covered his ears with his hands, and kicked Michael's face, leaving him to crash to the floor. Liam, still masking his ears from the loud sound, forced his way out of his bed. He saw Michael groaning as he held his bleeding nose.

"What the heck was that for?" Michael shouted as he grabbed a tissue and glared at him.

"Well, sorry. It was an accident, so it's not my fault, right?" Liam replied, grinning while combing his tangled blonde hair.

He's always trying to evade by saying sorry, Michael thought, shaking his head. Since his birth, when Michael complained about Liam being rude, noisy, and causing trouble, he always thought of many reasons to prove he wasn't doing anything wrong, like when Michael complained about Liam putting soap in Michael's mouth when they were little. Liam avoided punishment by saying that the soap looked like Michael's toothbrush. Now, however, the chance of him avoiding being punished was thin, because he was thirteen years old.

He probably did it on purpose, knowing that mom and dad were going to leave soon. Michael thought, but decided to just let him be, as punishments didn't really change his behavior much.

It felt like ages for Michael, waiting for his parents to come. In less than an hour, he was bored of reading books. Reading wasn't his favorite hobby, but he also couldn't play games on the computer because Liam was hogging it. Michael had a painful four hours of waiting until he heard the creak of the door being opened. When he opened the door, his parents came in.

Finally, thought Michael.

The first thing they said was, "Good news, kids! Your wish came true. You're not going to grandpa Peter's house,"

That brought energy into Michael again. *Yes! We don't have to spend weeks in that stupid, boring house!* Michael thought joyfully. Grandpa Peter's house was the most boring place ever to him. It had nothing entertaining. Grandpa Peter retired from his archeologist job about ten years ago, when he was fifty-eight, and had been living by himself since then. But the worst part about Grandpa's house was that he didn't have a TV. He only had a laptop to search up new things about history, and that laptop was a four-year old Chromebook. He was overprotective about his possessions, so he didn't let Michael and Liam close to it. "Then what do we do when you're gone?"

"Well, you're not getting a babysitter; that's for sure."

As soon as his parents said that, Liam opened his door, ran out of his room into where Michael and his parent were and shouted, "Yay! We don't have a babysitter!"

Michael's mom smiled. "No one was really available to babysit you, so we thought sending you to camp would be the best. It'll be a hiking camp."

Liam's face suddenly dropped. "I thought it would be some kind of fun camp, not in the mountains," he said and shut the door to his room.

"Well, if he doesn't like it, he will just have to adjust," said Michael's dad, seeming a little annoyed at Liam's behavior.

They started packing at about five o'clock in the afternoon. Liam grouchily forced his camp materials into his small backpack. The camp regulations for bringing materials were this: if you bring unhealthy stuff like chips and sweets, it would be confiscated. Michael knew that Liam wasn't picking the right materials to take to camp.

Michael looked inside Liam's backpack. He found Pringles, Hershey's candy bars, and all the things that the camp didn't allow. Michael tried to tell him that, but Liam just grabbed his backpack, rushed inside his room, and closed the door. Michael decided to let him be responsible for his actions, snacks taken away or not.

Packing was quite hard for Michael, due to his being unprepared. But he was lucky because campers didn't need to bring their own sleeping bags, as the camp provided them. So he only had to pack the usual things, such as sunscreen and clothes. And Liam still had the sweets in his bag. Michael decided to ask him about that.

"Hey, if you bring sweets and things like that to camp, they'll take it."

Liam made a "don't worry about it" gesture and said, "Don't worry, I'll take care of it myself."

Michael sighed and finished packing. Finally, it came time to catch the bus. As soon as Michael and Liam left their house, the camp bus arrived.

It was about six o'clock in the evening, according to Michael's watch. He remembered that his mom said that it would take his mom and dad about two weeks for them to complete their mission. *Two weeks,* Michael thought. *That is a long time.* The bus, being a small Benz van, was quite small compared to other camp buses, and it had quite a few people, about thirteen, when Michael counted. But when he counted, the people sitting on the back row of the bus seat, he noticed a familiar face.

"Josh!" Michael shouted, getting his attention. He also received some "be quiet" sounds, but he didn't care. Josh was Michael's best friend, and for Michael, being with him was better than anything because it was his first camp. Also, he needed someone to assist him. Josh also greeted him with a smile and began talking loudly. They only shut their mouths when the coach told them to, and five minutes later, they started talking again, making them a pair of unquestionable troublemakers to the coach.

The distance to the camp was way longer than Michael thought it was going to be. He knew it was going to be a camp for hiking and things like that, but there were loads of mountains around the city. And they had a lot of camping sites in them. When Michael looked out the window after about one hour, he realized that the bus was on its way out of the city, and still they were a long time away from their destination, according to the coach. Dizzy from the long ride, Michael put his hands on his head and looked around the bus. Everyone slept except for him. *How do people sleep with all the rumbling and curving in the bus?* Michael thought. However, in the next few minutes, he fell asleep, despite his spinning, dizzy head.

Pain stung his face as the sound of a slap reached his ear. Michael clutched his face, looked around, and saw Liam grinning. "What was that for again?" Michael shouted.

Liam shrugged. "Just to wake you up, I guess. Better than showering water on your face," he laughed.

"What? You could've just tapped me, and I would wake up," Michael replied as he searched for any red marks on his skin.

"You didn't wake up when I did it." Liam smirked, as they rose out of the seat and walked out of the bus.

Lies, Michael thought, wanting to punch him in the face, but at that time, he heard the sound of the coach's whistle, and all the members in the group gathered near him.

"My name is coach Scott. Call me by that name from now on. We'll be hiking to the camp from here," The coach shouted. Michael looked around the mountain. *Oh, now I know why we took so long to come here,* he thought. There were almost no buildings nearby, and also almost no sight of people, only muddy roads and farm animals walking along the grass. This was real countryside.

"Gosh, if we get lost in here, it'll sure be bad for us," Josh said, as he tied his blue shoelaces tight.

Liam nodded his head in agreement.

The coach motioned for the group to follow him as he pointed toward the forest of tall, humongous trees. "The whole mountain is going to be a forest. There's not many signs that tell you the way to go. If you get lost, well, if you have a phone, you can call someone. But if you don't..." The coach stopped. "Well, just follow the rules and stay close to the line, okay?"

The students nodded their heads. He gave each child a flashlight and then started walking toward the steep muddy trail that went up the mountain. Michael and others followed. Soon, they were in the forest. Michael shuddered from the spooky feeling of the trees that blocked the path from the sunlight.

"Coach Scott was right. This place really has tall trees. You probably wouldn't really see the sky if you go deep inside the mountain," Josh whispered to Michael.

"Well, it's already night, so it doesn't really matter," Michael replied. They continued walking in the bright beam of their flashlights.

"Coach, I'm dying! We have been walking for hours!" Michael heard a girl from the group shout.

The coach ignored her and kept walking. After that, protests came out from the kids one by one, and the coach made a surrendering face and settled down near a large waterfall. Michael and Liam, who were never good at athletics, yelled a sound of joy and ran to the waterfall, although it was really dark. Josh, whose shoelace was untied, slipped and fell toward the waterfall, making him drenched in the soupy mess. Michael, who could see Josh trying to stand up, tried to call the coach or the kids in the group for help, but they were already too far away for them to hear. Michael ran toward Josh, helping him stand up and clean himself up. Liam groaned as his brother motioned him to come, but when he stood up, Michael noticed that Liam's foot was stuck underneath a tree trunk sticking out of the ground.

When Liam pulled his foot free, his shoe flew into the pool of water next to the waterfall. Also, the trunk scratched him, leaving a patch of red on the skin right on the lower part of his leg. Liam winced, then hopped on one foot to get the shoe out of the water. As Liam made lots of splashing sounds trying to get out of the pool of water, Michael suddenly realized that there weren't any flashlights shining nearby them. Liam came out of the pool, his pants drenched with water. As the splashing sound stopped, Michael also noticed that silence except for the sound of the waterfall, unlike a few minutes ago.

Wait, what is happening? Michael thought, and called out, "Coach Scott?" No response came back to them.

Liam, now noticing what was going on, asked, "Where is the coach? I can't hear anything."

"What's happening? Did they leave without us?" Josh asked, his voice shaking. That set the mood for Michael. With a troubled face, Josh looked around the surroundings.

Michael also looked around for anything that could help them. There wasn't anything. He saw that a few meters down the trail, the trail suddenly disappeared because of a large rock blocking the passage. There was nothing that told them the way. Going back was not a choice because they had already walked at least thirty minutes on this route. They might have a chance of getting more lost than before if they turned back, because they had no idea where they were. "Hello? Anybody there?" Michael's desperate voice echoed through the air.

Liam tapped him on the shoulder. "I have an idea. Josh has a phone." Liam tapped on Josh. Josh gave him his phone with a sad look on his face. "Why are you so depressed?" Liam's face suddenly drooped when he pushed the *on* button on his phone. It didn't turn on. "Your phone's off?" Liam exclaimed with a look that seemed to say *please no.*

"Oh, I shouldn't have played games on the bus!" Josh shouted, covering his face in his hands. Michael shook his head, which was what he did when everything was going in the wrong direction.

"Let's check what we have right now. We might have something useful in our bags." Michael told them. After a few minutes of searching for tools and food, this was what they had: a pack of gummy bears, a pocket knife, and a bunch of other camping supplies, such as sleeping bags. However, they had no system of communication, and they were stuck on a silent mountain with no one nearby that could help them.

"Now what do we do?" Josh asked in a desperate voice.

Michael couldn't make any decisions about this accident. He was too shocked at what happened. *How did slipping in a pool of water lead to this situation?* Michael thought, looking at the dark clouds slowly covering the sky. "Let's just sleep for now, then decide what to do," he said and sighed. They got their sleeping bags, spread them out, and slept beside the waterfall, which made roaring sounds echo through the forest.

* * * *

Michael had a horrible nightmare that night. It was about the event that happened yesterday: being lost in the woods, but alone. He woke up with a start, and when he opened his eyes, he saw bright light shining through the tree leaves above him, and he blinked his eyes. Then he rose from his sleeping bag. Michael saw Liam and Josh, both with an exhausted look on their faces.

"Alright, let's go look for some way to get out of here..." Michael stopped talking as he saw Josh shake his head.

"We've been searching all morning. It's almost impossible. We tried to wake you up, but you just wouldn't," Josh replied. He sat on the ground, taking out his water bottle to drink.

Michael frowned. *There must be some way*, he thought.

"Staying here is not going to help anyone," Michael said, as he stood up. "*We* have to make decisions now. Nobody knows that we're here. Let's not just wander aimlessly deeper into the mountains. We have to make a plan." Despite Josh's complaints, Michael headed backwards, on the way down the mountain, and Liam followed. Josh had no choice but to chase after them.

There was no exact trail to follow through the mountains because of the heavy rain. They walked in the gloomy, cloud-filled weather until the sky showered rain so heavily that they had to find a place to hide themselves under a bunch of tall trees. As Michael looked around the place, he saw a big waterfall.

Wait, a waterfall? Michael thought with suspicion, and peered at its features. *Tree trunk, puddle next to waterfall…wait, that's the same waterfall!* Michael let out a groan of frustration, then paced around, making a circle, which was what he did when he ran out of ideas. He now saw Josh and Liam walking toward him.

"I can see the same tree trunk that I tripped on!" Liam told Michael, his face making a confused look. "Wait, so we went in circles for *hours?*"

Michael nodded."

Uh…" Josh murmured.

Michael looked at him. "You know… I made a mistake about the *no devices* thing. This is my school backpack, and I forgot to put my school laptop in my house, I guess."

"Well, it doesn't matter now," Liam replied, before Michael could respond. "You think there is a internet signal in this mountain, huh?" His voice got louder as he spoke. "Of course not! So stop giving people false hope!" Liam walked away from Josh, leaving Josh staring at him in shock, wide-eyed. Michael, too, was shocked at Liam's words.

How could he be like that, even though he's in a stressful situation? Michael thought as he glanced at Liam, who looked very angry. Then Michael went to Josh to comfort him. He talked about random things for a long amount of time. After a while, Liam stood up and started walking. Michael sighed. He had no choice but to follow his brother. He and Josh followed Liam. Silence fell for a long time.

Michael stared blankly into the sky, which was colored gray by the clouds. Soon enough, the clouds rained droplets of water onto his face, and when he stopped to look for somewhere safe from the rain, he saw only Josh standing in the rain. "Liam?" Michael shouted.

"He's gone," Josh said. "He was frustrated. Very."

Michael stared at Josh for a long while and then put his face into his hands. "Why does it have to be like this!" Michael roared angrily.

Josh put his hand on Michael's shaking shoulders. "Come on, there is no way we can find a way out of here if we keep on doing this. Let's go," Josh said with a cheerful tone. Michael nodded and pulled himself up, although his mind was filled with worry.

It had almost been two days since they were lost in the woods, and no one was coming. Trying to be optimistic, they started off, trying to find an exit out of the mountains again. But that wasn't as easy as they thought.

"Ouch," Michael groaned as he slipped off the rock that he stood on. "Man, this mountain is dangerous if there's rain."

Josh nodded his head. Josh saw that Michael still had his somber face, and he hoped that Liam would be safe. However, hoping is only hoping. Josh didn't understand Liam's decision of going alone. *Is there any benefit on going alone?*

The rain constantly dropped water on Josh and Michael, and to Michael it didn't seem like it was going to stop for a long time. By the time the rain finished, they were soaking wet. Despite the harsh conditions, Michael was determined to go down the mountain, which would take them to the exit. But what kept bugging him was Liam's absence. He was stuck in his cloud of thoughts when a scream startled him.

Michael motioned for Josh to come over to the sound. The sound was not far away, but not too close, either. They frantically ran around trees and over rocks. The sound was actually coming from the edge of the mountain, the part where people could fall off and get injured. And there he saw a person a few meters below them who clutched his knee with his hand right. Next to him a slithering creature slowly disappeared into the woods. Having a feeling that it was someone familiar, Michael squinted his eyes to examine the person. *Wait, isn't that...*

Michael put his hands on his face, very surprised. "Oh, no." It was Liam's figure that Michael saw. Shouting his name, Michael rushed over to Liam, whose body trembled. Blood oozed from a snakebite just above Liam's right knee.

"Ow," Liam winced as Michael touched his snakebite wound.

"Liam! Come on, can't you defend yourself?" Michael looked at Liam like he wanted to punch him. But Michael was quite relieved because Liam's wound had more than two puncture wounds. It wasn't likely that it came from a poisonous snake, Michael reasoned from his knowledge from his biology class. Liam grinned a boisterous smile, making Michael more frustrated at him as he wrapped a bandage around the bleeding wound, which was the only thing he had for treating wounds. Then he said something that made Michael very surprised.

"I'm sorry," Liam whispered, his facial expression showing that he really was. "I shouldn't have been so stupid. Now I regret it."

The anger slowly receded inside Michael.

"Now I can't really walk well, then... I got you all in trouble."

Michael even saw some teardrops glistening in Liam's eyes. "Yeah, I don't know how to solve that quickly, but...fortunately you don't have a poisonous snakebite."

"It doesn't matter now," Josh's voice came from up the slope. Josh pulled a long piece of rope out of his bag and lowered it to where Michael and Liam were. At the end, they were finally able to get up the slope. Soon they were all breathing hard, lying on the soil. Michael thought about the severity of the situation. *So, Liam is hurt, we don't know a way out, and there is nothing in sight...* Michael took a big sigh of desperation.

Suddenly, Josh announced: "I think I know what we should do."

"What is it?" Liam replied, dabbing his ankle drenched with blood with the tissue that Michael gave him.

"Somebody needs to be brave enough to go down the slope to the cliff and then look at our location."

"Well, who wants to do that? It's dangerous! We don't want to die, right?" Liam shot a strange look at Josh.

"I told you, we need to do it in order to get rescued or something like that!"

"Why don't *you* go then?"

"Well..." Josh stopped talking, looking like he was clearly out of words.

Michael, who was frustrated with the endless talking, stepped between them. "I'll go. Did you know that it is really frustrating to have you in a situation like this?" Michael asked. "Come on, man. I know that Liam's hurt and all, but seriously?" Michael stood up, readying himself to go. "You guys stay here. I promise that I'll find a solution to this."

Josh and Liam, both looking guilty, nodded. Michael, wearing a determined look on his face, disappeared into the woods.

"Good luck, Michael," Josh yelled.

Michael barely heard Josh's voice as he advanced into the forest. He stepped into the marshy region of the mountain, his boots making loud sounds as he walked along the tall trees. He sat on a rock, checking the supplies in his bag, which sharp rocks and branches had torn.

"Okay, I have a flashlight, a pocket knife…" Michael murmured to himself as he dug through his packet of supplies. Then sighing, he stood up, pulling the flashlight from his bag. He pressed the button on the flashlight to see if it still worked. The flashlight turned on with a click, illuminating a wide area. Then he groaned as his stomach growled for a meal.

So hungry, Michael thought. For a brief moment, Michael thought about going back to where Liam and Josh were to check for some food, but when he looked around, it looked like it wasn't a very good idea. It was getting very dark as the sun set, and Michael walked around for a long time without any clue where he was going.

"Oh, shoot," Michael said under his breath. "Now I don't even know where I started from." Panic rushed through him, but even after several deep breaths, he couldn't calm down. His heart thumped so loud that Michael heard it beating against his chest. *I can't go back now. I have to do something, or else something pretty bad could happen before we get rescued, or we might not be rescued at all, at least when we're not dead. I need to do this.*

Just as he thought about it, he was surprised at his determination and bravery. Before he went to camp, he didn't have the boldness to take risks. Whenever there were times that he had to, his parents took care of it for him. Michael also felt embarrassed that he relied on other people to do things for him. Suddenly, Michael felt his legs losing balance and sat on the rock close to him. Yawning, he pulled out the sleeping bag from his bag. Then he tried to sleep, trying to put away all the worries. Michael tried to think a calming thought. Then he fell asleep, exhausted from today's tiring work.

* * * *

Michael woke up to some rustling sounds. When he looked up, the sky was still quite dark. *What was that sound?* He thought, as he pulled himself out of the sleeping bag. The sound came from a certain direction. He also smelled something burning, like burning paper. *Something's going on here.* Michael stood and cupped his ears to hear the sound better. It was the sound of footsteps against fallen leaves, and it seemed like that there was a group. Suddenly, Michael heard a rough, low-toned voice.

"Here he is!"

"Go get him before the fire reaches him! Quick!"

What? A fire? Michael thought, thinking about Liam and Josh, who would be still there at the waterfall, waiting. "Oh, no." He was now with a group of two people, who were wearing the same rescue clothes. Michael felt hopeful, hearing that they were a rescue squad.

"Quick, kid, we need to get out of here before the fire strikes us."

Michael recognized the voice as that of the man that he first heard. He watched as the man pulled out a rolled up map from his bag and unrolled it. Michael, looking at the map, saw that he made a false move. He was moving upward, into where the top was, not the bottom. *Oops,* he thought, worrying about Josh and Liam's situation now. They could be lost, trying to find a way out and could be in very bad state, which could make them harder to locate. And another concern was the fire. What if the fire reached them first, before the rescue team reached them? Michael couldn't take the thought of that. He just couldn't. He had to do something before the fire got them. Michael first thought of convincing the rescue squad to help him get Josh and Liam.

"But… my friend and my brother are still in the mountain, waiting for you. And my brother has a snakebite. We should get there, fast." The man nodded, and Michael felt hope, but what he said was different.

"Yes, we can. However, the first priority of our mission is to rescue anyone that we see first. We need to get you out of here before we do anything else. Otherwise, we might lose all the people that we're rescuing."

Michael, frustration rising in his mind, shouted, "But you guys can do something, like, work individually and also rescue my brother and friend still lost on the mountain, right?"

The man made a wrinkled face that made Michael suddenly worried about Josh and Liam. "When we found you, we thought we had a way. But one walkie-talkie went haywire. We couldn't communicate with it. Now we only have one map and one working walkie-talkie, and there is no internet for us to call each other."

Michael's shoulder sagged. "I thought that rescue squads were supposed to rescue everyone they can and take whatever chances they had to…"

Michael murmured, shaking his head. "I'm going to get them out, even if you guys don't. But first, I'll need the map." Then, without warning, Michael snatched the map from the man's hands, and before the men noticed what was going on and came after him, he was already far ahead.

The wisps of gray smoke were already zooming in on Michael. *Where is the smoke even coming from?* Michael thought, as he coughed loudly. Faint sounds of "Hey! Michael!" He glanced at the map that he had taken from the man. It indicated that he was close to the top of the mountain. He glanced at the gray clouds that he saw not that far away. They were all rising to the sky.

Oh, no. Michael thought, as he started scanning the map for the waterfall. *Bottom of mountain, fire? Then the fire will spread to the top really fast!* Filled with urgency, Michael headed toward the waterfall, his stomach rumbling with hunger. But that wasn't his first priority now. His first priority was to get Josh and Liam and get off the mountain as fast as he could.

* * * *

"Gosh, finding the way with a map is really hard," Michael murmured to himself as he rushed through the forest of trees, pulling out a flashlight to light up the map in the dark moonless night. "This map just shows the outline of it, and nothing else, so I don't know what will get in the way."

Michael suppressed a yawn and then noticed that the flashlight was darker than before. He made a scrunched face and dug through his bag for more batteries. However, there was nothing. Michael decided to turn the flashlight off and continue as much as he could. He squinted at the map. Then he was surprised that he was walking right past the waterfall. He faintly heard the water falling quite a long distance away. Michael let out a sigh of relief. Now he could just walk to the place that Liam and Michael were.

They wouldn't be moving around, would they? Michael thought, squinting around the waterfall. He walked around the muddy puddles as he progressed closer to the waterfall.

"Josh! Liam! I'm here! We can get out now!" Michael only had to wait a few seconds until he heard a reply.

"Yeah…we're here."

Sighing with relief, Michael bounded toward the sound. However, what he saw wasn't pretty. Josh stood next to Liam. A sunken expression lined his face. Josh saw Liam in an even worse condition. Liam lay on a rock, wincing every time he moved his body.

"I don't know what's going on," Josh said as he rose. His face looked very pale. There's something up with Liam's snakebite, and I don't know what to do."

It really looked serious. There was an unordinary, yellowish color on and nearby the wound, and it covered a huge amount of skin on his knee. Michael gasped. He had researched this kind of infection before at school for an essay. If left alone, it could be serious.

"Um…Josh?" Michael asked urgently.

Josh, seeming to recognize the urgency in his voice, replied, "What is it, now?"

Michael's face turned serious. "How long has it been since his knee was like this?"

Josh looked at him. "Well… about a few hours. When we woke up, he was wincing in pain, and that was how it looked since then."

Michael nodded. It didn't seem really serious, but it would turn serious if not treated soon. "I have a map. Let's get outta here before things get serious," Michael said, then paused as Josh grabbed his shirt.

"Wait, where did the map come from?" Josh suspiciously eyed the map.

"Uh…" Michael stuttered, as he thought whether or not he should tell the truth or make some kind of excuse because Josh was a person that despised lies. After a few seconds, he made a decision that admitting the truth didn't harm anyone.

"Well, a couple of rescuers came, and they said that they would take me out first. I said no, and they wouldn't let me go get you guys. So I snatched the map from them and ran."

"Nice. That's what you should've done."

Michael was grateful for his understanding. Then he heard Liam whisper weakly to his ear, "Can we get out of here first, please…I can smell the smoke… "

That snapped him out of his calmness. He sniffed the air and coughed loudly. The smoke was getting closer. He nudged for Josh to stand up, and they both assisted Liam, holding him by his shoulders. Throats aching from the incoming smoke, Michael, Josh, and Liam determinedly but carefully proceeded to exit the mountain. However, they didn't think that the fire would face them straight on.

It was not long before Michael heard Josh, and especially Liam, complaining about being tired from walking. Michael couldn't help but get frustrated. He understood Liam, but Josh was just getting in everyone's way.

"Can you just *get on* with it? Seriously, don't be stupid and complain in a situation like this!" Michael shouted with rage, and Josh, clearly surprised, straightened his posture and walked on without saying anything. But Michael knew from his expression that he was hurt, and he suddenly wanted to take back his angry words.

However, when he tried to tell that to Josh, he just nodded and said, "Let's go," making Michael feel even more guilty.

Liam whispered, "Now's not the time," and he decided to apologize when everything was well and fine.

Michael looked at the map. They were on the edge on the map, which meant that they could get off the mountain soon. Feeling a gush of relief, Michael confidently looked around, and suddenly closed his eyes as a lot of gray smoke blinded him for a moment. Then, he heard something, probably a tree, fall with a big thump. When he looked at it, it was engulfed in fire, black and scorched. Josh grabbed Michael and Liam's shoulders and pulled them away from the fire.

"Run," Josh ordered, and they followed him.

The wind blew towards them fast enough to make the fire spread faster. However, they had no time to think about such things. They ran as fast as possible. The fire spread towards them like a strong gust of wind. Michael glanced at the map as he shouted which direction that they should go. He felt the hot wind coming at his back, and he ran even faster until Liam slowed them down because of his injury.

Instantly, Michael rushed to help his brother, who's sweat fell like beads. The heat grew more intense than before. Michael was also running out of energy now. Assisting Liam and running had taken its toll. Then he noticed a dark shadow looming over him.

Liam shouted, "No!"

A burning log fell towards him, and Liam wasn't fast enough to avoid it. Then, Liam made a surprised face as Michael pushed him away. He fell to the ground as Michael's body crashed with the log, falling toward him.

Michael, for a time that felt like forever, had a searing pain racing up his back. Then he blacked out.

* * * *

Michael woke up somewhere that he didn't know. He was in a dark room, and he was apparently on a bed. Then he remembered, as he winced as he felt the burned marks on his back. It was hard to move, and when Michael struggled to get out of the bed, a door next to his bed opened. Liam and Josh, rushed to him. Josh looked totally fine, but Michael noticed that Liam had a cast on his right leg. Michael grimaced as he thought of the infection on Liam's leg.

"Bad news, Michael," Liam whispered to him. "You're going to be stuck in this hospital for about five days, or whatever time it takes for your burns to heal."

What? No school? No! There'll be too many tests weighing down on me then! Michael lay down again on his bed, filled with worries about school. Josh tapped Michael's arm.

"Well, I better get going. Your parents are there."

Josh waved goodbye and exited out of the door. Liam punched Michael, saying,

"Why're you making that sad face?"

At that time, Michael heard the door creaking as two adults came in. Michael had to squint to make out their faces because of the dark light. Michael smiled as he recognized the faces. It was his parents!

"Oh, Michael, I was so worried about you!" his mom whispered in his ear. "You were unconscious for almost three days! Our launch was cancelled because of bad weather, and we were afraid that you would not be awake before we had to leave."

"You know how it was for us when you were like that?" his dad joined in. "Thank God you're okay. I'm sorry, we want to stay longer, but now that your are conscious, we have to return to NASA."

Michael's face drooped. His mom gave him his phone to contact her.

"Guess I gotta go, too." Liam smiled, and followed his parents. Michael sighed, and lay on his bed once again.

This is going to be really boring, Michael thought as he stared at the ceiling.

* * * *

Michael looked around the small, now-familiar room around his bed. He'd been stuck there for five days, studying and playing, etc. Now he just wanted to get out of the hospital. The clock next to him indicated that it was 2:30 P.M. He glanced in the mirror at his burns. Still red, but no aching when he touched it. Michael clenched his fist, clearly frustrated. *Why don't they let me out of the hospital?* Right then, the door creaked open, and Michael saw the doctor walking towards him with Michael's parents.

"Your burn is fine enough, by most parts. You can go back to your house now."

Michael jumped out of his bed, hollering a sound of victory and relief, then stopped when he saw Liam standing next to the door.

"What are you doing? It's Wednesday today!" Michael exclaimed. Liam made a concerned face that worried Michael about something.

"You're lucky, Michael," Liam said.

Michael looked a confused. "Yesterday, the teacher announced that the class will have a field trip to a mountain. Yeah, sounds really bad, doesn't it? Well, guess what mountain the class is going to. It's the mountain where we got lost."

Michael, clearly surprised, covered his mouth with both his hands.

"So the trip is not a 'if you don't want to do this, then don't do it' trip. It's because we are researching about forest ecosystems, and forest fires are included in the lesson. I couldn't go because of my leg, *sigh*," Liam explained, clearly relieved. "Going in there will give me nightmares, man. Josh, you, me, all."

Michael suddenly thought of Josh, and gasped. *Wait, what about Josh?*

Liam made a face full of pity. "But there is one unfortunate thing. Josh, who has no injuries, is going to the trip."

"Oh, no, Josh is gonna die of fright," Michael replied.

"Well, too late to keep Josh from going, because they already left for camp," Liam answered.

Michael's parents and Liam led Michael out the door and outside of the hospital, where fresh air greeted him. Michael instantly felt alive and fresh again. As they rode the car back to Michael's house, Michael prayed for Josh. He also thought he was lucky that he was in the hospital for a long time, and he didn't have to go on the field trip that would give him nightmares for the rest of his life.

Man, bad things always happen consecutively, thought Michael, as he looked out of the window of the car. Somewhere in the mountains, Josh was probably having a nightmare. *Good luck, Josh,* Michael thought as the car slowed to a halt in front of his house.

The Young Murderer and her Dog

By

Sooyeon Park

"Focus!" Jade whispered to herself, trembling. Every finger pushed against a note made her stressed and dizzy. The piano rumbled, increasing her breathing and the light-headed feeling that threatened her consciousness. The song she played was two minutes long, but to her, it felt like hours. Just as she strained her neck to relieve her body, she pressed the wrong key. It echoed throughout the hall, and everything was silent. To stop the silence, Jade kept on with the song, panicking at the same time. Because of the terrible silence she made, Jade suddenly felt the tension rising from the audience and the judges, and the beautiful melody she made from the piano started crashing down. The audience whispered to each other and the judges made faces at the music she played. Jade's heart beat fast and her body felt numb.

When is this music done? She thought with discomfort. Her teeth chattered, and her bare arms ached from the cold. She breathed heavily, as she awkwardly sped up her playing. The notes that were memorized perfectly in her mind started fading away.

Before she knew it, Jade felt a pounding ache in her head, pumping like her heart. Shocked by the sudden pain, she stopped playing, and her head dropped down onto the piano, which made a loud screeching sound. The audience gasped as she collapsed, and Jade saw some people running towards her. Everything happened all so fast. She felt somebody lifting her. She tried to speak, but her vision blurred, and she passed out.

* * * *

Jade woke and felt something unusual. She smelled all the medical equipment, and she recognized her surroundings as a health room of some type.

"What?" Jade said, looking around.

Hearing her voice, the nurse glanced up from her papers. "Are you feeling, alright?"

Realizing that she was in the nurse's room found on the first floor of the hall, she squirmed uncomfortably and answered, "Yes." But as soon as she lifted herself up, she gasped in pain that struck her in her head, and she fell back down onto the bed.

The nurse got off her chair to help her. Suddenly, the door crashed open. Jade turned her head toward the door and saw Betsy, her *only* friend, in front of the entrance.

"Jade, you alright?" Betsy cried in panic, running toward her bed.

"Yeah, I guess." Jade dug her elbow into the bed mattress, forcing herself up. The pain struck her on the spine, but she ignored it. Her head stung her and ached like it did on stage.

"I'm gonna go home. Can you come with me?"

"Jade, you're hurt. The competition just finished, and there are a lot of people outside," the nurse replied, sitting back in her chair.

"It *finished*?" Her mouth dropped open, and her voice rang through the small room. She struggled to her feet and staggered to the exit door.

"No, you have to stay. You're going to get hurt out there," the nurse called from behind her, but Jade ignored her and limped out of the room. She realized sounds coming from the entrance of the building. Hastily, Jade staggered to the stairway which led her to the entrance of the hall.

"Jade!" Betsy stopped her. "It's finished. People are leaving already."

She was right. There were people everywhere, and not only were they part of the audience, but the winners of the music competition were there too, holding onto their trophies. Leaves were scattered randomly on the ground, and the puddles made them look wrinkled and dark. Above the leafless trees, drizzle penetrated the thick veil of fog that surrounded her.

Jade stepped outside into one of the puddles, which made a small rim around her grey heels.

"Jade," she heard Betsy's tiny voice calling her through the noisy crowd. Jade turned around to see her friend's grey eyes, which had hints of sadness in them. Rain made her pretty golden hair damp and wet, and her eyeliner got ruined. Sighing, Jade walked passed Betsy and the crowd, trying to ignore stares.

Some people recognized Jade and whispered to each other loud enough for Jade to hear every word.

"Look, it's that girl. She didn't get to finish her piece."

"Oh, she must feel really bad right now."

"Shh! She could hear us."

Some of her competitors stared at Jade as if she didn't belong with them. One came up to her and hissed, "Look, this competition is *not* for beginners. It is for those who have practiced for years. Professionals. I think your parents should have told you that, already."

Jade clenched her teeth. "My parents don't know about this."

The young musician seemed surprised but shrugged and walked away, leaving Jade with her blood boiling with anger.

Jade remembered the first time she learned piano. She knew that she was never meant to be with one. However, it was not that she had a choice about it. Everyone in her class played at least one instrument. Some even played three. Jade was the only one who couldn't play an instrument in eighth grade, and she knew that if she didn't change in high school, she'd end up with no one to talk to. *All I wanted to do is be part of my class.* She always thought to herself.

"Let's go" whispered Betsy in a calm voice. She gently pulled Jade's arm, and they walked silently toward their neighborhood. The cold wind struck against Jade's long brown hair, and her ears froze and stung her.

"It wasn't that bad, anyway," Betsy whispered, dusting off lint from her sweater.

However, Jade didn't felt like talking. Her face didn't move a muscle.

"Do your parents still not know about the competition?"

Again, there was silence. As the two girls reached their homes, Betsy waved goodbye, knowing that Jade didn't see her, but Jade turned around and waved back, before entering her home.

Holding back the tears that were about to pour out, she closed the door behind her, and she heard rain droplets dripping from the sky. People outside opened their umbrellas for little kids who were screaming and laughing. From the open window beside her lonely piano, Jade saw the sparkling rain splashing onto the ground. She ripped off her sparkly wet dress and got her shirts and jeans.

Hearing absolutely nothing but her heavy breathing, Jade knew that her mom was not in the house and that she was too busy with her work as usual. Not only did she miss her mother, but also her father, who passed away from a car accident one day on his way home. Every time she looked at her classmates, she felt a rage against them for how they treated their parents. Tired, Jade shook her head to forget about these painful memories and threw herself down onto her bed.

Her hair, which was once tied into a beautiful coffee-colored bun decorated with a sparkly white hair band was now all loose and wet from the rain, and her dress was all wrinkled and ruined. Instead of reading, she just held the book in her hand and started falling asleep. It had been a long, tiring day. She wiped away the cold raindrop on her forehead, and her eyes ached, which gave her a sharp headache. She knew that this was the last time she would ever play or even touch a piano.

"Just forget about it," she told herself, as her eyelids slowly fell. She looked at her sore hand. "It wasn't that bad," Jade mumbled, moving her fingers as if she were playing the piano. Gradually, her fingers stopped their motion, and Jade fell asleep.

A few hours later, hearing a strange noise, Jade's eyes opened in a squint. It was night and, she lay still, hearing a strange noise that was repeating from hours ago. Lazily, Jade thought as she pulled her thick blanket over her all the way to her face. Then she heard it again, but it sounded very familiar. She forced herself up and opened the window. Before she could fully open it, she was startled by the sudden bark from a dog. The noise continued a few more times and it ended with a high yelp a puppy would make.

"Strange," Jade whispered to herself, still staring out the window. She never had seen a dog in her neighborhood, and not only was it in her neighborhood, but the sound was also coming from an empty house few houses away. Thick fog and rain covered the house, revealing only its old roof. Her leg ached, her whole body felt dizzy. *I left my piano book at the hall.* Jade groaned, as she knew that her mother would soon find out about the competition if she noticed that the book was missing.

Jade looked around for her mother. She was not in the house, so she decided to go retrieve the book. She saw that it was just 10:00 P.M. and that the hall was opened until 12:00 A.M. Jade grinned, proud that she knew every single thing about the concert hall. *But how will I get there?* She fidgeted with her fingers. She needed Betsy to guide her way to the concert hall like she did when they were walking home. She almost decided to go back to sleep and go there early in the morning, but she knew that her mother could come home anytime. She could be here even in ten minutes. Panicking, Jade grabbed her sweater and headed out of her room, her foot almost tripping over the dirty pile of clothes.

"I'll be back in five minutes," Jade told herself.

Before she knew it, she was outside her house putting on her shoes. The cool winter wind rushed through Jade's hair, and she felt her hands freezing. She looked around her, admiring the beauty her neighborhood hid during daytime. The fog blurred the street lights, and the street looked so clean without any cars or bikes parked on the sides. Some houses were already decorated with Christmas lights, even though it was the beginning of November, and they made her feel warm and cozy. She glanced at her wrist, thinking that her watch would be there, but she realized that she had left it in her bedroom.

"Nah, I don't need a watch now," she said out loud to herself. Her voice echoed through the air. It sounded very familiar. It sounded like the stage in the concert hall. She could almost hear the pieces she played ringing throughout the neighborhood. The thought made her smile and laugh softly.

Without taking her eyes off from the sky, Jade stuffed her hand inside her pocket and felt something. She looked down and found her phone. She turned her phone on to see the time.

Jade shrieked in horror, "11:00 P.M.!" Her mom must already home by now, and the concert hall will be closing in an hour. She looked around her vicinity. *Where is this place?* Jade wondered if she passed the road leading to concert hall while looking at the sky. Not knowing where to go, Jade started searching it on her phone. However, her phone ran out of power before should could use her phone's map app. Fog slowly appeared from the corner of the sky, as Jade struggle with her phone.

"Dang it!" Jade looked around her and saw a gleam of light in the distance. She ran towards the light, hoping that it would be the lights from the concert hall. As she zipped down the road, she saw unusual plants and trees surrounding street. She tried to ignore the peculiar looking plants around her, but as she went in deeper, the number of trees and strange looking plants started to grow. At last, when she reached the light, she realized that the light came from a tiny house with a lot of plants growing around it.

Jade breathed harder. The house was farther than she thought it would be, and she noticed the fog that was growing thick, with bits of drizzle patting her head.

Maybe I can ask people in the house for the direction to the concert hall, Jade thought in haste as she finally reached the porch. The porch made a creaky sound, and the wood bent in as Jade took steps carefully so that she wouldn't break the old wood. She quickly stopped a foot away from the door and slowly raised her fist to knock. She felt her hands trembling and her lips shut tightly.

Why am I scared of a house? Jade thought in shame. She looked at the house for a moment. Vines almost covered the walls of the house, and the windows were all open and bright from the lights inside. Not knowing what was going to happen next, Jade gulped and knocked the old door few times. Nothing happened.

Cautiously, Jade raised her hand to knock again, but a sudden loud screech that filled her ears and echoed endlessly in her head stopped her. Shocked, she jumped back and fell off the porch, landing on one of the steps.

Despite landing hard on the steps, the wood still held her. Jade slowly stood up and stumbled clumsily away from the old porch, back to the sidewalk. *Was that an animal?* Curiosity suddenly overcame her, and without knowing, she headed straight toward the place she heard the sound, the backyard. Seeing a car parked near the yard, she hunched over and raced behind it, using is as a shield. She sighed with relief. The entire yard was visible from her secure vantage point. However, her satisfaction didn't last long. Her heart dropped, and her eyes opened wide as she took a glance at it. It was a wounded dog, covered in fresh blood.

A man stood next to the dog, his eyes red and blurred. His right hand was tightly held into a fist, and his left hand held a whip. Jade decided he was drunk. However, that was not all. Without speaking, the man slashed the cruel weapon across the dog's ribs. The animal howled and collapsed on its side. Its face was filled with terror, and its eyes were wide open as if it was dead.

Jade winced as the man continued tormenting the helpless creature, who lay down on the ground silent with its eyes still open. It blinked each time it was hit, but besides that, it didn't move a muscle. Jade saw it breathing heavily as if it wanted to die. She saw the dog move its head toward her. Surprised, Jade quickly looked away but took a quick glance from the corner of her eye. The helpless animal's eyes pleaded to her.

"Help me," its eyes seemed to say.

Sadly, Jade knew that she could do nothing to help the dog. Quietly, rising to her feet, keeping the car between her at an angle where she could see the dog, but the man could not see her, she decided to head back to her house. Then she saw the man drop his belt. She stopped in her spot and watched him. He stretched and glared at the dog. Then he staggered back into the shabby old house.

When the door closed, Jade looked around to make sure that no one was looking. Then, without thinking, she ran toward the backyard. She didn't have any plan in mind. She just knew she had to do something. Her heart beating wildly. Jade dashed through the bushes. Thorns and vines rubbed sharply against her skin, but she ignored them, concentrating more on the dog. As she got closer, her heart beat faster. She had never seen anything so bloody and injured.

Jade saw that the dog was bigger than she thought it was. It looked like a small golden retriever but with straight ears. Dried blood covered the rich cinnamon-colored fur from the previous beatings. It's paws, even though ripped and bloody, were still round and plump. Then she noticed its tail. It was the only part of the dog that was unharmed. As Jade came closer, the dog's tail wavered softly. Its pearly black eyes opened and stared at Jade.

It let out a faint whimper and tried to stand up, but its wobbly legs couldn't hold its weight, causing it to fall back down to its bruised sides.

It yelped loudly from the pain. Slowly, Jade squatted next to the dog, her eyes rapidly looked back and forth between the house and the dog, scared that someone might see her.

"What's your name?" Jade whispered to the dog, trying to find its name on its collar. As Jade, ran her hand around the collar, she realized that it was made out of chains. "Buddy," she read. She gently unlinked the two ends of the chain, feeling the dog's rough and clumped fur. Her plan automatically formed, as she lifted the dog. She was going to steal him.

Buddy was heavier than Jade thought, so she had to kneel back down to carry it in a different way. She felt her sleeves wet from its blood. The dog obediently remained still as it lay in Jade's careful arms, and she stood up and struggled her way through the thorny plants with the bloody dog in her arms. She reached the open fence gate and looked back to see if her rescue attempt had been discovered. Her heart pounded in her chest at the unexpected, horrifying sight––the silhouette of a man coming out of the back door.

If he sees me, he's going to kill me. Not knowing what to do, Jade held Buddy tightly against her chest and started running as fast as her thin legs could take her. She heard the door open and saw the man's shadow standing in front of the door. *Please don't see me. Please don't see me,* Jade thought, breathing hard.

Buddy, too, was scared. He shivered as Jade ran faster. Jade felt its rapid heart beat and heard a person chasing behind her at the same time. Her legs throbbed, and she wanted to stop. She took a quick glance behind her and was surprised to see that a boy was chasing her, not the man. However, that didn't mean she was going to stop. She knew that that boy was either the man's son or at least a person he knew. A long weapon was in his hand, and he screamed like a drunken person.

The noises of crackling leaves Jade made as she ran later changed into a sound of a hard, solid concrete. The cold air rushed around Jade's slim neck. While taking a quick look at the dog, Jade saw from the corner of her eyes, a warm yellow light getting brighter on her left side.

"What the…" Jade turned around and faced a loud truck, rushing from her left. At that point, she felt her adrenaline exploding within her. She squeezed the dog tightly, placed her right foot in front of her, and jumped off the road. She landed hard on the sidewalk on her side and rolled all the way to the wall nearby.

As she landed next to the brick wall, she heard the truck screeching to a stop and a loud scream. Jade gasped when she realized that the dog was not in her arms anymore and forced herself up. She then remembered how it slipped as she jumped off the road.

"No," Jade said, shaking her head. She quickly turned her head to the road. The truck remained motionless with blood on its wheels and on the ground.

Rapidly, Jade got up and staggered toward the truck. *Where are you, Buddy?* Jade breathed hard like she did on the stage and looked around the road and towards the truck. A familiar figure caught her attention. It was exactly what she was looking for.

She quickly scrambled up to Buddy, who lay weakly on the ground, and held its head up gently as she could. *Is he dead?* Jade thought, scared. Its eyes automatically opened, and its tail wagged faintly as it looked up at Jade.

Jade smiled, hugging the dog gently to her shoulders. She felt its warm breath breathing heavily on her neck and heard it bark softly in satisfaction.

As she let go of the dog, Jade looked towards the truck. *Whose blood is that?* Jade squinted her eyes. She followed the blood on the truck tire, to the blood on the concrete, to the…

Jade gasped, her hands automatically covered her eyes. She backed away from the truck to kneel next to the dog. The mad boy, who had been chasing her, was on the ground. His fractured arm was covered his bloody face, which was not in its usual shape. In the truck Jade saw the truck driver, his head lying on the steering wheel, which was soaked from his blood. Jade looked away wide-eyed, but she could still him from the corner of her eye. She closed her eyes tightly shut and turned away. When she opened them, her eyes caught Buddy's.

A wave of guilt covered Jade as she saw Buddy's eyes peering into her eyes. *I have killed its owner,* Jade thought, wishing that this was a dream. Her legs felt weak and wobbly. Jade knew that it was all her fault that they died. She could see the pearly eyes staring at her from her left and the people she killed on her right. *Wait. Dogs don't know anything about death.*

Jade turned her head and looked at Buddy, who was still looking at her. *They're just clueless little creatures.*

Just as she put her arms around the dog to carry him, she heard a soft growl. Surprised, she jumped back.

"What was *that*?" Jade blurted at Buddy's face.

He stared at her, not moving any parts of his body. He looked like a statue. A statue made of pure marble. Jade tried again to lift it but was given another growl, this time louder. Its lips slowly curled up, baring its fangs.

Jade stood, stunned what she saw.

"I need to carry you so that I can feed you, okay?"

Silence.

Jade knew that Buddy didn't know what she babbled about. She was trying to save a dog, and now this was what she got back? An act of murder, and no matter how much she tried, that word would never leave her. She heard about some her age being murders. Being fourteen, she never thought that it would feel like this to kill someone. *I didn't actually kill him.* Jade tried to calm herself down. *It was the truck driver,* Jade thought, again glancing over at the truck.

Tired, Jade turned away from Buddy and walked away. Surprisingly, Buddy followed weakly. She stopped and bent down to pick him up. Surprisingly, he let her. She didn't know where her house was. Rain was thicker and so was the fog. Jade looked around but couldn't concentrate because of pressure. She had felt it while she was on the stage, and now she had that same feeling. *There's a dead person behind me,* Jade kept on thinking over and over. *And I'm the murderer.*

Her steps gradually got faster, and within a second she broke into a run. Jade didn't know where she was going. She just needed to run away from the world. Buddy in her arms bounced up and down, as she ran clumsily.

Under the street light, Jade ran, her shadows and her footsteps gradually disappearing at the same time. She ran until exhaustion forced her to stop. She found cover under a strand of trees and collapsed on the ground.

* * * *

She woke in the middle of the night. Buddy sniffed the grass near her.

She almost forgot what had happened the day before, but remembered when she saw Buddy's deep shiny eyes. Jade realized that she was on grass. Familiar thorns and vines surrounded the area around her. *It must have been minutes I've been asleep.* She looked around her as she sat up, wondering if anybody saw her sleeping on the wet grass.

"Ouch!" she shrieked, jumping up, when she accidently leaned against a long thorn. Hearing her voice, Buddy looked in her direction and walked towards her, not noticing one of his crooked leg that hung to his side. He greeted her with a lick on her face, and she gave him a tight hug, wondering if Buddy still remembered how she killed his owner.

Jade didn't know where she was. Perhaps it was because of the dark. The streets lights were far from where she was, and she knew that her arms would fall off if she continued carrying the heavy dog.

"Where are we?" Jade asked Buddy, slightly scratching his chin. Buddy tried to close his eyes, but his eyelids wouldn't budge, allowing Jade to only see the whites of his eyes. He struggled with his crooked leg. As Jade studied the dog, she realized that his side was all ripped, and his face was dirty from the scars and blood. She knew that she couldn't do anything to "sew" the dog's skin back together.

"We need a vet," she grumbled to herself. She took out her phone, which was barely hanging out of her pocket and tried to turn it on.

No battery. Jade frowned at her phone and looked around. Vines hung deftly over an old tree, and the sky was clear without any clouds. Out from a distance, Jade saw lights flashing and heard a police car dashing on the road. Hearing this, she jumped up, grabbed Buddy, and ran toward it. She felt tired of thorns and vines. She needed help to go back home.

"Help!" Seeing that there was an open window for the officer to hear her, Jade screamed at the car as it approached. As the car passed by her, Jade dashed through the thorny bushes and trees with Buddy held tightly in her arms.

As the car finally stopped, Jade tripped over a firm root and landed painfully on her side. Buddy, who fell out of Jade's grasp, shook himself and limped slowly toward the people who got out of the police car, his eyes wild and shocked from the sudden fall.

"Buddy, come back!" Jade whispered loudly, struggling to get up. But, of course, Buddy ignored her and continued making noises. Tired of the disobedient dog, Jade ripped the thorns and vines that were blocking her view and launched herself towards him, grabbed Buddy by the stomach, and landed on something like a wet bag.

When she was on the ground, she heard the cops behind her, gasping in surprise.

"Get the doctor; get the doctor," she heard one of them say.

Jade, disgusted at what she landed on, took out her hand and saw pure blood on it. Shocked by the view, she stood up and saw what she had landed on. The cops, again, gasped at Jade's loud shriek.

It was a dead person. Not only that, but she also knew who he was. It was the boy who got hit by the truck, while chasing Jade.

Seeing this, Jade felt nauseous and fought to keep from vomiting.

"There's no need to throw up," a cop with a thick, red beard came up to her, not knowing the real reason why Jade was feeling sick. "See if the truck driver is still in there," he ordered the other cop. This made them clump together around the truck, which was all crunched up by a tree that has fallen on it. There were a lot of talking and flashings of torches. After studying the truck, one of them ran to the cop with the beard.

"We assume that the truck crashed into the tree while it was trying to avoid this boy."

"The truck driver is still in here," Another cop remarked. "He's also out."

Jade froze.

Seeing her expression, the cop with the beard said gently, "Don't worry. It must have been an accident."

He doesn't get it. Jade rubbed her eyes and realized that there was blood stained on her face, too.

"Are you lost?" one cop asked, looking around. "I don't see anybody else around here."

"Yes, my dog and I are lost," Jade quickly replied, pointing at Buddy, who was now chewing on the thin grass under him.

The cop made a face when he saw Buddy.

"Is it okay?" He scrunched up his face, as if he had never seen a dog before.

Jade took a glance at Buddy. *Whoa, he does look pretty sick.*

"You can come in our car, and we will take you home, but we can't take the dog," the cop finally said after a long pause.

"What? Why?"

"He will have to go to a veterinarian. Call pet control," he ordered the other cop.

Jade looked at the cop in disbelief and then turned to Buddy. His eyes were still dark and glossy, and his neck was all covered in scabs. In one word, he looked creepy.

"Can I at least borrow a phone to call my mother?" Jade asked. She knew that her mother never used the phone, but she fortunately had enough money in her pocket to pay a taxi driver. *I'll pay extra, if they don't let Buddy in.*

"Sure." The cop reached in his pocket and took out his phone. It was a cheap kind, but it still worked.

"Thank you."

Jade took the phone and called a taxi.

"Wait," she turned to the cop. "Where is this place?"

However, he was already speaking to one of the cops to cancel the call to the pet control. Jade opened her mouth to repeat, but the police interrupted her.

"We have an emergency. If you are going to use that phone, make it quick."

Hearing this, Jade sighed and gave him back his phone. She then looked at the road where the truck was. She saw the dead body.

I killed him. Jade thought, and she could feel her face redden.

"Don't worry about it." The cop saw what Jade was staring at. "We'll find out more about this incident."

Jade gasped quietly. *No, no, no.*

"Okay," she whispered and faced the road. She took Buddy in her sturdy arms and headed for the road behind the truck.

"Wait," the cop called from behind. "On our way, we will drop you off by the vet. Get in."

"No," Jade sputtered, then lied, "My mom can treat him. She's a vet. She'll know what to do."

The cop looked suspicious, but he answered, "Ok, hop in."

Grinning, Jade climbed into the comfy seat and placed Buddy next to her. One of the cops got in. Jade told him her address, and the cop nodded.

"The one near the concert hall, right?"

"Yes," Jade answered.

The cop started the car, and it moved unexpectedly fast on the road.

The car ran roughly over the clumpy road, which made Jade feel sick. She remembered the piano books she was supposed to bring home. She knew that she would have to forget about them until she arrived home. The beautiful music, which she had once played, faded away into the air and was now forgotten by its player. She was a murderer.

Once a person murders another person, the killer would forget everything around her. That was Jade. She forgot the pieces she played on stage and even forgot some notes. *How did that song go again?* Jade closed her eyes and imagined how the actual song went. *First, the song started with an A. The low one. The next note was…* Jade opened her eyes. She knew that she would gradually forget about the whole thing called "classic." Buddy would be more important. Cops seeking the truth about the incident would be another problem. Jade sighed. *The cops will soon find out about this. What's the use of pondering about it?*

* * * *

Jade thanked the cop, as she got out the car and ran toward her house. Buddy ran at her side with his tongue hanging out. This made Jade smile. It felt like years she had not been home.

Buddy sniffed the air as Jade put her hand on her door knob.

"Unusual, isn't it?" Jade glanced at Buddy, who was studying the house door with his nose. Jade took a deep breath. She didn't know what her mother would say about the dog or the way she went missing all night. She would have to deal with whatever her mother would say to her.

She slowly turned the door knob. It was tougher than she thought it would be. She jerked it harder, but it wouldn't budge. Jade pushed Buddy aside and held firmly onto the doorknob with both of her hands. She used all her strength and turned the doorknob. It finally twisted with a crashing sound, and the door finally opened. Buddy's ears perked up, and he cocked his head to get a better look inside her house. Hands stinging, Jade rubbed them together and held Buddy back while she fully opened the door. The jacket she left on the chair was still there, and the cushions were all over the floor like when she left. *Why didn't Mom clean this?*

She carefully stepped in and looked around, picturing her mother waiting for her on the sofa, or calling the cops to find her; however, her mother couldn't be seen anywhere on the first floor.

"Mom?" Jade called, wishing there would be at least somebody here. Her arms around Buddy loosened, and Buddy wandered around the house. She walked to the living room, got the house phone, and dialed her mother's number.

"Hello? Mom?"

Jade sighed when she heard her mother's phone ringing on the kitchen table. She slammed the phone back into place and stood up.

"Buddy," Jade called. "We're going to the cops."

* * * *

There were people crowded in the police station. In fact, there were so many of them that nobody realized that Jade was the only teenager with a dog following by her side. Her brown hair was wet with sweat, making it look darker. She thought about calling the cops from her home, but she wanted to show them the proof, using Buddy. As she approached an old looking cop, she felt herself getting nervous and her breath getting harder. The old cop, seeing Jade, squinted his eyes, surprised to see someone so young at this time of night.

Jade ignored the look and kept on with her walk. She felt very small and weak compared to the crowd she around her. There were big sweaty men complaining about their hurt friend, and parents crying about their kidnapped children. *Why did I even come here?* Jade felt her head aching, but she knew that she belonged here. She was one of them.

Soon, she reached the old man and sat down on a chair in front of him. He had white hair, and his cap was slightly tipped to its side. Jade felt her cheeks burning and her mouth sputtering for words. "Um," Jade hesitated. "There is a problem." Jade cringed at her awkward self, but the cop nodded and smiled understandingly. Despite his intense-looking face, his smile was warm and genuine.

"We're here to help," the old man said. "So tell me, what is it?"

Jade opened her mouth to speak, but right at that moment she bumped one of her shins into the metal chair leg, making her gasp in pain. Confused, the cop leaned closer to Jade.

"What did you say?"

"Nothing!" she spat out, knowing that she was making a fool of herself. Then she took a deep breath and faced the cop. *Let's just finish this. They're going to soon find out anyway.*

Jade started then took another big breath. The cop wrinkled his forehead.

"Don't worry, little girl. We're not going to hurt anyone, but there are other people waiting. You gotta hurry it up, and I'll listen." The cop smiled again.

"My mother's missing," Jade said, shaking. However, she knew that there was also another reason she came to the police station. The cop opened his mouth to talk, but Jade interrupted.

"And..."

The cop stared at her.

"I also murdered someone, I think," Jade mumbled.

This made the cop nod slowly. "And when was this?"

"A few hours ago."

He nodded again. He took out a pencil and started taking notes. "Name?"

"Jade Dawson."

"Did you only kill one person or more?"

Jade stopped. She remembered the truck that ran into a tree because of her and the boy.

"Two people. A boy and a truck driver." Jade forced the last words to come out. She suddenly got this feeling that someone was staring at her from a distance. It was from her peripheral sight. *He seems pretty familiar,* Jade thought and took a quick peek at him and gasped. It was the cop with the red beard whom she met a few hours ago. His eyes were wide, and Jade could see his lips that were mouthing the word: "You?"

Shocked, Jade turned her head quickly, but she could still see him standing, fuddled.

"Jade Dawson," the old cop repeated her name. "How did this happen?"

Hearing her name, Jade quickly turned back, sighed, and decided to tell him everything. Her voice trembled as she talked, but the cop listened to her thoughtfully, nodding to each sentence she said. While speaking, she could feel the red-bearded cop staring straight at her.

"It was an accident," Jade finished. Her voice had a crack in it.

"I understand," The red-bearded cop said, suddenly interrupting. Jade's wide eyes turned to him in surprise.

"Something similar happened to me when I was your age," he started. "And that's what made me a cop." He laughed softly.

Jade nodded, slowly patting Buddy, who slept patiently on the floor next to her.

"So, all this happened because of this dog?" the old cop asked, leaning over to look at Buddy.

"I had to help him," Jade whined. The scene of Buddy getting beaten flashed through her head.

"I see," he replied. He cringed when he looked at Buddy's wounded body. "I bet he has to go to the veterinarian."

Jade nodded. The shiny name tag on the cop caught her eye. James Winston.

Jade glanced back at the red-bearded cop, who rubbed his lips against each other nervously. *He must have found out that I was lying about my mom being a vet.*

"So," Jade started. "Are you going to call my mom about it?"

Officer Winston sighed. "Yes, we will need her phone number." He passed her a pen and a post-it note.

Taking the pen, Jade reluctantly wrote down her mother's phone number, knowing that her mother's phone was left in the house. The ink smudged as Jade ran her palm over the rough, old paper, and she handed it back to the officer.

Nodding, he picked up a telephone in front of him and took a glance at the paper. Nervously, Jade petted Buddy as she shifted in her chair. The dried blood flaked off as Jade scratched Buddy behind his ears. Buddy looked up at her and gently licked her hand.

"Hello?" Officer Winston said roughly into the phone, his gentle voice gone. Then he hung up, stared at the smudged phone number, and redialed.

Did I write the wrong number? Jade peeked at the yellow note on the officer's busy hands. The numbers were blurred a bit, but it was still right.

"Hello?" He tried again but ended up hanging up the phone. After that, he turned to Jade. "Are you sure that this is the right number?"

"Yes," Jade replied almost at the same time he ended. She saw the slow suspicion rising within him. Trying to change the subject, she quickly added, "But I don't know where she is either."

"Hm," Officer Winston sighed, taking a small notebook from his back pocket and writing in it. Jade sighed in relief that all the tension was all gone and turned her attention to what he would ask next.

"How about your father?"

"He passed away when I was six."

Officer Winston looked up in surprise from his notebook. He looked directly at her and asked, "Then who were you living with this whole time?"

"With my mother." Jade squirmed uncomfortably, fiddling with her fingers that were covered in dog fur. She saw the officer still staring at her for a clear answer.

"After the truck accident, I went back to my home with Buddy and saw that no one was there," Jade stopped to take a breath, then continued. "Everything was left unmoved, and my mother left no notes."

"She left without you knowing it?"

"Yes."

Officer Winston frowned softly and rubbed his lips. "Okay, you'll have to wait at home for a while until we finished

Jade received another post-it note and wrote her phone number and made sure that she didn't smudge it.

"We will call you if we hear anything about your mother," the officer assured.

"Okay, thank you." Jade got off the chair. She picked Buddy up and headed out the door. The morning sunlight shone down her face, as she called for a cab.

* * * *

Buddy lay down breathless on the house sofa. Jade sat next to him and rested her phone, charging next to her side. She, herself, felt breathless. As she stood up to get water, a familiar figure stood on the right side of her. It was her piano, left untouched for days. Jade, without knowing, started to walk slowly toward it, She realized the tiny dusts particles between its keys and the fading color of its wood. She ran her thin fingers on the cold, solid keys, remembering the moment she played on the stage in full view of the audience.

Jade pressed a key. Its sound almost echoed throughout the house. When she lifted her finger out of the key, dusts were covered on the tip of her finger, and she realized that her fingernails were too long. Ignoring her nails, Jade pressed the next key to the song, this time together with her left hand. That sound, which she hadn't heard since she met Buddy, popped the next set of notes in her mind, and she played it.

From the faded reflection from the piano, Buddy was barely visible. Jade saw that Buddy's head was raised and cocked to its side and at the same time, watching Jade, as she continued with her notes. After a long pause on one note, Jade took a breath and dashed her fingers through the rest of her song, and within a minute the whole neighborhood was echoed with the famous "Moonlight Sonata" and it was in its 3rd movement. Because of the rapid movement in her finger and the strong concentration she used, she didn't even realize that she was standing.

Because of the sudden volume and change, Buddy suddenly started panting and gasping, his mouth forming into a smile. Jade smiled back.

How did this song came out so bad in the competition? This question suddenly shot Jade like a bullet and stayed there until she felt a hint of discomfort like she did on stage. She felt her finger joints gradually hardening and her muscles tensing in pain. Sweats rolled down her forehead, all the way down to her neck.

And there it is. The part you started crashing down. Jade felt somebody whispering these uncomfortable words close to her ear. In a few seconds, like she did on the stage, she lost her beat, and her stiff fingers started pressing random keys.

The faces she saw on stage faded into her mind. One by one, their faces cringed at her music. Some whispered. Some covered their mouths with their hands. Some looked around in confusion.

Jade silently groaned, as her head continued aching. She saw Buddy's reflection from her piano, showing no signs of discomfort from the music. Frustrated, Jade threw her hands off of the piano keys, and let them hang by her sides as if they were boneless. She had enough feelings and pressure from the performance, but at the same time, glad that at least a dog enjoyed her playing. She, then heard Buddy stand up and run towards her.

Crack!

As she turned around, the loud noise of shattering window glass made her shriek and lose her balance. On the other side of the window stood a familiar man with a whip in his right hand and a smoking gun in the other, pointing at her, as she fell.

She fought hard to breath as she lay on the cold ground. Her chest felt like it was underneath something heavy and furry. Smoke drifted under her nose. *What's happening?* Jade thought, as her chest continued being pressed. She found herself harder to breath, when she heard footsteps coming nearer.

When they came close to her ears, Jade forced her eyes to open to see the mad man looking down at her.

His mouth slowly turned into a grin, as he bent down next to her.

"Gotcha," he sneered between his teeth as he reached his hands towards her.

No! Jade thought he was going to hurt her; however, to her surprise, something was lifted off her chest, and the smoky smell disappeared, leaving Jade panting hard in confusion.

When Jade opened her eyes, she was surprised that the man was heading away from her. *What?* Jade blinked hard at the figure that was lying weakly under his right arm.

"Buddy?" Jade whispered. Her voice had a crack in it.

His tail hung lifelessly under the man's arm as he walked. On the side of his neck was a bullet wound with blood pouring out from it.

Jade felt her chest. No bullet. She looked at Buddy's bleeding neck again. Her face burned, and her eyes stung.

Buddy had saved her.

Jade remembered how he lay dead on her chest, and how he jumped in front of her right before the gun fired. Tears ran down her face as she realized that she failed in trying help the poor dog.

Broken window pieces stabbed her hand, as she forced herself to stand up.

"You will regret this," Jade screamed. She grabbed her fully charged phone and dialed 911.

Hearing this, the man turned around. Jade was shocked by the view. He had tears in his eyes too.

"My son was *everything* to me," he started. "Before my wife died, she wished for one thing. Just one thing!"

Jade felt her face redden.

"She told me," he hesitated, "to take care of her son. But *you!*" He pointed his gun at Jade. "You ruined *everything.*"

Jade opened her mouth to speak, but no words came out. Her throat throbbed. "I just tried to save Buddy," she finally said, softly.

"Buddy?" he sneered. "He is no longer Buddy now." It was true. He was just a dead dog. With that, he turned around and headed out with the dog under his arm.

"I'm still going to report you," Jade choked, as she held out her phone. As she turned her phone on, she squinted her eyes at the various unread messages that suddenly flashed into her eyes.

"I hope you have a great last day of school!" One of the messages said. It was from her mother few months ago.

Hastily, Jade scrolled through the texts. Most of them were missed calls.

Crack. Crack. The sound of the man's footsteps heading out echoed into Jade's ears. She looked back at the screen.

"Jade, I just wanted to tell you that I have an urgent meeting. I have to make sure that you're reading this" Another text read. Then there were more missed calls.

Shivering, Jade scrolled down faster, skipping some. It was sent weeks ago.

'Sorry Jade :('

What? Jade kept scrolling.

'I don't think I'll make it.'

This made Jade's heart beat hard.

'I should have told you before I left for the airport'

Why? Jade shoulders ached. *Why did you go?*

'The plane is shaking harder than usual...'

And that was all. Jade tried to scroll down for more, but there were none left. That was her mother's last text.

Jade looked up back at the man. Her face froze. She failed in everything.

She failed the music competition. She failed in trying to save Buddy. She failed in trying to keep her mother after she lost her father. Above all, people would soon find out about the incident and misunderstand that she killed the boy on purpose.

In front of her, the man turned around and walked silently through the road that was covered in broken glass.

Crack Crack

Jade couldn't help but stare at Buddy, who hung under the man's big arms. His scab covered body, his lifeless ears, his ruffled fur, and his beautiful face. Her closest friend, her brother. He was gone now. Jade dropped her arms weakly beside her, her legs feeling weak at the same time.

The warm orange light from the sun flashed dimly through the tree branches as the street lights flashed on. The man's footsteps got quieter as he walked farther away. Jade stood there, her eyes peering straight into Buddy's. His eyes never closed or blinked and neither did Jade's. Her eyes concentrated on nothing else but Buddy. *It's all my fault,* Jade thought angrily.

Her emotions took her back to when she was in the concert hall. Her hands shuttered, and her heart beat fast. She was one of the audience applauding the young musician who had finished his piece. Around her, people clapped and clapped…until the next musician walked up the stage. *W-what?* Jade's hands came into an abrupt stop, as she saw a girl in familiar clothes and recognized the face of the person walking up to the piano and sitting down.

Isn't that…? She gasped. Her hands covered her mouth, as the girl started her piece. It was the "Moonlight Sonata". The song she played in the competition.

The girl kept playing and playing, her hands smoothly gliding against each key. Her body moved along with the beat, and her shoulders stood squared. Jade stared at her wide eyed, as if it was someone she never knew. Then, she looked around her vicinity. Betsy sat in the front. Her eyes her sparkled in admiration at the music. Other musicians sat in a row next to the stage. People were mostly parents of the young performers. People were scattered everywhere.

A sudden strange note startled Jade's thoughts. She quickly turned around and saw that the girl was hesitating. Her shoulders shivered, and her eyes rolled. Then, she collapsed onto the piano, and the sound echoed throughout the quiet hall. Within a second, everyone stood up from their chairs, and shouting and talking filled the cold air. People ran towards the girl, shaking her weak body to wake her up.

Jade stood with wide-opened eyes. Her vision slowly blurred. Then, she was back standing on the road. Shattered glass was all over the road, and everything was still. Buddy and the man were no longer visible. The sound of his footsteps was gone. Jade stood there alone. The streetlights gave her a shadow that reached out to the roads.

From a distance, she heard faded music ringing in her ear.

Could it be, Jade thought, as the wind froze her cheeks, *the music I once played?*

The music gradually disappeared, as if it was just an echo from far away.

History

By

Xavier Rose

In 300,000,000 B.C. in Mexico, there was a god named Shawn, and he demanded the early humans to build a temple on the Moon like the pyramids with stairs around it, and because the Moon used to be part of Earth, they were able to build it. Later Shawn dropped an emerald on top of the temple which became a portal to a golden universe on the top floor. The people called it the Star. Then a god named Cattana came from the darkest part of space and demanded war with Shawn. Shawn picked up the Moon and threw it at Cattana. A cavemen, however, put feathers on a stick and poured mud on it. Later the mud dried, and they dipped the stick into a pit of mud and wrote what's happening on stone.

Cattana was sent flying into space. Later Cattana wasn't allowed into the golden universe anymore because Shawn put a nuclear field around the temple. So Cattana realized if he wasn't allowed to go into the golden universe, then nobody else would be able to, either. He was however able to get into Earth and other planets but not the Star. Part of the Moon broke off from the Moon with the temple and became another Earth, in another galaxy.

In 1525 A.D in Spain, a shepherd looked into a telescope in an astronomy tower and found the star above Mexico. In 1527, the shepherd lead twelve men on an expedition to Mexico, and found the cave writings in Spanish which was evidence that the temple existed. Three men died from snake bites and wild animal attacks. The shepherd went back to Spain and wrote about the temple and called it "The Lost Star." Three men were afraid of the star, so they threw some of the evidence into a volcano and died from an eruption. In 1528, the leftover people who knew the star existed died because of war.

In 1862, the North Americans built a rocket to find the star. Then a group of five were selected as the crew for this project, but the youngest member of the crew named, Andy, who was related to Randy, wanted to record this moment, so he wrote everything that happened in his diary. The crew came back with evidence, but they disappeared. The people back on Earth who were involved in this experiment were later captured and killed during the Civil war. There was still very little proof that the star existed. The evidence was stolen by a South American solder and taken to Spain where he buried it.

In 1906, in Spain, a mining crew went digging and found the paintings and the diaries with some camera men.

"Listen you remember what happened fifty years ago. This trash will not hurt anyone," complained the lead miner.

"But we can't just burn them," replied Randy's great grandfather, Greg. The lead miner ran off with the remains of the painting. Greg ran after him and knocked the painting out of his hand. Greg took the book and the film and didn't tell anyone and sailed to America and started a family in 1907.

In 1956, a man found the film on the star from 1906. He ran into a television studio and interrupted a Three Stooges episode to get the word out to everyone. The cops found him and arrested him and threw the film into a volcano.

In 1996 in America at six o'clock at the dinner table in Randy's dad's house, his father pointed his finger at Randy. "Listen you kids can't find out about my great, great grandfather's diary, or your kids will go after this garbage!" boomed Randy's grandfather as he leaped from the table slamming his fists down.

"OK, now sit down please, William gates III is here," answered Randy's dad. (William gates III was one of the richest men in the 90's)

Dawn of adventure

In Washington D.C 2016 on June 23, the last day of school at 3:30 P.M., the substitute we had was crazy. She squawked all day about the "Lost Star." My dad told me my story could be about it.

"What fantasy," I exclaimed as I walked out of the classroom. My name is Tom.

"Yeah," answered Dave as he juggled a soccer ball in the hallway.

"And the Earth couldn't have been with the Earth," replied Mark as he was speed reading his geography textbook.

"I believe it," complained Steve, as he followed his logic. I am glad the summer is starting because the whole year was nuts. We walked out of the school and to our neighborhood.

"Hey, we should go to Burger Queen tonight, but on our bikes," suggests Steve. We all start talking. Wham! I crashed into Randy. We both fell and dropped backpacks. Randy was a kid in my neighborhood, and he was carrying a stack of books along with his backpack.

"What was that for? I need to pick up my motorbike fast!" shouted Randy. I don't know how he got a motorbike license though. We picked up our things. I see a little book on the ground, the title was *Launch 1862*. I grabbed it and went on with the guys. At eight thirty we rode our bikes to Burger Queen and sat at table next to a table with guys in suits and a little rich kid. I could tell because he was playing on an expensive phone. Also in case something happened, we all had baskets in front of our bikes which had crazy stuff in them.

"Hey guys, remember when I crashed into Randy?" I asked the guys.

"Yeah," they answered.

"Well, he dropped a small book," I tell them as I set it down. "It talks about…

"Lost Star," the guys interrupted me.

"Are you thinking we should go after the Star?" Steve asked.

"Yes, I heard there is a new launch pad we could use," I told them.

"Wait, don't you remember what happened in 1956? I don't want to go after the star," Mark told me.

"But just think; we could go to the Star and live in there forever," I tell the guys.

"Alright, we leave tomorrow, but we need to tell Randy," Mark told me.

"Done," I told the guys.

Then the little rich kid said in a squeaky voice, "I want that book."

We then got chased by the guys in suits and ran out of Burger Queen. We then rushed to our bikes and took off. The guys chased us and got into a car and came after us. We rode into our neighborhood, and the guys were still chasing us.

"Throw the stuff in your baskets," I yell. We threw money, pie, happy meals, cake and confetti. Suddenly, everyone scattered. Now, I rode off a giant wooden ramp onto a house's roof. *Wrong roof*, I thought, but my house was in front of this house. I put my kickstand down so I could put my feet down. I pushed my feet down and jumped off the roof on my bike, hoping to land in the window that led to my bedroom. I was not going to make it, so I quickly stood on my seat and jumped off my bike and crashed into my bedroom window. And my bike rolled off my roof and landed on my front porch. I set my alarm clock and fell asleep.

Next morning came too fast. Ring! I wake up and throw my alarm clock out the window. Wait the window was closed and the glass shattered. I thought what happened was a dream. I packed up my huge backpack with my things like a C.D. soda in bottles, Mentos, water balloons full of gasoline, matches and lighters, a phone, etc. I went to Randy's house to ask him if he wanted to go on our adventure.

The rocket and aliens

We go to a space station. This was awesome because we were going on a three-hundred-million-year-old quest. We put the Mentos in bottles of soda, and threw them at the security guards. We walked farther and found out we had to climb a fence around the launch pad.

"Stand back," I tell everyone. I set the gate on fire and threw a gasoline balloon at the fence. It exploded the fence, and we kept walking. When we reached the door to the launch pad, the door to the launch pad had a huge lock. I tried to figure out the password that opened the door. Wham! Dave just slammed his head right at the door. The door breaks. It's 9:30 in the morning, so no one was in the building and the building didn't open till 10:00.

"Let's go, also I have a black blanket, and the floors black so get down and keep yourselves in the blanket, or we will be caught on camera," I whisper. We get on the floor, and I put the blanket on us. We all crawl into the vents. Mark goes first, I go second, Steve comes in third, Randy comes in fourth, and Dave comes in last.

"Tom I am stuck," whispered Mark.

"Dave catch the blanket and crawl out and help us," I commanded Dave. We go shooting out of the vents. We climb onto the top of the elevator that leads to the rocket. Then a scientist's comes into the elevator. The problem was that the roof of the elevator was made of glass.

"Hey what are those kids doing on top the elevator," said a scientist in the elevator.

"Beat them up," I tell Dave. Dave elbows the roof, and we fall into the elevator. We pushed the button in elevator, and the elevator took us to the rocket. We got out in front of the rocket. Oh no, there was a hand scanner that opened the rocket.

"We didn't come prepared for hand scanners," I whispered. Then from the mighty heavens, a god (Randy) puts a glove on the hand scanners.

"Where did you get a glove from," I asked Randy.

"Remember when got past the guards, I stole one of their coffee mugs," He explained.

"Also, Tom when I got out of the vents I brought a leaf blower into the vents, and push a button on it that said reverse," explained Dave. When we entered the rocket, they had a pool table, an air hockey table, ping pong table, foosball table, a normal table, arcade machines, food and drink dispenser, chocolate fountain, a T.V. and couches, a Mini Golf course, baby basketball, Internet, a bowling alley, a shuffleboard, hot tub, trampoline, and a dart board. Then Randy disappeared.

Then he talked through a microphone. "Good afternoon, gentlemen. I will take you to the Star. Also if we crash, well I can't tell you, because you are under the age of three, just joking about that last part, and right now it is 10:30." The bad part was everyone at the launch pad station heard Randy through the microphone. I looked out the window and the guards were shooting guns at us.

"Here we go," Randy said through the microphone.

"Wait no...Ah!" we all shouted as we flew off.

We fell on the floor and were stuck because of the gravity. The bad part was the machines start moving, because of the pressure. The rocket turns and we all end up rolling together. Then the pool table moved toward us. And the other stuff. Then the darts fell out off the dart board, and come at us. Then when all hope is lost we land on the moon, and the ship tilts back ninety degrees. And everything goes back to where it was. We got so mad, and we went to the top of the spaceship to punch him, but he was gone. There was a hole in the window, and there was a green liquid oozing down the control panel. The control pane started to melt. I take a fork from the food and soda dispenser, and poke at the liquid. The fork started dissolving.

"Everyone go downstairs and put on space suits," I command. We head down and put on space helmets, and we went outside. And Steve brings a water bottle with him.

We see a small lab. As we walk closer, it gets bigger and bigger. And then Steve threw his water bottle at the door. The door starts melting and the I realize that aliens and their technology melts with water. So, I head back to the rocket and take out water guns. Then we put on virtual costume and disguise ourselves. Then I stole a map and look at the map and we get to the dungeons. Finally, we find Randy.

"Well let's go," barked Dave.

"But we don't have any fuel," replied Randy.

"What if we steal the thing that powers the lab?" Randy suggested.

We head over to the center of the lab. Now the hologram runs out of battery. Then all the aliens look at us. All of a sudden everyone pulls out their water guns and starts shooting the aliens. I pull out a lever from this giant beam. Now the aliens attack us. We start shooting them. One of them shoots something at me. The alien misses and hits the rocket. Oh no the doors start to close, and they catch fire.

"Everyone grab onto me!" I yell. They do, and I take a new version of a fire cracker, called Death Ray, and it blows up. We fly thru the hoop and the door. Then we fall and run to the rocket and flew off.

The problem

(Hour five in the rocket) "Guys one of the engines blew up!" shouts Dave. We rush to get our space suits in the control room. The lights turned off. We walk down the stairs a little. We see an alien that looked like the ones from earlier. So, get under the pool table. Then we crawl into one of the vents. It feels a little warm. Wait are we in the part that's...

"Fire!" shouts Dave. Great were near the engine. We claim all the way up the vent. We all see some suitcases. We split and hide in different suitcases. Dave gives us all walkie-talkies.

"Guys remember when an alien shot something, well he missed and hit the rocket," I tell the guys.

"Well the explosion was green stuff," Mark tells us.

"Guy's maybe this is not just their hang out area, meet me by the ping pong table," I tell them. Then we hide under the table.

"So why are we here?" Steve asks.

"I found this manual, and the eight ball is a code, and the ping pong ball, and the bowling ball, the puck on the air hockey table, the golf ball, and the baby basketball. We have to put them in a special place," I tell them. We think and we know what to do. So we get all the balls.

"O.K., now what?" Steve asked.

"We need to find a place to put them in," I tell them. The alien approaches us. We put the balls in place fast enough, but a trap opens right where we are standing. The trap door we were on lead us into a slide. Now we're on a secret floor. Steve screamed through the walkie-talkie.

"Maybe I can hack into the computer of the spaceship," Dave said.

"Randy, fix the engine and wear this helmet; it's a camera. Tom supervise Randy though this camera. Mark, you and I are going to fight these aliens." Then the camera turns on. Turns out space does have gravity. It's like bungee jumping in space.

Randy gets to the engine and fixes it. Randy swings himself into a one of the rockets windows. He is stuck. I help him get thru the window. Dave talks thru the walkie talkie, and the aliens are defeated. Suddenly, the rocket crashes into another planet, and we crash into the window, land seven miles, away from our rocket. This is a weird snowing night time planet. I look for all the other guy's. I give the give the guys jackets.

"Are we at the North Pole?" Steve asks. Dave smacked him.

"This is planet X," Mark explained. "I went to Egypt to learn hieroglyphics, and then I found a rock in the pyramid that told me that this is planet X."

I have a helium pump, balloons, cardboard, and a fold out cardboard box. I set up a twenty-person tent. And on the inside set up mini-stove, mini fridge, also a setup table, I cook burgers and, French fries and pizza. While the guys build the kart. (An hour later) there our flying kart is complete. We put our bags into the flying kart. Zoom!! Something hits one of the balloons. Oh no, some of the creatures on the star landed here. Cavemen start chasing us. The box is stuck to the ground.

"Tom, burn it with your lighter!" Dave yells at me. I melt the ice and were free. All of a sudden Mark falls out. I grab soda and Mentos from my bag. I make myself a jetpack out of the leftover soda and Mentos. I jump out, I put the Mentos into the soda and grab Mark.

"Hold on!" I shout while grabbing his hand. I throw him into the kart. I am out of soda. Then I spill gun powder and drop a match, and they run. Randy fixes the rocket. I run in, and we fly off.

The Star

"Black hole!" Randy shouted. Everyone ran to the escape pod. Then I ran to the control room, but on the way my lighter fell out of my pocket, and set the rocket on fire.

"Escape password denied," the computer said to them. I was listening to them through the walkie-talkie. Then all the bowling balls rolled into the control room, and caught on fire and came at me but hits the window. I take a fire extinguisher and I sprayed water at the window and it froze. I also sprayed it at the fire.

Crash! That was a hard landing. The black hole was to protect the second Earth I thought to myself. I get up and look around this other Earth.

"Gentlemen, I give you the Lost Star!" shouted Randy while standing on a cliff. It was awesome because we're on a cliff looking at everything. Rumble! What happened. Then the cliff fell. Crack!

"Ah!" we shout as we fall. We end up in the bottom of this swirling water from under the cliff. I am stuck in mud under the water. I am about to drown. Dave swims to me and I hear a noise which was a bell. Dave pulls me out of the mud.

"Tom follow me," Dave mumbles in the water. It's the guy's, they built a submarine, from what we have. It looked like a torpedo with a giant with a plane on top of it. Dave opened the door to the Sumerian.

I get in and then the lights turned off. Then the submarine shook.

"Oh no, there's explosive rocks!" I shouted. I followed the guys to a ladder in the submarine. And we started climbing the ladder.

"Where are we?" I asked them.

"We are in an escape pod with three rooms," Dave answers. Boom!

The engine blasted us out of the water and into the air. Then Randy goes up front. Then Randy speaks through a microphone.

"Everyone this is your captain speaking. If you're wondering where we had the supplies for this, Mark found the supplies in the rocket before we all died, bad news we're crash landing do to the fact that some Indians are shooting us with arrows,".

"Ah!" we shouted. I fell into one of the rooms. Hold on this was a gun room. I had an idea. I take a pistol and a bazooka and two machine guns and a machine pistol. I put the machine guns into my backpack. I open the door that would let us out. I shot the bazooka out and it blows up some of the Indians. I leave my backpack in the gun room. I leave that room and go to the front of the escape pod. I see a button that's labeled parachute. I pulled it and ran to a window. Great the parachute was ripped. All of a sudden one of the Indians got into the ship.

"Everyone get into the front of the escape pod!" I shouted.

I punch him and kick him. He grabbed me by my shirt. My pistol fell out of my pocket and shot. It shot directly toward the control room. I punch the Indian so hard his face crashed into a window and fell out. All of a sudden, I fell into the gun room Crash! The escape pod lands directly into a sinkhole. It was so dark. I reached for pocket and pulled out my waterproof phone. I only had four percent battery left. I looked around the ship and I saw a box labeled in need of fire. I opened it up and it had pinecones, paper, wood, and smoke masks. I started a small fire, and my phone died. I used the light from the fire to find the door but it was on lockdown. I tried to open the door. I heard a small voice.

"Charge!" shouted Dave.

Wham! The guys put tape around eleven pool cues and smashed it into the door.

"Where did you guys get pool cues?" I asked.

"Randy stole them from the spaceship and used tape to stick them together," explained Mark.

"Also, a bullet hit a button that ejects everyone in the front," Steve told me. I grabbed my backpack. The sinkhole led to a cave.

"Ow!" I shouted. My mouth felt numb. I saw a tiny arrow on my lip. Oh no. I turned around and saw hundreds of guys that looked like Indians.

"Run!" I shouted. The Indians shot Mark with tiny arrows, then Randy and Dave.

"I––am h––it," I said in a slow-motion voice. I fell onto the floor.

Where was I? Was I dead? Wait I was in a cage. I got up. Wait were in a cage. I look above the cage and see that rope is holding us above fire.

"Tom, long story short, you were in a cage above fire, and those tiny darts had something to put you to sleep," Mark told me. I looked down and see the Indians cheering and dancing around us.

"Where is Steve?" I asked.

"No idea," Randy replied darkly.

We started to move down into the fire. Then we stopped.

Now Steve cut a hole into the cage from the roof. "Hold this and grip it tight," Steve orders. I don't know what this is. Then he took a match and burned the object in Steve's hand.

"Wait, it's a firework!" I shouted.

The firework was facing up.

"Oh, give me that," commanded Steve while he took the firework and pointed it in different directions.

We landed directly next to a canon completely made of fireworks and two cardboard boxes and a hang glider.

"How did you do all this?" I asked.

"It's a super long story," Steve told me. "And I left a cannon that shot fireworks, so we got into some cardboard boxes. We could only take two people, so I took a giant cardboard box and added wings to it, but there were two."

We got into a cardboard box, and Steve got into the other one with wings. And Steve put the cardboard boxes into the canon.

"Get in," Steve told us. We got in and had no idea what was going to happen next.

"So, it's going to work like in that movie where the astronauts got in the rocket, and then people shot it out of the giant cannon," Steve explained. Oh no, in the movie the astronauts got into a bullet shaped rocket and were shot out into space.

"Wait! Fire!" Steve interrupted me. We flew off toward the temple. Crash!

"I am never flying with you again," I replied angry and dizzy.

"Also, do any of your walkie talkies have problems?" Dave asked.

"Nope," we all replied.

"See the temple," Mark said while pointing at a large building. We walked to the temple.

We walked up to the first few steps. Then two Indians came at us with spears. Then, they took us to their leader. Then, they took us to a little stick hut. Their leader was sitting on a throne made out of solid gold.

"Humans, you are to leave this planet and never come back!" boomed their leader. Behind him were some stairs up the temple.

Then Steve looked directly at the leader's face. "He is wearing a mask!" Steve shouted. His mask started to fall off. He is Cattana.

"Get them!" shouted Cattana. I know some karate, so I knocked out some of them. We ran out along with Cattana and his men chasing us. I stopped running then, and I reached for my bag and pulled out a CD. I held it as if it was a dangerous weapon.

"Stand back, or I will throw it," I demanded.

"How will that harm someone?" Cattana replied in a high-pitched voice.

I threw it at a tree, and it fell to the ground, and I remembered I only had one C.D. Then an Indian grabbed Randy.

"Run!" I shouted. We ran to the stairs and started running up. Then I heard a conversation between Randy and Cattana on my walkie talkie, I listen in.

"All right start talking. Tell us everything you know," said Cattana.

"I beat Muhama Alai, punched a gorilla in the face, sang along with Justin Bieber, threw an A.T.M machine off the Grand Canyon, invented dogs, and I even burned $300,000,000 that I won from the lottery!" Randy shouted with confidence. He is the most insane person I ever met.

"I just remembered I have dynamite and a tent," Steve told us.

"Heck no, I know what you're thinking," I replied.

"No choice!" Mark shouted.

"OK!" I shouted at everyone.

"Guy's stop running and help me build a vehicle!" I shouted.

They came over, and we set up the tent and got in and lit the dynamite. We fell down the stairs for a while. Then our tent caught fire and blew up. We flew above the stairs and up the temple.

"Ah!" we all shouted. We crash into more Indian guards. We flew over the portal and now were falling. I pulled out a match and threw it at the temple, along with a water balloon full of oil. There was a huge explosion, and the portal fell on us. I pulled out trash bags and made a parachute. I grab onto the everyone's hands, and the portal fell on us.

Whoa, we were in this yellow space world. I saw Dave and I ran to him. Unfortunately, I could only use swimming moves to get to places. I swam to Dave and the rest of the guys. "Hey, Steve how did you escape the Indians?" I asked.

"I had a pistol and shot the roof of the cave, and the Indians ran away, but I dropped it," Steve answered.

"I am Shawn," said Shawn. "I am here to tell you to bring what you need to reach Earth," Shawn continued. "Now go and make your world better."

I was thinking a question mark, and it literally showed up. "Everyone, imagine magic wands!" I shouted.

We grabbed our wands and went back to our world.

"Everyone follow me. I know where the comet's myth is," commanded Steve.

We ran down to the go kart.

"Wait, what about Mark?" I ask.

"Let's go get him," Dave said.

"I have machine guns," I tell everyone. I give Steve a machine gun.

"Guys get to the go kart. Me and Steve will rescue Randy," I tell everyone. Me and Steve go near Randy. There were no guards protecting Randy. We freed Randy and walked to the go kart.

"Hey, while we were in the rocket I found this grenade," Steve told me as he pulled out the grenade.

"Do you think that thing is real?" I asked.

Steve pulled of the ring.

"Throw it that way!" I shouted while I was pointing at a random place.

Steve threw it, and there was a huge explosion. Then a piece of metal came our way. I looked at that piece, and we just blew up the comets myth.

"Guys, the comet myth just blew up," I told the rest of the guys.

"Randy, you know how to fix things. Do you think you can fix the rocket with these old metal parts from the comet's myth?" asked Randy.

"Yes, you need to take me to the rocket," answered Randy.

Three hours later we finally were there. My gun broke and spilled gunpowder on my hands.

"Ready to go!" shouted Randy.

"Guy's get in the rocket. Because if you look to your left, you'll see a giant active volcano!" yelled Mark.

"Guy's, it says in the diary that the star was going to be destroyed in the year 2016 by an active volcano!" I yell at everyone.

Everyone got in. I grabbed a parachute in case something went wrong. I also grabbed my bag. The rocket tilted, and I fell out the window. I pulled the parachute tag. Bam! There's a hole in my parachute.

Wow, Cattana has a riffle. He aimed it at the rest of the parachute. Bam!

I pulled out a trash bag and blew into it. I land right next him and the trash bag in front of me, and land on it. I hid behind a rock and pulled out a folded-up golf club. I jumped out and smacked the gun with the golf club, and the gun looked like it was cut. He pulled out a sword.

"Oh, I forgot to tell you. I had a visit to the 1700's, and I made the cavemen hunt you down and the aliens, and I made the black hole!" yelled Cattana. We dueled, and then I pull out a ball. Then Cattana took out a pistol.

"Take dodgeball," I yelled. I threw it at him, and he shot the ball. There was an explosion, and he flew backwards. Turns out the ball caught a small fire before I threw the ball. Then the guys picked me up.

"How did you know where I was?" I asked.

"Tracking device, I put it on you when we were in the cage," explained Mark.

Leaving the star into time

Wow, there's a worm hole.

"Guys, I can't control the rocket," shouted Randy.

We fell into a wormhole. What was going on? Then I found a book on wormholes. Were supposed to be traveling seven thousand five hundred and forty years into the future. Then we went so fast we pass out. We woke up.

"I still can't control the rocket, and it's the year 9546 A.D," said Randy. Then spaceships flew by us. Suddenly, we were in a giant metal ball.

"Guy's go to that storage room. Go to it," Dave whispered.

We went to the storage room. I found and pulled out a hologram projector. I played it, and it told us they had enough technology to recreate "Star Wars." That explained why we were in a giant metal volleyball. We looked up and saw vents.

"Everyone start claiming through that vent," demanded Dave. When we reached the end, I smacked a weird button. It was an airlock button. We hid under the control panel. Everything was being sucked out into space. I pulled out the most dangerous thing I had, a five hundred thousand volt Taser. It was dead.

"Guy's, I need a way to recharge my Taser!" I yelled.

"Take this!" Mark shouted, tossing me an extra-large battery. I pulled out the old battery and put in the new one.

"Guy's, get next to me!" I boomed. Everyone held onto my shoulder. I put the front of the Taser into the control panel. I zapped the control panel. We flew backwards out of the control room, and gunpowder came at me. I threw the Taser.

"Why did you throw it?" Dave asked.

"I had gunpowder in my hand," I said.

"Everyone run to the rocket," commanded Steve.

We got into the spaceship and got back to our time. Randy then let me be his co-pilot. Then we got sucked into another wormhole. We ended up eight thousand years into the past.

We ended up in some sort of forest. I looked at my wand, and it was glitching. We got out and walked through grass at the rocket. Finally, I couldn't tell it was there.

"What year is it?" Dave asked.

I calculated the years we traveled back. "1527!" I shouted.

Then a hunter walked by. "Es mejor que esté es en casa y qué lleváis?" A hunter asked. Then the hunter ran off.

"He is talking in Spanish. He asked, 'You kids better be home, and what are you wearing?'" I told the guys. "Luckily, I take French, German, Russian, Chinese, Vietnamese, Japanese, Greek and Spanish," I tell everyone.

"Я поставил вам 10 долларов, что ваш не здесь?" Randy asked. That means in Russian, "I will bet you ten dollars that you're not here.'"

"Don't try that trick on me," I told Randy.

"Focus, the hunter is right. We can't look like kids from 2016. Also the ship is broken, and we need metal to fix it," added Mark.

"Hide and I will make us leather clothes," I told them. An hour later, I met up with the guys. "I went hunting and made these cloths," I told them.

"How did you make these cloths?" asked Randy.

"I used vines to keep the skin together, and you can guess where I got the skin," I answered.

We got dressed and went into a village. It started to rain. Then we walked into someone's two story home.

"Jack, Mike, Arthur, Richard y Tim, vayan a sus cámaras de cama!" a woman yelled at us in Spanish.

She said, "'Jack, Mike, Arthur, Richard, and Tim, go to your bedchamber!'

"I think she thinks we are her kids," I said.

We walked upstairs to the room. The room had a window and a bed made out of hay.

"Guys, if you look out the window, you will see a blacksmith shop," I told everyone.

"All right, Tom make sure no one is watching us while we steal some metal," Dave commanded. We jumped out the window, and I saw the shepherd who wrote the myth. I walked up to him.m He just standing in the middle of no writing into a book where

"Guys, get the metal we need. I need to ask the shepherd a question," I told them. "¿Vas a escribir una historia sobre un templo, y alguien llamado Cattana?" I asked. That means, "Are you going to write a story about a temple, and someone named Cattana?"

"Si, como sabes eso?" he asked. That means "Yes how did you know that?'

"Soy del futuro," I answered. That means "I am from the future."

Then time started over from when we jumped out the window. It could've been that I spoiled the future. I avoid the shepherd. The guys went to the shop and waited. Then knights grabbed me. They took me into a castle. The king just finished his lunch.

"Usted será lanzado en las mazmorras porque todos robaron metal," the king told us. The king said, "You will be thrown in the dungeons because you all stole metal."

"No, hice nada," I tell the king. That means, "I didn't do anything".

"Dave me dijo que lo planeaste todo," said the king. That means, "Dave over there told me you planned it all."

I pulled out a machine gun and dropped it, and it shot everywhere. I take one of the wooden spoons, lit on fire, and threw it at the king. It missed and burned the castle. I hid under the table the king ate his lunch on. The gun stopped firing. I went to it and picked it up. It still had rounds in it. Then one of the knights came at me. I shot him right in the chest plate. I used up all the rounds. Well his armor was bullet proof.

"Guys, get to the rocket!" I shouted. I hit the knight on the head with a chair and took his armor. I ran out of the castle to the rocket with the guys. I broke down the door. And we all got in. Then the wormhole took us to a different year.

"Great, it's twelve o'clock midnight, in the year 1862!" I shouted. I saw a man with a mustache. He wore a top hat and was dressed in a suit.

"That's my super great grandfather," Randy told us.

We followed him and saw people putting his journal on a string and lowering it onto a bonfire. I grabbed a rock and threw it far. They ran away. I took another rock and cut the string. We gave Randy's super great grandfather his journal. Then we flew into space and back to our time.

Back on Earth

Once we got past the atmosphere and were flying over Washington D.C., we ran out of fuel. We were going down. I panicked and ran to the back of the rocket. I found some sort of zip line launcher. I shot it out of a window, and it hit the launch tower. It turned out our parents were waiting there. And they were playing cards.

"Everyone come here!" I shouted. Everyone came to me.

"What's going on?" everyone asked. I told them what was happening. Then everyone took a parachute, except me and Randy. Then Randy grabbed a selfie stick and put it on top of the rope and held onto both ends of the selfie stick. The the rope snapped.

I jumped out with a pencil and quickly tied the pencil to one end of where our rope snapped. I do some back and front flips without holding onto the pencil. I quickly grab the pencil before falling.

Then dave grabbed my left foot. Oh no, the rope was too close the the engine. Then Randy gave me a grappling hook gun from his pocket. I shot it at the side of the rocket. I dangled from the grappling hook. I got closer to the side of the rocket. I elbowed the side, and it broke down. I got in and grab all the things we needed: a giant bucket with a lid and some pillows.

Randy let go of the rope.

I jumped out of the rocket as well. As I fell, I put the pillows into the bucket and Randy saw me and got in, and we closed the lid.

Crash!

"What the heck are you guy's doing?" our parents yell at us as we crash into the launch pad.

Why are there so many computers in here, I thought to myself.

"Go back to playing your card game," I replied.

"Oh oka––wait a minute." the people told us.

The guards blocked all the doors. Then our parents walked to us. They nod at each other.

"You're all grounded for a year. We had to go to court because of this!" They all yelled at us.

I zapped one of the computers with my wand.

"What did you do to the computers?" my mom asked me.

"I fixed them," I answer. Then I made the computer fly in three seconds.

"It's just an illu–it's flying?" my mother asked.

All the people check for ropes.

"Yep," I told them. "And we discovered another Earth, and magic, and the comets myth."

"Also, you owe the launch scientists five billion dollars," my mother told us.

I wave my wand and all the damage was fixed.

"Alright, you guys are no longer grounded or owe us money," our parents told us.

"Yahoo!" we all shout. This was the best adventure ever. We all celebrated.

"Also, our lawyer showed up late and threw a chair at the judge," My mom told me.

I thought that if I hadn't stolen that diary, none of this would've happened, and we all went home.

I am The Criminal

By

Ryo Sasaki

It was a cloudy day that we headed to the country. We went there to work on making videos and having fun. The cottage that we headed for was on a little mountain. It took a while to get to the small cottage because the road was rocky and slippery. After we arrived at the cottage, we had a small party. Everybody drank beer and ate junk food because we decided to celebrate the first day of staying in a cottage.

"I'm going out to veranda to see the moon," I said.

Then annoying Andrew said to me, "What?! You are already, up? Huh, you are not a big man!" I went upstairs, not caring about Andrew because he was always like that. I looked at the stars and thought they were beautiful, and I thought this vacation would be the best vacation ever until I heard the door opening. I looked back to the door and saw Sophia standing behind me. Sophia was a person who didn't really like to be crowded. "Oh, you scared me so much. You don't like to be with them?" I asked her.

Then she said, "No, I have something to say you." She opened her mouth and spoke my secret out loud. Then she said, "We shouldn't keep it a secret."

Fear and uncontrollable anger seized me. I grabbed Sophia's shoulder and swung her toward the veranda's rail. The rail caught her, and she leaned backwards, her eyes opening in terror. With one quick shove, she flew backwards over the rail.

"Sophia?" I was afraid. I went back to my room, and terrified thoughts about what I had done filled me with apprehension. I curled up on the bed and slept.

"Guys! Wake up!" Aiden shouted. Everybody rushed outside and saw Sophia dead on the ground below the veranda.

While everybody looked at Sophia with tears they were struck with fear. I looked calm and stared straight at her because one feeling ruled me that could make me look at her calmly, the feeling of "I don't want to be caught."

"Sorry to call you guys this late time. I called the police. They said they it will take at least four days to reach us because the weather is really snowy, and they can't use cars to get to the cottage," said Lucas. Lucas was a smart guy. He was the kind of a guy who stood for the leader of a group.

"We are talking about Sophia's death, right?" said Aiden. Aiden was my best friend. He was very nice to me.

"Come one, why? My colored nails came off! I just put it on yesterday!" said Elena.

Elena was a selfish girl. It was obvious that she liked Lucas, but nobody said so, probably because she is scary when she gets mad.

"Why did she die? I am scared," Emma said.

Emma was a nice girl. She didn't speak much like Elena did, but her advice about the video was really correct.

"I bet the criminal is Michael," stupid Andrew shouted with his eyes staring at my eyes.

I didn't know why he thought I was the criminal, but I was scared already that Andrew figured out that I was the criminal.

"Why do you think the criminal is me?" I said calmly.

"Of course, it is you. You left the living room first; then Sophia left the living room! How dare you murder Sophia!" Andrew shouted as loud as he could.

"But everybody left when the party was over right guys? Also, I think that making me the criminal would require that I have a reason to kill her," I said even though I was the criminal.

"Yes, he needs a reason to kill Sophia, and without that you can't make him the criminal, Andrew," Lucas said it like a person who wanted to protect his teammate.

Thank you so much Lucas. That will probably close Andrew's stupid mouth, I said mentally.

"How am I supposed to know? I assume that Michael had some trouble with her, right Michael? Just spit it out!" Andrew demanded. His face started to turn red.

"Please stop! I don't want any blaming here. I don't think there is any criminal here," Emma shouted.

It was unusual for her to shout like that, but her outburst helped silence Andrew.

* * * *

The next day I went to Andrew's room. I knocked on the door, "Can I come in?" I asked quietly, pretending to be a gentleman. But there was no answer to it, so I pushed the door open and quietly entered his room. And there was Andrew standing by the door.

"Hey, I am not forgiving you. You are definitely the criminal because nobody could kill her except you!" Andrew said, spit coming from his mouth.

"It is not me! Trust me. I have no reason to kill her, and I think it was an accident," I shouted, acting like I was serious.

Then Andrew walked right past me and left the room.

I didn't think this was a really good thing to do, but I started to search for clues that I could use to make him shut his mouth. I searched his closet, his bed, his table, and his bag. When I opened his bag and took a look at his wallet, I found a weird thing.

"Maybe this will do," I thought. I found many pictures of Sophia. But the weird part of the pictures was that Sophia was not looking at the camera. Then I thought maybe he was taking pictures from somewhere without her knowing he was taking a photograph of her, so maybe Andrew liked Sophia. This could be the information I need to make him keep his mouth shut! Maybe, if I said some lies and made him the criminal, most of the club mates would believe me rather than believing Andrew.

"I would like to start the gathering," Lucas said later that afternoon after calling everyone to meet in the den.

"Well, let's tell the police that the criminal is Michael," Andrew said it like yesterday.

"I didn't do it! But I found this in Andrew's room, and it might be helpful." I showed everybody the pictures of Sophia.

"I think these are yours, right? Andrew?" I asked to silence him.

"Where the heck did you find this?" Andrew said.

Then Emma covered her mouth saying, "Why did you take photos of Sophia, secretly? Were you stalking her?"

"No, no, no, no. Whatever. The criminal is Michael!" Andrew shouted so loud that nobody could talk.

"So, what the motivation for me to kill Sophia? Maybe, you asked Sophia can you date with me, and Sophia says no?" I said it directly to Andrew.

"No, no, no, no," Andrew said nervously as his face started to sweat.

"Why are you saying no? There is nothing with you and Sophia right, Andrew?" As Lucas said this, everybody looked at Andrew like he was a creepy guy. Then suddenly Andrew said, "Let's stop making someone the criminal, right? We should be peaceful."

"What? You are the one who started talking about this," Elena said emotionally.

"Or is it like you murdered her? And you want it to be hidden, so you are trying to make Michael the criminal?" Elena said directly to Andrew.

Only for that time I felt thankful to Elena.

"No. Nothing like that, please trust me," Andrew said, and everybody looked at him in a strange way. So did I. The gathering finished, and we all went back to the room.

Then Andrew came to the room and said, "Sorry, but trust me. I am not the criminal."

"Don't worry, I felt the same way. But I trust you. So, no blaming and peace, Okay?" I asked him as kindly as I could.

"Okay. But then who killed her?" Andrew said.

"Maybe she died because of an accident? I have no idea at all," I said.

"An accident might make sense. Good night Michael." He left, still looking at me suspiciously. I slept with the idea about how I could trick people without getting noticed by other people.

The next day, there were three days left until the police came to the cottage. I was more frightened than yesterday because I had never killed people before, and I was very afraid that the police might find out what happened and catch me.

In the morning at breakfast, we talked about Sophia's death. I really wanted to get out of this place, but if I did, then that would look suspicious.

"Well I bet she died because she fell off the veranda," I said it because I knew what happened.

"Hey, how do you know she fell off the veranda," Emma stared at me. I could tell by looking at her face that she thought I was the criminal.

"I don't know, maybe because she was right under the veranda. So maybe she could have tripped and fallen off and died? I can't tell for sure because I didn't see her die," I said impatiently. I got up and suddenly went up the stairs to my room. I calmed myself down and said, "I have to make a plan that can make Emma think she died because of a trouble she had or something like that. Wait" Something popped in my head to make Emma the suspicious one and to also prove that I was *innocent*.

I knew there were better decisions to make, but that was the only way I could make her trust me for a truce. I went to her room and searched while she chatted with Andrew and didn't even notice me going into her room. I started to search for Emma's weakness, one she doesn't want anyone to know. "Wait a minute." I found a paper that said, *I don't get why Sophia bullies me all the time. I don't remember doing things that would make Sophia a bully. Mom, can you please help me.* I think she wanted to show this to everybody because I heard that Emma was bullied by Sophia, and she hated being treated like her slave. Maybe this could help to make her the suspicious person.

At the second day of gathering, Emma started talking. That was very unusual for her, so everybody skipped her and started discussing. I couldn't trust what I just heard and saw. Emma sat on the table like a bossy king shouting to everybody to be quiet. We all became quiet in a moment. When we stopped talking, she started to talk like a boss. "Listen up people! Michael is the murderer!"

"Wow, chill out, Emma. Why do you think I am the criminal? I proved it was not me when Andrew said I was the criminal," I said confidently.

"I thought you were more honest and responsible. I thought you were a person who said things that are true! You are evil!" Emma said angrily.

"But do you have any proof? If you don't, then you can't prove that I am the murderer. Also, even if you have something you call proof, I would probably ask you if that proof is real," I confidently continued.

"I do. I don't wanna waste time saying that you are the criminal without any reason. Remember when you said she fell off the veranda? We never knew that she fell off the veranda, but you somehow knew that she fell off the veranda, so I thought you pushed her off the veranda. Isn't this true? I am not going to let you say that this is not true! I know you killed one of my best friends! She died for no reason. Why did it have to be her!" Emma shouted.

I became quiet for a few seconds.

"Say something, Michael!" Emma demanded forcefully.

"Why are you assuming that I am the criminal? I just said that she fell off the veranda because she was right below it. Maybe that was just an accident. Are you assuming that I am the criminal because you want to blame the crime on me?" I replied a little bit rudely because she knew too much. I now kind of regretted complaining about what Emma said because I said it so emotionally that everybody looked at me like a murderer who tried to hide the truth.

"What? There is no way. Why would I want to kill my best friend. Are you saying this nonsense because you don't wanna be the one who will be treated as a criminal?" Emma argued.

Since she argued, everybody looked suspiciously at Emma.

"No, Emma. I am not trying to be that offensive. I think Sophia was not your best friend. Was she?!" I said, staring at her eyes.

"I don't even know what you are talking about! She was my best friend. There is no reason for me to kill her. Stop saying things that don't even make sense!" Emma shouted it with sweat on her face. Everybody's attention was on Emma because she was being so emotional.

"But there is a reason for you to kill Sophia. Do you know what it is? You can't hide it anymore," I said, pointing my finger at Emma. Emma didn't respond so I continued, "So Emma was being bullied by Sophia. There are a lot of people who murder bullies because they were bullied." I turned to the group. "I just thought Emma pushed Sophia out of the veranda. I didn't mean to say these things, but I had to because I wasn't the criminal, but Emma tried to make me the criminal," I said it pretending like the victim who was about to be accused by the true criminal.

"Hey! Michael, that is enough!" Lucas shouted at me.

At the moment, I thought, "What? What did I do? I did nothing!" Then I looked at Emma. She was crying! I thought, "Why do you have to do this to me..."

"Wow, making a girl cry! The worst thing you can do. Learn some manners man!" Andrew stared at me. Now, it looked like I was the *bad* one because I made Emma cry!

I said sorry to Emma and went to my room. The next day, I awoke and went to Emma's room to apologize about the things I said yesterday.

I knocked the door, slowly pushed it open, and said, "Sorry about yesterday. I didn't mean to be that offensive and make you cry. I just had to protect myself because I didn't kill Sophia," I said looking at the floor, thinking that I was getting better at acting.

"It is alright. I guess I was mean, too. I just thought you were the criminal because you can never tell if she fell of the veranda. But it looks like you aren't the criminal," Emma said staring at my eyes.

At least she understood that I wasn't the criminal. But I had to be careful to not tell any specific things that happened. So far, I had tricked Andrew and Emma. I hoped nobody else would find some sort of proof that might make me the criminal, but there were still two days, including today, until the police arrived. I had to be ready for any possible things that could happen. I nodded and left quietly, spending the day in my room, only leaving to get meals.

At the meeting that night, we surprisingly didn't argue about who was the criminal. It was a good thing for me.

"Well, we better get ready to tell everything to the police!" Lucas said to everybody, like the best leader in a gang of a really a bad people.

"I agree with him because if we keep on blaming people, then that is just a waste of time. Probably if there is a criminal here, the police would notice because they are professionals," I gently, pretending like a guy who was serious.

"Me too. It could have been an accident," Aiden said calmly.

We had no trouble that tonight, but that didn't mean I was safe. The next morning, I woke yawning. I looked at my phone, and it was 5:30 A.M. It was early, so I was about to sleep again. Then Aiden rushed in my room.

"Why are you here?" I asked, hoping it was not something to do with Sophia.

"I am here to ask you if this is really you!" Aiden shouted at me, holding Sophia's phone. I had a bad feeling about it. It was the problem with me killing Sophia.

"What do you mean, is it really me?" I said in a confusion, even though I knew it would be about Sophia.

"Look!" Aiden said. "I picked up her phone in Sophia's room! It's a message."

I took the phone from Aiden and read the message. It said, "I have to confront, Michael," I freaked out.

"Sorry, but I have to show this to everybody in the meeting tonight," Aiden said.

I couldn't say no because that would make me more suspicious, so I said, "Okay, but I will prove I am not the criminal."

Aiden wryly grinned at me.

After he left my room to talk with Andrew, I went to Aiden's room and started searching. I searched his bag and found a sheet that said arrest warrant. It was given to him four years ago, but I never heard that he did some sort of a crime. I continued to read the sheet then at the bottom it said setting a house on fire. I decided to grab this warrant and when he was about to show the message, then I could show the sheet to everybody. I went back to my room until Lucas called for an early gathering.

"Guys! Today I would like to have two meetings because I want to talk about Sophia in the afternoon and have fun at night!" Lukas said.

"Sorry, but I have to say something to you guys. I have a proof that made me think that Michael is the criminal," Aiden interrupted Lukas. "Take a look at this." Aiden showed the message to everybody.

"Is this true?" Lukas asked.

"I can't believe it, Michael!" Andrew said.

"Wow, I didn't think Sophia's death was a crime!" Elena said.

"This can't be true!" Emma said holding her mouth.

"Sorry Michael, but I had to do this," Aiden said staring at my eyes.

"Well, I have something too to show you guys! Aiden, four years ag..."

Aiden recognized the paper I pulled from my pocket. He suddenly held my mouth and started talking. "I actually don't think he is the criminal because he is my best friend, and also he is a nice person. He couldn't have killed a person!" Aiden said it in a hurry.

"Why did you help me?" I whispered in Aiden's ear.

"Give me back what you were about to show the others," Aiden whispered back.

"But you were the one who started talking. Why did you change your mind so quick?" Andrew asked Aiden.

"Because there is nothing to prove that this is the message to us to tell that Michael is the criminal," Aiden said looking at the corner of the room.

"Okay, so I guess the afternoon meeting is done. We will have a meeting night at our normal time." Lukas concluded this meeting.

After the meeting, I went to Aiden's room and showed Aiden what I was about to show everybody.

"Oh, good thing I stopped you! But you have trust me! Somebody else started the fire that destroyed the house and blamed the crime on me, just because I was walking by!" Aiden shouted at me.

"Okay, calm down. Can we have a deal? I will not say anything anybody, and can you hand me the phone," I said, putting my hand out for the phone.

He handed me Sophia's phone. I deleted the message. Then I took it to my room and searched her phone to see if there were any more clues that proved I was the criminal. When I opened voice mail, I found something kind of suspicious. I played the recording.

It said, "Michael..." When I tried to delete the recording, it continued, "Please help, Aiden... Aiden? ... *Bang*," then the recording ended. After hearing the recording, I had hope that I wasn't actually the guy who would be suspected of killing Sophia. I was happy, but I didn't show my feeling on my face because that would make me look like I deleted the clues that made me the criminal.

At the nightly meeting, we gathered in the first floor's living room. As usual, Lucas started talking, "This is our last meeting, so I guess we will have to talk about what we will tell the police about Sophia and after that we can have some fun, right?"

"Sorry to interrupt like this, but I found a clue that leads us to the real criminal," I said, showing everybody the phone.

"Really? This is the last meeting; let's have fun man!" Andrew said staring at me.

"No, this is serious," I said as I pressed the play button on the phone after Sophia said my name. I knew what I did was not following the deal with Aiden.

"Please help, Aiden... Aiden?... *Bang*," I played the part. I looked at Aiden. Aiden was looking down to the floor.

"Aiden, will you tell us all about what you did to Sophia," Lukas said as he held his chin and stared at Aiden.

"Okay... I was trying to make Michael look suspicious and show definitive proof to everybody could make the Michael criminal. But it didn't work as I thought it would. Sorry Michael, even if it worked I would still feel bad."

"The reason why I killed Sophia is because four years ago, I was blamed as a criminal doe starting fires that destroyed a great deal of property. Sophia somehow figured it out. She said if I paid money to her monthly, she would keep it secret. I paid half of my part time jobs salaries, but I started to have less money since I quit one of my part time jobs. When we came here I didn't have enough money to pay her. Then do you know what she said!? She said, "Who cares?" That made me mad and made me decide to murder her. I was outside looking for a good place to kill her. After she fell off the veranda, I grabbed a rock hit her head," Aiden cried.

I decided that Aiden had a really hard time because of Sophia. I was not the only I only one who had a reason to kill her.

We waited until the police came and watched Aiden going with the police officer. I ran to him and said, "Thank you for being my best friend."

Then he replied, "Sorry for being a friend like this."

The feeling of guilt filled my heart. I was the one who should have been caught. I would never forget this feeling for my entire life. It was all my fault. I couldn't believe how cruel and guilty I felt. I couldn't stop my feeling. I didn't know what to do, so I just watched Aiden leaving here in a police car.

One month later Lucas decided to put together another trip. I really wanted to quit this club, but there were a lot of memories. I decided to go on one last trip with this club. Hopefully I wouldn't murder a person again. Because that last trip was the worst memory ever in my life, and it will be forever. As I got ready for the trip, I guilt overcame me. I decided to go to police and confess what I have done to Sophia and Aiden.

Since I had decided to go to police myself, and I told the court that I pushed Sophia off the veranda because she was blackmailing me, the judge sentence me to prison for only five years. It was still a long time, but it was short for what I have done. I could have gotten up to twenty years.

After I got out of the prison, I went back to my house. As usual my parents were glad that I was back. I didn't completely feel refreshed, but I hoped I would never do such a thing again!

When I was walking down a street to buy some food, I saw Aiden buying some vegetables. I ran up to him. I said, "Hi, I am sorry about the things I did to you."

Then he said, "No, I deserved it. I actually killed her. I never thought that I could cancel what I had done," Aiden said, looking at my face.

"Hey, could I be your friend again, like I used to be?" I asked.

"We can, if you are willing to accept me," Aiden said looking sad.

"Of course. Why wouldn't I accept you. You helped me a lot when I first got in the video making club. I wanna help you; I have to help you," I said smiling.

"Thank you," Aiden said looking away from my face.

I promised to myself that I was going to help cure him from his depression.

Three months has passed since I helped Aiden. He was working in a really big company and sometimes looked tired. Sometimes, he called me, but most of the time he was fine. I got a job working in a cafe. All I did was serve people drinks and food, but I liked the job. It was fun. I still didn't think that I compensated for things I had done, but at least I was helping Aiden. That was the best compensate that I could do for now.

I sometimes wondered why I had to do this for Aiden, but whenever I feel like that way, some reason gave me energy to do anything for him. My mom usually said, "Is your friend doing fine?" before asking me if I am fine.

But I was fine with it because my mom said, "You don't have to carry it all. I am your family, parent, I can help you."

I decided to go to a park with a lot of cherry blossom and picnic with Aiden there. I promised myself to talk everything that I kept secret. I still didn't know how Sophia detected my secret. When we arrived at park, I put the mat on the grass and went to find the bathroom. I came back with some food from convenience store.

"I was really worried about you. I was just thinking that you were taking so long for just going to the bathroom," said Aiden with a worried face.

"I have something to say to you. And also a question," I said handing out a can of a beer.

"What is it? I don't mind, even if it is about me," he said smiling at me.

"Don't worry. It is about me and Sophia. Sorry for dragging this topic up after so long a time. But I feel like if I just spit it out, I might be free from what kept me back for the whole year," I said seriously.

"Okay," Aiden said, but he stopped smiling.

"My secret was that I was once caught by police for kidnapping someone. But I didn't actually do it! I was just there because I was buying sandwiches in the small mart. But the guy who actually did it was caught, too. Then he said, 'He is my teammate.' I looked at him in shock. The kidnapped boy was found dead. So, I had to stay in the prison for long time. And I knew if my club mates found out that I would have to get out of the club. I actually loved the club until Sophia started collecting money from me to make her keep it secret." I spoke out my old secret to Aiden. I didn't even care now, but I was surprised from what Aiden said to me.

"Sorry," Aiden said looking at me. "I found that out. When I lost my wallet, I went to the police office and signed the papers to prove the wallet was mine. Then, there was a poster that said, 'The ways you do not get kidnapped.' Then I saw your face on the poster. It was at that moment that I knew that you had some trouble with kidnapping. So, I told that to Sophia. Then she said we could get money from you. I was confused, so I asked Sophia how. Then she said she would tell you that she knows your secret and say if you want her to keep it secret then you had to pay fifty dollars each month. And half of the money will be mine," Aiden said looking down at the ground.

"But, why? Why did you?" I asked, confused.

"Because I am not kind of a nice guy you think I am… I was happy that I got twenty-five dollars every month for doing nothing, but deep inside me there was some guilty feelings. Then few months later, Sophia found out that I had a criminal record for setting a house on fire. She started collect money from me," Aiden said, not even looking to eat the food I gave him.

"Well, I didn't know you were having hard time. Maybe if I knew I could have helped you," I said.

"Nah, I am okay," Aiden said with a smile.

"The conversation became kind of dark, but let's have fun. Time keeps on going. We can't waste this time! We shouldn't regret what happened and what's over already. Nothing is going to change," I said, eating sandwiches.

After few months, Aiden succeed in his job and had to go to France. I was still in America working as a waiter in a cafe. But I had some fun there.

The picnic we had at a Cherry Blossom Park was the last time we met. The memory had of being a criminal is now in the back of my heart. For sure, it was not a fun experience, but that experience gave me a chance to look over my life."

I learned an important during this time. I should do things I really wanted to do, and I shouldn't do anything that made someone sad.

When Bombs Drop

By

Samuel Stein

Fear gripped and tore at my heart. The wind sent the biting, frosty air through the window in sharp gusts, and the billowing mushroom cloud on the skyline told me that we had achieved nothing but failure. Rachael's trembling hand took mine. Yes, the world being torn apart terrified us. The massive, looming cloud helped to drive home the hard, cold reality that yesterday--a day began like any other—was the end of an era. Rachael and I sat in our living room watching TV with the world at our feet, thinking ourselves invincible––young hacktivists––programmers who ambitiously stood unblinking in the face of danger. The dark shadow overhead notified us that we were sadly mistaken.

* * * *

It began around five-thirty in the afternoon, a bead of sweat trickled down my forehead. I brushed my long hair out of my face and resumed typing. Rachael's keys clattered away into oblivion as I focused on the last string of code. The numbers taunted me, and I tried to enter the commands. Rachael and I worked as reporters for the local newspaper. Everyone's business was our business. There was no secret email we couldn't find, no scandal, and no lie. My concentration broke as I bypassed the firewall. Just another scandal. I tried to justify in my mind how I could live with myself for causing so much mistrust in people. I shrugged off the feeling, as I had grown used to doing.

After some Chinese food, Rachael and I settled down to watch TV. I started to fall asleep, but just before I drifted off the audio cut and grew fuzzy. A static sound echoed through the dark apartment and then darkness. Creepy, a tingling crawled up my spine, and I inched closer to Rachael. Suddenly, a voice rang through the silence and made me jump. The head of a figure wearing a black hood and a voice modulator spoke slowly, without expression.

"We have taken notice of your work June Templay, Rachael Powers. Only you can save the world from what is coming." Footage of tanks, a mushroom cloud, and then soldiers marching in file along a wide hall. The voice continued," In Maine, 53.7 miles from your location, is a military base, created with the sole intention of controlling all the world's nuclear power at once. This operation is being run by a man, Lieutenant Johnson, commander of the top-secret operation known as Operation Blackthorn--a program designed to overthrow the U.S. government and America's military strength in one fateful blow. You must infiltrate the base and upload a virus onto military servers, shutting down this organization and the nuclear power they're harnessing as their own. You can download the virus at https//:www.putlocker.io. The bombs will start falling in two days' time." As suddenly as it had been taken, our power returned, and, the familiar sound resumed on the TV.

Hours later, Rachael and I were still arguing over the virus. I was firm in my belief that we should go. Rachael, however, was not so sure. "June, it's too risky! We don't know!"

"Rachael, do you want to take the chance? They hacked our firewall. They must have resources, and that means they're not joking around. If a stranger called your mother by her name and told you that she was in trouble, would you check and see?"

"Yeah." she muttered reluctantly.

"Good, now let's get ready."

All that was left to so was to download the virus. This seemed simple enough. It turned out to be the opposite of simple. The clock slowly ticked away the hours. The download required active assistance and constant permissions which led to many long, dreary hours of hard work before the download was completed.

The golden sun slowly started to brim over the horizon; and I awoke. The download was complete! I went to wake up Rachael, and found her passed out on her keyboard, her eyes wide open. It always freaked me out that she did that.

After a quick, unappetizing breakfast, I tried, with the help of Rachael, to find the fastest route to take to Maine. Rachael's parents had loaned her their Prius so we started the hour long journey to what Rachael insisted was our doom. Our voyage was silent and tense because neither of us had anything to say.

We arrived at the place where the GPS trail left the road, and Rachael parked in a small clearing nearby. The glitter of snow was hypnotizing. Rachael was enthralled. However, our lovely, fairytale hike was cut short as we neared the ominous bunker. Tall and dark, casting a looming shadow that spread darkness over the brightly lit forest. Two stories high with two sub-levels, according to the blueprints, downloaded with the virus. There was a tall fence with several coils of barbed wire running along the top, no windows, and only one door. Rachael shivered uneasily.

To encourage her, I strode confidently toward the looming gate. Rachael didn't move. "Rachael! Come on! You can't chicken out now."

Rachael just shook her head and walked away. I couldn't believe it. That Rachael would leave me to explore this danger alone. My mind was set. I couldn't go with her, no turning back now. I trudged towards the dark gate.

* * * *

The air stifled my lungs and forced short, quick breaths. A light flickered and grew steady, making shadows dance on the walls. I was faced with another door further down the hallway. The knob squealed with reluctance as I turned it slowly. I resisted the urge to panic as I continued down the corridor. For a brief moment, I contemplated going back the way I had come; but the thought of proving Rachael right was not an appealing one. I had shut down the cameras for thirty minutes, giving me a short time-window and them a reason to be looking for me. In addition, I was equipped with only a small penlight, a pocketknife, and a chocolate bar, but I knew that my job was fairly simple: get to the servers, insert the USB with the virus onto the right modem, and leave.

I turned left into the hall heading towards a maintenance closet. A shadow flittered across the back hall and made me jump. Nothing. "Phew." I swallowed the lump in my throat and kept moving. The idea of running into the deadly arms of some silent figure made me tremble. I quickly gathered my thoughts and tiptoed down the hall as the gray walls closed in around me. I continued walking towards the maintenance closet, keeping a sharp eye on the ever-wavering shadows. I turned the next corner into blackness.

* * * *

Cold steel bars greeted me when I regained consciousness. My cell was small, holding only a steel-framed bunkbed, with its moldy mattresses and torn blankets, and a small toilet with a broken toilet seat. A stifling smell enveloped all. I rose carefully to my feet. At least I still wore my own clothes. My head hurt. I tried to look through the bars to get some idea where I was, but I say nothing in the dim lighted hallway except a row of empty cells and a heavy steel door at the end of the corridor. I saw no way to escape and lost track of time as seconds turned to minutes, and hours slowly ticked away.

A light grew gradually brighter at the end of the far corridor on my right. The silhouette of a man appeared and curiosity, fear, and anger took hold of me. I screamed, "Who's there?"

The silhouette vanished as the man turned the corner. A blindingly bright beam penetrated my eyes and spots blotched my sight. A massive, bulky figure stood in front of me and all my anxieties returned when he spoke in an inhuman voice.

"Get up!"

I hastened to obey and scrambled to my feet. The door of my cell opened and a second, smaller figure cuffed me. I noted the gleaming firearm each one carried. As I was being bound a familiar voice whispered in my ear, "If you want to leave follow my every move without any question and you might live!"

It was Rachael! A wave of relief washed over my body and I felt almost delirious until I realized that I was being hustled along the narrow passageway again without time to process the sudden turn of events or reason for them. Rachael marched in strait file behind the main officer. I surveyed her closely looking for any signal to run. We neared the end of the hall towards daylight, and emerged into a noisy bustle of what looked like office workers. A brightly lit glass dome surrounded us, and trees and blue sky showed through the clear glass ceiling. The computer operatives talked over each other into microphones and hurried about carrying important-looking papers. Rachael pretended to stumble and crashed into one of them; knocking him over, and amidst the chaos I ran back the way we came, Rachael hot on my heels.

A few sharp turns and false alarms later Rachael caught up to me. "We've lost them for now, and I downed the cameras, but we have to keep moving!"

"Rachael, I'm so sorry; how did you find me?"

"Not now! We have to go!"

I raced down the hallways with Rachel close on my heels. I made a turn and entered a room with a small desk, computers, and rows of filing cabinets lining the walls. A woman sat at the desk typing, and jumped and screamed when we burst into the room.

"Ahhhh! Intruders!" She reached and pulled out a small handgun from her waist holster and trembled, "D-Don't move a muscle!"

I backed into Rachel, slowing moving toward the doorway.

She was an elderly woman with green eyes. She wore a sharp navy blue suit. I could tell she didn't want to shoot us, but I wasn't ready to take any chances and calmly said, "We aren't intruders." I noticed her name tag. Carefully formulating another lie in my head, I said in a calm, firm voice, "We were ordered the search every room Mrs. Wattson." I saw how the gleaming firearm seized Rachael with fear, so I continued, "We were just looking for them, have you seen anyone come in or out of this room?"

Mrs. Wattson holstered her gun and said, "Senator! Senator Wattson, and you two don't work here or you would know that." She paused and then continued in a moderated tone, "I think we can help each other. I was taken prisoner six months ago by these traitors. I know the way out, and I have a car, but I can't move like I used to so I need your help."

"June, I know the way, and she'll probably just turn us in in the end."

"Please! They have my daughter; they'll kill her!" the senator sobbed and drew long breaths.

Pity conquered reason in my head and I said, "Rachael she needs our help. we can't leave her."

I helped support the senator out the hallway, with a reluctant Rachael following. Soon we were at the exit with bright daylight flooding the passageway and enveloping us at the end of the corridor. I breathed in the fresh, crisp air, taking time to appreciate it as I didn't know what would happen next.

The senator led us to her car. It was parked not far away in the compound we had entered through. It was an old navy blue Cadillac. Rachael and I had to lie down in the back seat to hide from the guards at the checkpoint.

"June, what's happening up there?"

"I think something's wrong." I said. As I leaned forward; I could hear the conversation.

"I'm sorry Senator, but we cannot let you go through. There's a strict policy on Tuesdays ma'am!"

"My pass credentials are here, you fool! Now let me through!"

The young guard's voice shook as he said, " I-I'm sorry Senator Wattson! We can't let you through without the proper credentials!"

The senator noticed we were listening and slid her card back to us, Rachael and I knew what to do. We slid out the back of the car with the senator keeping the guard busy. There was a long white booth in which the guard stood. It had two windows through which we could see the keycard swipe. The guard was too involved in his heated conversation with Senator Wattson to notice Rachael's stealthy hand reach in and swipe the card. As soon as it as swiped a noise emitted from the machine distracting the guard. His eyes were fixed right on us!

"Hey!"

ZZZAAAP!! Before he could move another inch, he stood still in his tracks shuddering as if he were cold. He fell over.

I noticed the Taser in the senator's hands and smiled ruefully at Rachael. Then I climbed back into the car with Rachael following, and soon we pulled out of the compound onto the open road. A silent voyage home granted us time to think about what had happened, and Rachael recounted how she got back into the base.

"I had only gone few miles down the road before I realized I couldn't leave you to potentially die, so I followed the tracker on your GPS. After I saw you were out cold in your cell, I knew the keys weren't going to be sitting right next to the door, but they were! How convenient is that, right? They must really trust their security. I also found a couple of spare uniforms in the maintenance closet, and you know the rest."

Then the senator told her story, "I am, as you know, a US senator, but I have access to something in the governmental database, I don't even know what, that makes me an asset. They kidnapped my daughter and husband."

When she had finished she was almost in tears again, and Rachael comforted her. The rest of the trip home no-one said anything, afraid to, lest they hit a raw nerve.

* * * *

When we reached our apartment, we discussed what to do about both the Senator's, and our own situations. I no longer had the virus, and the senator no longer had any creditability.

"The nukes are supposed to go off tomorrow evening, according to the message, and we have no way of stopping them!" I said, not because anyone didn't know, but because I needed to reassure myself what was happening.

Rachael came over to me with tears in her eyes and silently showed me her phone screen, displaying recent news.

The senator crept behind us as we read the news and looked at the screen. "That's my husband!" She burst out into sobs and threw herself on the couch.

The News read," RECENT MURDER FINDS MAN DEAD IN THE WOODS OF NORTHEAST MAINE"

"They must have realized I escaped!" moaned the senator as Rachael tried to calm her down. She hurriedly signaled me to go to the other room and then said in a hushed tone," If the Senator was a prisoner, how did she have a gun, let alone a car or any pass credentials!"

Before I had time to answer a cold voice cut in," I think I can answer that for you." The Senator let a green canister clatter from her hand onto the floor, and everything grew hazy. I sank into a cold, restless sleep.

* * * *

I awoke with a jolt, a tingle racing frantically up my back. Sweat dripped down my face, and my breath came in heavy, short bursts. Rachael sat in a corner, her eyes facing outward into the gloom. We were back in my cell! A small figure emerged from the gloom and came close to my cell. My heart pounded like it was beating a hole through my chest. My heart pounded a hole through my chest. In the dim light, I recognized Senator Wattson. The expression on her face told me something was wrong.

"Senator! You're here!" Rachel said.

Before she could continue, the senator interrupted. Oh, yes, I'm here."

It was not the senator's voice.

"Senator, get us out!" Rachael's voice cracked.

"I can't. The door seems to be locked." She laughed a little at her own humor.

"What about your husband? You were being blackmailed. We stood up for you!" I shouted.

"Oh, that dreadful old fool? He wasn't my husband."

"And your daughter?"

"She never existed." The senator seemed reluctant, this time pausing before answering.

She continued," Who do you think runs this place: The government? The military? Me?" She pulled the USB with our virus out of her pocket and played with it in her hands. "No," She concluded slowly. "The people who sent you this drive, this disease."

"Who are they?" Rachael asked.

"That was this organization. W needed this drive-in order to begin our nuclear testing. When plugged into the main server, this drive is deadly, but when controlled by me, I can access anything on it.

She came closer to the cell and showed us the back of her neck, revealing a USB port implanted in her spine. You want to know what asset I present?" She shoved the USB into the back of her neck with a sharp cracking sound that forced me to cringe. "I can access any database, computer, server, or motherboard I want, using only my mind. For example, an email, an Instagram post, or a nuclear launch, could be triggered with a thought"

She abruptly turned away, giving us no time to respond, into the gloom. Behind us we heard a noise, then saw a red flash, and then, fear gripped and tore at my heart. The wind sent the biting, frosty air through the window in sharp gusts, and the billowing mushroom cloud on the skyline told me that we had achieved nothing but failure. Rachael's trembling hand took mine. Yes, the world being torn apart terrified us. The massive, looming cloud helped to drive home the hard, cold reality that we had failed. Failure pulsed through my aching brain. I stood there helpless. The mushroom cloud forced all other thoughts from my mind.

* * * *

A few hours later, the sky was dark and Rachael and I hadn't said a word, only an atmosphere of silence engulfed us and consumed everything. The air still alive with dust and debris still affected by the explosion, was thick. *Not anything could be worse* I thought grimly. I thought of my family, my parents, and cousins. Rachel's intense silence told me that she also thought about lost family and friends. I sensed her terror as an inhuman voice rang in our ears, and a hulking figure moved in and out of the shadows.

"I'm sorry you had to see that." This time, the voice was sympathetic, kind.

"Are you the one behind this?" Rachael spoke timidly at first, but then anger overcame her fear, and she shouted, "Are you responsible for the death of millions?!"

The figure stepped forward revealing a tired, sorrowful face. "Don't worry. It was just the test bomb, detonated 250 miles above the Canadian wilderness. I'm not responsible. I'm being blackmailed by that beady-eyed little senator, she says she has my son. So, no, I'm not here to kill you, only to help you."

Anger burned in me, for the first real time in my life I had been vulnerable to the whims of others. I had been manipulated, by one I deemed less capable than myself. Outwitted.

The figure expressed his story in detail. "I was in Vermont with my son when I got a call from command to come to Maine for a "special assignment." I was a general in the military and was, of course, reluctant go with my son to a military base about sixty miles in the middle of nowhere, but I thought it was a sign from one of my previous contracts. I thought it would be good for him. They just performed a surgery and implanted this in my spine. He showed us the back of his neck, displaying an ugly looking scab and a USB port rammed into it.

"I still don't know what it does, but they said I'd have to continue my work for them, the military that is, or at least I think, or they'll kill my son. I don't know if they even have him, but I'm not willing to take the chance."

"We know what it does," said Rachael. "We can help you if you can us out."

The man obviously didn't need further persuading. He quickly unlocked our cell and led us out into the hall, up a stairwell, and around a corner where we came face to face with the entire computer database.

"My name's Johnson by the way, J.J. Johnson."

"I'm Rachael, and this is June," said Rachael. "Why are any of the computers working after the NEMP?"

"This place is shielded. These people are smart, and if it comes to it, they can survive here for years after the world is destroyed."

Rachael and I got to work going through all the files on the nukes and what was going on. However, there was not much to gather, only that there was enough nuclear power to cause global extinction sixty-two times, which did nothing but motivate us further to find out what to do about it.

"That USB port in your neck can, when activated, allows you to control any executive commands on the drive. So at any time, the Senator…"

Johnson cut Rachael off abruptly, "We should probably go, because there are about thirty soldiers coming this way."

Rachael continued somewhat hurriedly. "Either way, with merely a thought she could set off a nuke and kill millions. The sooner we get what we need, which is the virus that when implanted into the servers will send all of the nukes out of the atmosphere and into space, as well as kill anyone connected to the system."

I cut in saying, "This is all assuming we find the virus saved in one of these files."

Rachael responded, "I already found it, and I'm downloading it now.

June, we really need to get new computers. These are so much faster. The download only takes five minutes!"

"We don't have that time, they'll notice you're gone any time now," Johnson sounded very doubtful of the plan.

"I can shut down the cameras, and that should buy us at least twenty minutes. Once we're done, they won't know where to look. We'll be fine," I said reassuringly.

* * * *

Five minutes of minesweeper later, the virus had been transferred. We ran down flight after flight after flight of stairs. The air grew dense and thick. It felt as if I could grab it in my hands, like some sort of jelly. Rachael looked like she was about to pass out, and Johnson seemed indifferent. The lights, wires, and noise of the servers made it look like an alien world. The bright lights dazed Rachael, making her sway for a moment, then regain her balance.

The sever we were looking for stood right in front of us, but it took several seconds to find the right insertion port. Just then, we heard footsteps of what seemed like hundreds of soldiers. The hundreds turned into five–– heavily armed. Johnson pulled out his pistol and hid behind a server, covering us. He fired a warning shot, and the enemy soldiers quickly took cover. They returned fir and bullets ricocheted off the servers.

Rachel handed me the disk, and I moved to slide it into the computer when I realized the significance of my next action. "Johnson!"

"What?!" he shouted over the gunshots.

"If I put in the drive, it'll kill you too. You're connected, so if I insert this drive, you'll die, as will everyone on the base. You all have ports in your necks."

"Do it." he shouted, "And if you ever find my son, please help him."

"No!" My hand trembled inches away from the computer port. No matter how hard I tried, my hand did not move closer. I simply didn't have the courage, and I knew it. I turned to Johnson to respond, but the Senator appeared from behind one of the server and with one, well-aimed shot, she disarmed Johnson. He lay there, holding what used to be his wrist, unconscious from the pain.

There was no noise. No one moved. The Senator slowly strode towards us, and Rachael began to panic. We hid behind a server, but I felt the eyes of the Senator boring into me, melting me. In the next moments, I don't really know what happened, but the cold of her barrel was chilling my forehead.

Rachael screamed, "June!"

The Senator fell in spasms on the floor. Her body convulsed rapidly. She twitched violently. Her hands clenched tightly. Her mouth opened, but no sounds came forth. Silence filled the room. No one spoke. The soldiers lay motionless on the floor.

Senator Wattson still breathed. A red glow emitted from her eyes, and as we looked at her face we saw the half of her face that didn't have skin on it. It was metal! The light in her eye sputtered and went out. An eerie gloom fell over the entire bunker. Everyone was shut down. Two hundred seventy-three nuclear missiles launched simultaneously shaking the foundations, as rubble began to fall.

I wasted no time trying to contemplate what had happened. Rachel followed me as I raced outside to the top of the bunker. We sat and watched as the sky filled with the orange-red color that one sees when a candle dies. The nukes launched into space where they detonated, luckily nowhere near any satellites.

* * * *

The next morning the news read: CYBORG SENATOR FOUND DEAD.

I never did find that boy, but a newspaper headline three years later noted a child's body found in the Maine woods. I kept good to my promise with Johnson and honored him and his son with a memorial in later years. The US claimed to have launched all the nukes to space as a token of peace. Other than that, the entire incident was covered up.

One thing can never be covered up. The ones who die for the common good of the common populous can never be shaken from history with physical things, for they will be set down eternally in the hearts of those who knew them.

I'll be Okay

by

Ha Trang Tran

The summer of Junior year was highly anticipated. No more restless nights, staying up until 3:00 a.m. to study for meaningless tests, no more stuck up teachers with their boring lectures, and no more arrogant jocks who thought they were better than everyone just because they were on the football team——well, for the next two months at least.

Noah lightly shook his head to flip his dark brown hair away from his piercing grey eyes. He'd been wanting to get a haircut for the last month but never got around to it. He threw his head back to study the patterns on the ceiling, trying his hardest not to fall asleep. But it was difficult. His eyelids were slowly closing themselves halfway, only to open them again with his fingertips. Noah looked quite silly. It was as if the wooden table and chair sets that had been in the boring dusty classroom, for who knows how long, were singing him a lullaby, as he slowly drifted off into dream world.

"Just for a little while," he thought to himself. He couldn't help but to let out a yawn that turned out to be a lot louder than he expected.

"Mr. Martin! What do you think you're doing yawning in the middle of my class?" Mr. Collin barked. He seemed to have gone from boring lecturer to a psycho angry protective mother of two, really quickly.

"I'm sorry you're boring?" Noah whispered under his breath.

"Would you mind repeating yourself?"

"I'm sorry you're boring," Noah's voice trembled a little, but he made it clear that he wasn't going to back out of the battle that should've been resolved a long time ago.

Noah never put up a fight his entire life. He had enjoyed being a pacifist, or in other words, not caring. But enough was enough. He knew that Mr. Collin never liked him. But somewhere along the line of false cheating accusations and unnecessary humiliations in front of the whole class, he had had enough. Noah could easily write a one-thousand-word essay on why Mr. Collin should have been fired a long time ago.

Mr. Collin just stood there, his face slowly turning into a ripe tomato. But before he could say anything, the satisfying sound of the second to last day of school bell ringing sliced through the dull air of what seemed to be the endless dark pit of Geometry. Noah would think they'd put something a little more interesting for the last period of school. But high school schedules always defied logic, so adding a boring class like Geometry came as no surprise. Noah sprinted to the classroom door as fast as his long, skinny limbs could take him.

As he stepped from the classroom, Noah easily noticed his best friend, Aria. She was definitely not the teacher's pet. She wore a black a leather jacket and black boots. The perfect aesthetic for the "rebel" type. Noah looked into her deep, dark eyes––eyes that melted into warm and bright glowing circles that appeared as if they could suck the soul from anyone. They almost looked like circles of an eclipse. Little freckles sprinkled across Aria's nose. Her cheekbones and jawline carved in perfectly, and her messy, dirty blonde hair fell perfectly down her back like a waterfall. And her lips––they're definitely her stand-out feature. They were full and plump, like billowy clouds floating in the sky. She leaned against one of the lockers and as she spotted Noah, what must've been a smirk curved up from the corner of her lips. There was no reason for Aria to have a backpack, it wasn't as if she actually did school work.

Aria and Noah had been friends from the beginning of time. Wherever Aria was, anyone could trust that Noah would be there, too. They even knew each other back when Mr. Jones had hair, and everyone knows that was a long time ago.

"Sup," Noah hummed.

They both swiftly headed out the door and walked to some end-of-school party that was supposedly the best thing ever on the face of the

Earth. Noah never went to parties, but Aria wanted to crash. It wasn't as if they had anything better to do.

Once outside the closest thing to prison, also known as school, it seemed as if the fresh Oregon air celebrated summer as well. Sunlight pierced through the gaps of trees, who were busy salsa dancing with the wind. Noah jumped on his bicycle that was supposedly "ruby red" but, throughout the years, worn out to the shade of dirty bricks.

As they pedaled through the empty streets, the sound of their rickety old bikes was the only thing heard that broke the silence. The sun was setting at the horizon, and the streets turned almost grey. The chilliness made Noah almost wish that he had brought a jacket or at least something to keep him warm in that starry summer night.

The houses on the side were lined perfectly, each with their own courtyard and garages and the same old identical design. It was all just the same—the same old people going to their same old work with the same old outfits, all going to that one grocery store with the same old clerk who seem to hate his job more than anything. That's why Aria always appealed so much to Noah. She was interesting, new, and anything but ordinary. She had her own life, and she made his life fun.

Noah heard the raging music of the party from a block away. He always saw parties as energy vacuums. He felt as if everyone secretly judged him in the back of their mind. Human interaction wasn't necessarily Noah's forte anyway. "Awkward" would be the appropriate term, he supposed, but Noah always preferred, "socially challenged."

Noah never felt the need to go out and make friends for the sake of it. He would much rather spend time alone with a book or a video game. Social events were just unnecessary and boring, not to mention apprehensive and stressful. People expected him to socialize, but it just drained all the life out of him. The people there were always masked with smiles, and everything was so plastic. There was not one bit of genuineness in birthday parties or family gatherings. But high school parties—they were always different.

Noah and Aria parked their bikes in the huge front yard of Amy Miller's house and entered. It was somewhat of a mansion. The entire house was made from marble. Everything looked luxurious, but that wasn't the first impression of the party. Sweaty bodies moved to the raging beat of wild music while everyone had a cup of what Noah hoped to be fruit punch. The lights flashed into a burst of neon colors. The room was dark but at the same time lit. Familiar faces looking like they were having the time of their lives, dancing without a care in the world. It was crazy rage.

Noah stood there at the doorway, with an expression of shock on his face. He stared at students completely letting go. I thought I knew these people, Noah thought to himself. They looked like they were actually having fun for once. In the world that tried to make make them robots, carving out their opinions before they were even born, they rebelled. They rebelled by understanding that life wanted them to grow up and go to college and get a good job and pay bills, but they still chose to enjoy the moments that they had. Noah wouldn't have ever thought that anyone in this seemingly dull town could have any bit of spark of happiness. But they did.

At that moment, Noah wanted nothing more but to belong there, to devote his soul into this group of a couple of dozen of dancing teenagers. He slid his body through the crowd, making his way towards the middle enough so that he was surrounded by a good amount of people. There he just danced, letting his mind and body be devoured with the atmosphere of this place. For so long he had to worry about finals and late assignments, staying up late biting his fingernails, hoping that he would do well on some test. For so long he'd let himself be defined by letters and percentages. But that didn't matter anymore.

Dancing the night away, sweat droplets rolled down Noah's back. Drenched in his own excitement, Noah looked down to his wrist to see his watch showcasing that three hours had already passed. Then, the thought of his best friend flashed through his head, like a spark of light dashing through his mind. Where could he possibly be. Noah's mood fell. He walked through the crowd aimlessly, bumping into faceless bodies, not knowing where he would end up. He felt a sudden burden on his chest. His throat froze, and his entire body was exhausted. It was as if he were drained of all the energy he had left, and now all he wanted to do was go home and snuggle with a nice cup of hot chocolate and a good book.

Noah somehow found his way out of the door and ended up right near the doorway. Without even thinking, his body drifted outside to get some air to breathe. He walked down the enormous stairway to the front yard. At the bottom, Noah saw about a dozen kids spread out socializing. Some bounced to music. He gazed up at the sky and saw a myriad of stars. It was like heaven for his lungs. They expanded, taking in all the air they could get. He finally felt a sense of space. He breathed in the sweet scent of freshly washed grass and autumn leaves.

He wandered into the back of the house and spotted two figures. Noah moved closer. He saw Aria speaking a tall guy wearing a jacket that nearly covered his bald head. Tattoos covered every inch of visible skin, and a dark aura, highlighted by a pale complexion that made him seem white, followed him.

"It's not a big deal. It's just smoking." The boy's thin, crusted, pale lips curved into the words. He smirked a little from the edge of his mouth, as if it was funny that Aria would find the act of smoking bad.

"I'm not sure. What if we get caught?" Aria's voice shook with nervousness.

"We won't," once again, he smirked. The boy acted as though he found Aria's rebellion entertaining to watch.

Noah stepped a bit closer to grasp the situation. Aria's hands slowly drifted towards the direction of the half-full pack of cigarettes in the boy's palm.

Noah stepped out from the shadows. "Hey, Aria. We need to go."

Two pairs of eyes turned to Noah's silhouette, glittering in the starlight.

"Get, ready. Let's go," he repeated himself. This time his voice firmer than before. Aria froze, wide-eyed; she looked at her best friend in disbelief.

Impatient, Noah grasped Aria's wrist and tugged. Aria tripped over herself as her best friend physically dragged her to the gate. The guy just stared at them, shaking his head lightly with disbelief.

Aria struggled, finally pulling back and stopping Noah.

"I didn't ask for that," Aria said. "You know I can fend for myself. Gosh, those guys probably hate me now."

Noah paused for a moment. "Since when did you care about being liked? And plus, I thought I was doing you a favor. You were in a bad situation and I got you out of it. Thank you works, you know."

"It's just smoking. Big deal. I'm a teenager. Noah, let me live," Aria struck back.

Noah thought his explanation was much easier that is was. "You seemed hesitant. You shouldn't let anyone push you into doing something you don't want to do."

Aria stared at the ground, avoiding eye contact. "I wanted to do it. I was just afraid because it was my first time…"

Noah fought back anger and kept himself calm and collected. "What do you mean, you wanted to do it? Aria, smoking isn't good for you, and you should be smart enough to know that! What's next, drugs?"

"One cigarette won't kill you, for goodness sake. I'm young. I need to live my life to the fullest. I know you see me as this friend who needs protection, but I can take responsibility for my own actions. It's not my fault I actually have a life, and friends, and emotions. You should try it sometimes. All you do is make the right decision and never have any bit of fun. When you're eighty, you're going to look back at your life, and not know that you've actually lived it or not."

Aria seemed to have held in these words for a long time, and now they were just bursting right out of the cracks between her teeth. Like a lava from a volcano they exploded, attempting to burn every bit of Noah's self-esteem.

Noah fought back anger and kept himself calm and collected. Clutching his teeth, he couldn't find the words to say, so he just stormed off, away from the party. He got on his bike and spend away from the confrontation.

"Finally," Noah murmured to himself, the sound of his raspy voice was mixed with a soft sigh. He had always loved blasting his music to the point where everyone near him heard every single word while biking. He felt as if the louder the music, the deeper it seeped into his soul. His dad always hated that he could hear Noah's music from a mile away. But what did he know? He's too busy out drinking with what were supposed to be his "business partners." If only he was in a business, maybe their family could afford a roof that did what it was supposed to do—not leak.

Noah tried to convince his mother to divorce that pig countless times, but she never listened. She was too afraid for Noah's and her own safety, and parts of her were still in love with the person his father used to be: the kind of man that would buy her flowers and open her doors, one that loved her unconditionally. A person whose touch sent shivers up her spine and whose voice was softer than a breath of spring. But young love could only take one so far, and she had to learn the hard way that marrying at eighteen might not be her best decision.

Sometimes the abuse got so bad that Noah heard screams of horror in the middle of the night coming from his own mother's hoarse throat. He heard the sound of things breaking, shattering glass and his own father calling his mother things that a woman should never be called. But as long as Noah kept silent and told himself that it was all just a nightmare, he felt that nothing bad could ever really happen.

Noah loved his mom. He loved her so much. They had the type of bond that even the sharpest knives couldn't cut. She was all he had, really. Within his world where nothing matters, she was the one thing that did. He loved her when she worked extra hours to keep him alive. He loved her when she would skip meals to make sure he had enough to eat. He loved her when he fell asleep on her lap as a child, with her hands in his hair, tugging at the roots. He loved her when he held her after many of his father's rage attacks and watched her being torn inside out––something that made a part of him die.

Noah didn't understand why his mother couldn't just leave. Maybe she didn't know. Noah thought maybe it was the fact that she didn't see him for what he was, a monster. She just shrugged it off as an illness, just a man who had a disease and struggled to keep up with it. At first, he would make her feel bad for him; that he didn't mean to hit her and that he was sorry. But he crossed the blurred line at some point and now, no apologies were given, no words of comfort were heard, and no sign of humanity was shown. Sometimes Noah desperately searched for any spark of his mother standing up for herself, and for all the screaming terrors, he found a dash of hope only once, and it had a disastrous result.

It was a Thursday, or a Friday. It wasn't really what Noah was paying attention to considering every other disastrous act that happened that night. Noah came home late, from hanging out with a group of guys that he barely knew. Stepping into the hallway, he could already hear the loud distinct voices from his apartment. He walked slowly to the door and jerked it opened. The scene he saw was something out of a horror movie.

His dad towered over his screaming mother, her hair tangled in clumps and littered with pieces of what appeared to be glass. Her forehead bled the blood of her broken soul. Unending red drops rolled down her cheeks as if they were tears. Clusters of glass spread over the floor, and her mother's cries echoed down the hallway. Eyes of what could only have been the devil looked at Noah. Then his father turned and stormed off with rumbling footsteps filled with frustration and anger.

Running as fast as he could he to be with his mother, he crouched down and scooped her up into his arms and sat her on his lap. He cradled her, stroking his hands through her hair. His body warmed her pale, icy flesh. She dissolved into a mess of indistinct groans. "Shush," he whispered into her ears. "It's okay. You're okay."

Her cries slowed and came to a stop. Her heart stopped racing, harmonizing with Noah's heartbeat and slowly blending in with the moonlight.

A passing car brought Noah's attention back to the present. He turned onto the street the street that housed his apartment complex and peddled a little harder. He parked his bike in the rather dark garage with only five cars and one old motorcycle, wondering what could potentially be camouflaged in the dark shadows that hovered over most of the garage. The apartment's lighting situation wasn't necessarily preferable.

After struggling to fit the fifteen-year-old key into the lock and jerking it open, Noah stepped into the overpowering smell of smoke that, not surprisingly, surrounded his father. His father lay slackly on the food-stained couch, his white tank top curtains his inflated stomach from the overdose of alcohol he had drunk. After getting past the obvious sense of smoke, the smell of his father's distinctive smell of not washing for five weeks overtakes Noah's nostrils. His dark hair almost looked white due to the layers of dandruff and grease that stared straight into Noah's eyes, straight into his soul.

His father was out cold, not even slightly noticing his son's timid existence. Noah didn't bother to awaken the beast from its slumber for greetings, so he just walked through the dusty hallways to his room. There, he threw his bag on the floor and collapsed on his bed. He thought that he, too, deserved some rest. Noah closed his eyes and drifted into a dreamless sleep.

Noah loved sleeping. It was always his thing. Not in the stereotypical potato couch way. It was his way of escaping from reality. When he closed his eyes, he felt as if nothing else mattered the slightest bit besides the soft mattress and the comforting warmth of the blanket wrapped around him––not the math exam due in two weeks, not the ignorance of his father, not the coldness and deadliness of the world.

From what he thought was just a light nap, to his surprise, he woke the next day to the sound of his cellphone vibrating through the cloth layers of his backpack. It was Aria, her voice escaping from the telephone's speakers trying to tell Noah something about––actually, Noah didn't know what it was about. With one eye open, he responded with inaudible murmurs that he couldn't even recall. And in the foggy atmosphere that came after twelve hours of sleeping, he went back to sleep.

He woke about an hour later to the noise of obnoxious construction next door, which seemed to go on forever. He took a short shower to wash off the sweat that drenched his body from the un-air conditioned building. He dried himself off with a stained towel from who-knows-what and grabbed his computer to catch up on some emails. Then he proceeded to head out for some breakfast. He went on a search mission for any sign of food, and succeeded in finding an apple and a half-spoiled milk carton that he managed to chuck down only to find that it wasn't worth it and threw it away.

His dad was out doing whatever; Noah didn't care enough to figure out. His mother was not home, either. He guessed she was working. Noah's phone rang again, and the mild sound of vibration faded into the air and wandered somewhere to the back of Noah's mind and became a kind of background music at a raging party. Everyone knew it was there, but no one really bothered to do anything about it. Noah collapsed on the couch and searched for the remote to turn on the TV. There, he sat peacefully staring at the screen.

Noah's phone rang again in the afternoon, this time more overbearing than ever before, waking him up from an afternoon nap. He pushed himself off the couch and had to physically drag his feet to his room to pick up the phone. It was an anonymous caller. Little did he know, this phone call was a raindrop that would become a hurricane.

An unfamiliar voice picked up. "Noah Johnson?" It was a woman.

"Yes, who's this?" Noah felt a cold breeze pass through his body, but there was no wind. He sensed that something was wrong.

"We're calling from the JLVA Hospital. It's your mother. She's been stabbed. She was brought into the emergency room." The nurse's voice dripped in empathy.

Noah's heart squeezed, the poor organ contracting and pushing against his ribs like a bird crying to be free from a cage.

"We've tried calling you this morning, but it's more serious than we've expected. She's now gone into a coma due to injuries to the brain. Apparently as she fell and her head…"

The phone left Noah's hand in one swift motion. It hit the ground, shattering into pieces. But Noah couldn't have cared less. Those words sent a rollercoaster of emotions racing through his veins. Like poison, they crept into every cell and buried themselves in his synapses. He felt numb, as if tiny sharp icicles grew from each nerve, piercing through his thin flesh. His brain froze in utter terror, as did his body. He swore his heart could've skipped a beat. It felt as if an elephant sat on his chest, weighing down on him. But at the same time, his head was blank. All that was there was pure whiteness. He couldn't think of anything else but the agonizing words that are "she might die."

He then snapped out of his own mindlessness. She was still in the hospital, alive, maybe even struggling to breathe. The next moments felt like seconds. The hospital was only a few blocks away, so Noah ran as fast as he could. Sprinting to the front desk, Noah was already out of breath. He must have looked as if he had just run a ten-kilometer marathon. "My mom…My mom, Marie Johnson. Where is she?"

The lady at the counter was old, wrinkly, and almost squishy. Her thin gray hair was tied into a neat ponytail with strands falling down, outlining her face. The bags under her eyes looked as if they carried all the sleepless nights she's gone through. She looked up at Noah through her circular glasses. To her, he must've looked like a total loony. She looked down, searching through a pile of papers.

"Room 309," the lady mumbled.

Noah ran through the white hallways, sensing in the smells of antiseptic and medical gloves. Finally, he spotted it, the sign of room 309 above the door. Fear overtook his body for what might lie ahead on the other side of the glass door. He ran the entire way, only to take approximately two more steps to get to her. His brain had to physically force his tightened muscles to move.

There she was, lying with a nurse by her side. Her long blonde hair scattered over the white pillow case. Even with what seemed to be five hundred machines hooked onto her pale body, she still looked so beautiful.

"Mom?" Noah tried to keep his voice as stable as possible.

The nurse spotted Noah immediately. She looked like she would be in her mid-twenties. She had raven hair that went down to the middle of her back. Straight and conditioned, it was obvious that someone had to take good care of it. She had a pale face, with squishy cheeks and eyes that were big, brown, and prominent. She stared at Noah through them with a look of surprise and confusion.

Noah went to the bed, sitting himself down next to his mother, and holding her closer than ever. He never wanted to let go and wished with all of his might that this moment would stay forever, scared of the events that may occur next. But as time went by and with the possible secretive judgement from the nurse, Noah had to let go. Sweeping her soft bangs away from her face, Noah cupped the sides of her cheeks.

"Tell me what happened," Noah asked the nurse, still studying the lines on his mother's face.

This wasn't a question, it was a command. The nurse looked down, toying with her own fingers, and sighed softly.

"It was your father. I…" she paused. Her voice was soft and gentle, calming Noah's repetitive heartbeat. "I'm not sure what exactly happened. Apparently, he got into an argument at the diner and, in a rage, stabbed your mother. Someone called the police, and he's been arrested. Your mother was taken to the hospital right away. She's in a coma now. We tried everything we could. But…" She paused again, regaining the strength to go on. "But we're not sure if she'll make it through the night."

Noah stared at the nurse, stunned at how she could say those words. "She will," Noah whispered, telling himself that everything would be okay, telling himself the lies he needed to hear before he could look himself in the mirror and say the cold dark truth. He looked straight at the nurse. "She will be okay."

She nodded, not sure how to react. The nurse rose from her chair and walked out of the room. Her footsteps blended into abyss, disappearing like a black cat in the night. Noah sat there, forcing himself to breathe in and out. He was fighting sleep even though it was only the afternoon and finally surrendered. He nudged himself up next to his mother and allowed his eyelids to rest.

Noah woke up to the noise of the heart monitor beeping slowly. One, two, three, and then one long never ending beep. Noah may have been oblivious to the world around him but he had watched one too many K dramas to know what that meant. Noah stood up, expressionless, kissed his mother's forehead, stepped out of the hospital room, and left completely. He felt nothing––but not like a bored nothing––just a complete and utter void. His mind was a total blank. He saw a group of nurses and doctors rushing into the room, their faces painted with fear and anxiety, not knowing what might come their way.

He walked through the hospital hallways and through the door. He settled at a small cafe right next to the hospital and sat down. The cafe had a comforting and quiet feel to it. It had a bar that curved at one corner of the space and rows of wooden chairs and tables scattered everywhere else. The scent of freshly made bacon and egg floated in the air. There were picture frames of magazine covers and nature on the walls. Noah stared blankly into space with nothing on his face, not even one tint of emotion. A waitress came over and asked him if he wanted something to drink.

Noah looked up at her, forcing himself to look fine. "One black cup of coffee, please."

"Alright, anything else?" the waitress asked.

Noah went off in a daze for approximately seconds, and then looked at the waitress again, "It's a nice place you've got here, you know. I should've taken my mom here sometime; she'd have loved it here."

The waitress smiled, genuinely, something that Noah had hoped he could do, and went off with his order.

That was all he remembered about that day. He didn't even remember how he got home. Noah's phone didn't stop buzzing the next day or two, messages, voicemails of friends and family sharing their grief. He didn't have much family, and they lived far away.

Noah didn't care to reply and just left his phone to bleed out its battery, percent by percent. He occasionally tapped on it, to scan through the messages. But that was it. He locked himself in his house, with the comfort of his couch. He bundled himself up with blankets and popcorn to go through all the old movies that had been living in the cabinet for who knows how long. He took short breaks to nap once in a while. People came over at times, scanning Noah's face, searching for any sign of damage. But they would fail. Noah was his usual self, not too happy, not too sad, and only speaking up when a question was asked.

Around the second or third day, Aria came over. It wasn't like Noah was keeping track. She said that leaving a bajillion messages on every media platform wasn't working, so she gave up on asking for permission and setting a meeting date and took matters into her own hands. The banging of the door had sent sound waves through the cold-blooded apartment. Noah had jumped, almost spilling his half empty bowl of popcorn onto his sweat-stained blanket.

"Noah!" Aria yelled. "Open the door, dang it."

Noah couldn't even react when Aria jerked the handle enough times to fling the door open.

"I should probably get that fixed," Noah said. There was no other word for the action. He didn't exclaim. He didn't sob. He didn't scream. He just said the phrase.

Aria ran up to the couch to try to give her detached friend a hug. Noah didn't resist, but he just shook himself a little to escape from Aria's grasp. She got the hint, and backed off to look at her friend, who was busy looking at the ground.

"Hey, you. Look at me. What's going on?" Aria had never been more concerned.

"Nothing."

Noah slowly put his blanket around his body again, making a shield from himself and the world. He sat on the couch and continued with his movie marathon, like nothing had happened. Aria inched away from the couch, distancing herself from Noah. Just like the others, she scanned every inch of Noah's face. Nothing.

"Noah, stop it. I can't take it anymore."

"Stop what?" His eyes remained glued to the screen. Staying away from all the emotions he had bottled up, from all the tears he had been running away from."

"Stop pretending as if everything is okay," Aria inched closer to Noah, but strangely, the closer she moved to him the more distant he seemed to get. She held out her hand, her fingertips shivered with fear that she might have lost the closest friend she had. She was scared. She was scared that Noah's ears couldn't hear her words anymore, that his heart had been caged for so long that it would never know how to feel and that he might've floated so far away from reality that he might not be able to come back. Aria broke. "Please, let yourself feel something."

Noah looked up, shocked. Aria's face was bright red. Her eyes filled, and a single tear dropped and carved its way perfectly onto her cheeks. From all their years of friendship, Noah had never seen Aria like this. She was always fun, wild, and the most care free soul he had ever met. But there she was, crying.

Just like that, the chains that were on Noah's door shattered, and he immediately held his broken friend in his arms, closer than ever.

In the breaks between Aria's sobs. Noah finally heard the words, "Please, let yourself break. You don't have to be so strong all the time." Before he knew what was happening, Noah sobbed as well. He buried his tears into the sleeve of Aria's t-shirt. His cheek pressed against the crook of her neck. His body shook. Their cries blended into one another's.

"Maybe," Noah took a breath. "Maybe if I was there for her more, maybe if I was there to protect her, things would've turned out better. Maybe if I was there to protect her and held her a little tighter. Maybe this is all my fault," his words collapsed on one another. Every bit of his fractured heart fell from his chest.

"No. Don't say that. It wasn't your fault. She's in a beautiful place now, Noah." Aria said in a manner that comforted her as much as Noah.

Noah looked Aria straight in her eyes, fighting to control his tears. "How could this be God's plan for me? Please, tell me how."

"Because sometimes, things happen to us. Things that are horrible beyond belief. But you grow from that. You never forget it. But you learn to accept it, and you become stronger than you ever thought you could be."

Noah paused for a long moment and nodded. "I'll be okay," he whispered.

Those words seeped into Noah's brain and settled themselves into his heart. His pulse stopped racing, and little did he know, those words would stay with him forever. At the time, he didn't understand how, but he grew more than ever. Throughout the rest of high school, college, and when he became a lawyer and had kids of his own, those words were a part of who he became.

Printed in the United States
By Bookmasters